"If th

So starts Neil's edgily compelling tale-within-a-tale of Mars - the Red Planet. A Mars marinated in human blood since before the dawn of time. A tale quite unlike any you've ever read before. Told in a way that'll take away your need for caffeine ! Yet keep you wired for a lot longer.

Once again 14 year old Neil Lee puts the pedal to the metal, right from the very first word, and takes you on another breathless ride, squealing the tires and blasting the horn, right through a dark and dangerous teenage mindscape of sweet innocence, endless war, gruesome violence and confused loyalties. All highly spiced with action and all expressed in the slightly twisted, yet strangely insightful, way that this unique boy -author, with his serious learning disability, has suddenly become so famous for.

This gifted kid at 14, long before he's allowed to have a driver's licence, once again drives us madly, but skillfully, right along the edge of the precipice and scares the living bejesus out of us with his fresh but darkly exciting visions.

If you're a kid who wants to hear the most amazing voice of your own generation, or, if you're a geezer who wants a guide to "Generation Duh", pick up this book, hold your breath and come along for the ride. Right down the Highway to Hell.

Come on !
The door's open - and Neil Lee is revving up the engine.
And grinning his terrible grin.

Two fascinating stories of humans on Mars - 400 years in the future - and 25,000 years in the past. Both bloody brilliant and redly compelling !

Faster, funner
and even more mistakes

Neils last book had glaring mistakes on every page. And this second book, ***Only Human***, which has more pages and more complications, likely has even more.

In our efforts to bring you Neil - completely raw and unabridged - we admit that you will find a great many spelling and grammatical errors in this book.

Our intention, since Neil has a learning disability and uses words in ways that no-one else ever has, is to bring you exactly what he writes in the exact manner he writes it.

Since he does see everything in a slightly different light, he has a truly unique voice which we think should be heard - so we practice minimal editing.

As a result, there are likely some real clunkers in here that even Neil didn't intend - but hey. After all - we're only human

If you find any, please drop us a letter noting the page and mistake. When we print the second edition, we will include your name in it as someone who helped out immensely.

Write to: **NOGGIN**
Galactic Headquarters:
PMB Penthouse 880
289 South Robertson Blvd
Beverly Hills CA 90211

Only Human
Martian Independence

by

Neil Lee Thompsett

2/17/00AD

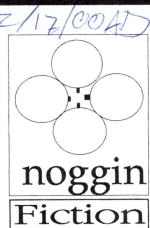

noggin Fiction

Only Human

Martian Independence

ISBN 1-892412-88-8

COPYRIGHT © NEIL LEE THOMPSETT, 1999

ALL RIGHTS RESERVED

FIRST EDITION - NOVEMBER 1999

Published by
noggin
PUBLISHING & STUFF

Galactic Headquarters :
PMB Penthouse Suite 480
289 South Robertson Blvd,
Beverly Hills California, CA 90211

To order
Copies of this book are available for US$12.00
(includes shipping and handling in the continental US).
Write to the above address and include payment in full.
(Don't forget this last part). Make out cheques to: Noggin
Or surf to: *nogginshop.com* to e-order
(Prices subject to change without warning or reason)

Warning
No part of this publication may be copied by any means
or for any reason, without the express written consent of
the copyright holder and the publisher. Or else.

Weasel words
This is a work of fiction. Any resemblance to any person, living,
dead or unborn, or any locale or event in the past, present or future
is entirely coincidental.
And any attempt to claim otherwise is just plain stupid.

I dedicate this book to my poor little Heum-brother Jonnic Thompsett because he has had to put up with all this " lousy book " stuff for years, and has had to endure being known as "Neil's brother" for almost as long.

Jonnic, I hope you don't get drafted.

Notes for non-geeks
(Who don't understand Sci-Fi stuff)

There are two very different, but very similar stories being told here. Both at the same time. Both are about Mars. Both are about loyalty. Both are about violence. And so, both, ultimately, are about human nature.

<u>The First story:</u> This is the story of the first time humans were on Mars, 25,000 years ago. They didn't originate on Mars but were brought there from another part of the universe, by Aliens (who we call 'The Civilized Races'). Humans were brought here because the Civilized Races hoped to quarantine them until they grew out of their infectious disease of violence, and could become civilized.

This story is told through playbacks of recordings made by Marsolla - the Recorder or Planetmind of Mars.

So whenever you see the word: 'PLAYBACK', you know that the Recorder is playing you a recording of what happened with that first human civilization on Mars, thousands and thousands of years ago.

This Recorder, whose name is Marsolla, is a giant intelligence who is the brain of the planet Mars. It knows everything that happens on the planet and records it all. It speaks telepathically to certain humans and can influence events to some extent on the planet.

According to Neil, every planet has an intelligent PlanetMind like this. And who knows. Maybe he's right.

Notes for non-geeks
(Continued)

The Second story: This is the story of the second human civiliation on Mars, which takes place 400 years from now, in the 25th century.

This is the main setting for the book and so, when you see the word 'RECORDING', it means that we have switched to the future story - and the Recorder is recording it as it happens.

This story is told by a young boy on Mars who is drafted to fight in a war - much like the American War of Independence - except it is Mars fighting to be free of a tyrannical Earth.

Over the course of the story, our nameless young hero grows from being a child, to being a man. His loyalties change and he matures - but, even as an old grandfather, he still can't escape his essential human nature.

This story is also the prequel to Neil's first novel; <u>Becoming Human</u> - and shows where many of the characters in that cult classic novel got their start.

Acknowledgements

My mom went over everything and helped me to make it all a lot clearer. Thanks Mama.

Jonnic Thompsett invented the phrase "Generation Duh" on Thursday, October 28, 1999 at 7:45 am on the way to school. He graciously let me use it on the cover. He also helped with the photos

I invented "Jolt Music" in 1998 and used it in my first book Becoming Human. It's all mine.

I also made the sculpture "Militiaman" which is used on the front cover.

I'd also like to thank:
Ryan Ford
Jim Youngman
Will Ferkodic
David Lechtman
Erica Volk
Carol Whikman
and the entire Beverly Hills High football team (the Normans) for constantly mocking me and keeping my head the right size.

(Extra small)

This is a war story.
If you do not study war,
if you do not wage war,
if you do not love war,
read no further.

War is no place for tourists.

"War always starts at home"

— Neil's Secret Journal

Chapter 1

(PLAYBACK - 23,500 BC)

If there was ever a Golden Age for humanity, it was when they lived on Mars - the first time - 25,000 years ago. When the sweet water was here and the fresh air was here and all the dreams were possible.

Not like now. They've come again, but this time with their foul chemical vapor factories and water-crunchers and pole-melters to try and make the planet liveable again.

Back then they were gods, bold and shining, fearing nothing. Capable of anything.

Now they're like sad little insects, burrowed deep into a toxic waste dump and clinging to life as they fight one another for scraps.

I was there to watch the humans then and I am here to watch them now.

I am the Recorder - the Mind of Mars. I will explain myself later, but in the meantime, all you need to know is that I record. I playback. I watch.

And I tell you now, only one among the current crop of humans is even worth watching . . .

(RECORDING - 2398 AD)

It was 40 minutes until I was to to be dropped to invade the city .

I was 40 miles up in the cargo ship, tied down in the small Offense Capsule which I was to be dropped in.

As the belts wrapped around my hands and gun tighter, I became more terrified, knowing that I would be spooked by the drop and knowing that the gravity would be working against me as soon as those cargo doors opened up.

I couldn't look to my friends for comfort since they were strapped down tight as well.

All I had to calm me down was my sameness to everybody else. Same uniform colored grey, same helmet, and same multi-pro goggles which I am not allowed to take off at all during combat. I was nameless. Faceless. Personalityless. How could I be singled out to die. There is great safety in sameness, I thought.

Even so, my teeth started to chatter as I felt my blast pants getting drained of the weight liquid. I was trained to use the liquid as weights to protect against g-force surges while we were in the stratospheric cargo ships. I don't know how it worked, but it did.

"20 MINUTES !" said the communications personnel in my headset communicator.

I went back to my one-of-many way of thinking. My uniform was just like any old uniform you'd see

ONLY HUMAN - MARTIAN INDEPENDENCE

here: adjustable chest armor, plastic - slash - graphite shoulder pads covering the whole shoulder, armor cloth from the 20th century which seemed obsolete, but worked well enough to keep using.

I also had my lightweight three foot plastic air tank; just in case I have to swim or go through poisonous gases or if I survive a flaming , my boots; designed to run in the snow or to climb the tallest mountain and last, my trusty old helmet, which had its own communications system connected to it. It was made of black metal and able to connect to your left shoulder pad for better circulation of the circuitry. Or whatever the hell they told me in training. I wasn't paying much attention.

This uniform could take a full four shots in the same area before allowing bullets in. Any more shots after four in the same area, would result in being wounded and most likely dead with the new types of bullets around today. So the trick was not to get hit more than 4 times in any one spot.

As I looked up to the cargo ceiling I felt more scared. My theory wasn't helping me.

Then it happened.

The sirens went off, the glass top shot up and covered my whole body. I was like a bullet being loaded into a big rifle.

Then the cargo doors opened up and the vacuum of space did the rest, sucking my capsule out of the ship and into space.

I felt the neck-snapping jerk towards the planet

as gravity ruled.

Seeing the atmosphere from so close amazed me, then I realized that this was the drop I'd been dreading so much. So far it was beautiful.

The gravity of the planet pulled me faster towards it - desperate to get closer.

I looked to the bottom. Seeing the clouds shooting by me at incredible speed, but with no sounds whatsoever scared me again. I knew that the clouds weren't moving that fast, it was me.

Suddenly I saw the outer surface of the glass light on fire. There was a special coating designed to take the heat and burn off, but that was no consolation when the burning was two inches from your face.

The gravity was now working strongly. trying to smash my body to the top of the capsule. Luckily I was tightly strapped in .

I was terrified beyond my mind, and, still looking down, feeling all my nerves tickling all at once, I saw the ground coming fast.

Suddenly I felt the parachutes blasting out of the top.

I felt another jerk throwing my head down and back up. Whiplash.

I felt sick and thought I was going to hurl.

Then I hit bottom, and there was no time for it.

The glass top shot off, the belts wrapped around my body all snapped off at the blink of an eye.

I knew what I had to do now. I had trained for this till I could do it in my sleep. My time had come. I didn't even think about it. It had been made into an instinct. As soon as the belts snapped clear I grabbed my gun and turned on my multi-pro goggles.

I ran out of the capsule, my only purpose in liferight now was to acquire a target

I saw the other troops landing and running out, but dismissed them as targets.

All I did then was run, having my trigger finger tense and converting my bullets to explosive. My goggles pointed out the way to my target, all I did was follow the tracks.

It was night-time, well that's what my goggles said.

I ran with the other troops who were anxious to see some action.

Suddenly they all stopped.

I did not understand what was going on. I started to pant from the long run towards here.

I then saw the platoon leader .

" There's the base," he whispered, pointing out towards the glowing lights of the city.

I pushed my way through to get my own glimpse of it. I made my multi-pro goggles zoom into the defenses. I recognized the city from old videos of my youth. It was famous. Its Twelve Towers and its beautiful architecture were known all over the planet. I had always hoped to visit and now, finally, I was here. But not to enjoy it. Probably to hurt it - probably to level it to the ground.

It wasn't a city of beauty anymore. It was an

enemy base. Which must be taken at any price. Slowly my vision crept up onto the defense walls of the city. There were gunners on the top of the famous CityWall, using 50 caliber Atmospheric Chain Guns, and they were all probably convertible to explosive. I knew, out of sight, there were hundreds of soldiers all hiding behind walls and synthetic grit bags. Walking on the plains and mincing from side to side, like giant crabs freed from a market tank and mad from it, were the bloody drone guns. (mobile chain guns, radionn controlled and dangerous.)

I quickly zoomed out before anyone saw my head sticking up or picked up my radar visions.

I looked at the Sergeant .He quickly picked up his rifle and connected the second clip onto the side.

" First Twenty go with me, then you all charge !" he whispered.

He pointed at the first few people around his presence. I was one of them.

I knew that he had doubts of getting out of this one alive. But being the brave Sarge he was, he charged with the soldiers. I ran with the first Twenty with my finger feeling itchy to pull the trigger. To do something. Anything but think about things.

I watched the soldiers from the back, knowing that if they died, I was the one to get what was left. My share of glory would be coming soon. At 3000 feet a second.

I ran faster. Might as well be first.

The shots started to fire. I saw them starting the

first few rounds towards us. The tracers seemed to be coming in slow motion. And so pretty in the night.

We were at the plains now, running like mad horses right into the rain of bullets. Thirsty for it.

Our soldiers started to fire at the same time. Screaming. I was too.

Bullets coming like lead walls to us.

I knew that if they were going to hit us at this distance, they would have to use the standard bullets since the explosion ones wouldn't go far enough. And I could take 4 standard hits anywhere if I had to. Maybe more if my armor was overspec.

The other soldiers of my Twenty became scattered around as the bullets started coming,

The first man went down, his head flying off. Of course, with 50 caliber slugs, sometimes you couldn't take 4. The head armor was never very good.

I was scared of being shot the same way, but luckily I was a good runner. I could outrun my fate, by rushing towards it.

I heard the second team right behind me. I guess that I should of felt safer but I didn't. If my first team got in trouble then the second team would run right into that trouble without a chance.

The man right beside me must of been thinking the same thing. He became jumpy and started to run faster , screaming and howling. He started to fire. The sound of his gun, shooting at anything he saw, sounded like a demon itself.

" Ahh ! They're all around me !" he cried.

A nutter.

He then turned around to look. Always a big mistake in a hot zone. Suddenly a bullet hit his air tank on his back. He started blowing pressurized air and it sent him around the ground like a failed rocket until it blew up. It probably killed him right away, but even dead he kept on making trouble.

The men around him got hit with the sharp plastic of the tank and the force of the air shooting out of it. He knocked down three of us. I was hit on the side of my arm. Then the dead man shot right into the air, his tank still venting. His air ran out and he fell onto me knocking me over and dripping blood and gore on to my uniform.

I pushed him away seeing a sharp piece of something sticking through his belly.

I rolled on the floor and stopped a minute, seeing the soldiers of my Twenty getting mangled in the worst possible way.

A man jumped over me holding his gun over his head. The next thing I heard was his yell and his arm flew back to land right in front of my shocked face, spraying blood all over my helmet and goggles.

I stood up and was immediately hit in the head. Whump!

Then I was down again.

That's when I lost my mind. Or at least my marbles. That's when I forgot my name. And that's when I started hearing voices.

I thought at first it was just my head ringing from

taking that blow. I actually thought for a minute that my head had been blown off, and this is what it felt like, but I could still feel my hands and feet waving like a turned over crab.

I lay on the ground hearing that continuous bonggggggg and thinking that it was all over for me. But then I heard the most sweetest thing a man could hear: the enemy's fire power stopped. They were converting to explosive bullets.

That was the chance. The eternal 5 or 6 seconds.

"ENCORPSE YOURSELF !" said a voice in my head over the ringing.

Good idea. I quickly stood up, and using the low gravity and the extra strength the armor gave me, grabbed the body of a nearby dead man and holding his gun in my left hand, I ran with the corpse hugging me, its back to the enemy.

The other soldiers got up and ran with me, following my mad plan.

I was now in the front of what was left of the platoon, I was close enough to see the drone gun running towards me and the chain guns of all angles of the base aiming for me. I knew then that I was going to go down in combat. If there was any way for me to survive this I would of done it already but there wasn't any.

No time to weep about it.

I gave a yell and started to fire out of the arm pits of the corpse wrapped around me. My gun on one side, his on the other. I felt the explosions on the corpse's back as the enemy sent standard rounds at me. Incoming rounds were ripping the corpse to shreds, but they weren't 50's or explosives. Must be something else.

Drone gun I realized.

I shot at the drone gun running towards me and shooting crazily. I shot the eye then the bottom engine of the drone gun. Drone no more.

The other soldiers charged with whatever they had with them. I slowed as I saw the chain guns become operational. They created the wall of lead once more, continually shooting at the corpse I was clinging on to. I kept saying to myself, like a prayer, what the ArmorMaster had told us. "4 direct hits. 4 direct hits. 4directhits. Ford Erect Tits " as I continued to return fire.

The other Twenty took advantage of us holding the enemy from changing to explosives. They ran in throwing grenades onto the drones and chains. I kept shooting at the defenders.

I looked up and saw the next sweetest thing.

It was the second platoon coming through the atmosphere right on top of the city, like giant fireflies from hell.

The chain guns that were left turned around and started to fire up on the burning capsules, maybe not knowing that they were unattackable. It was a mistake that cost them the battle.

While they were looking up, we shot them down.

The enemy soldiers that were left then got

desperate when the descending cages weren't affected. They gave up their guns and started to fire the flame torches at us, hoping to clean us up quick and then get to the reinforcements who were falling like burning snowflakes.

They could have killed us all with explosive bullets if they had only not panicked. If they had been able to take that 4 or 5 seconds to change - but they didn't. And wiping out flamers was much easier than wiping out gunners.

Knowing what was coming, I quickly threw down the mutilated corpse and started to run back a bit holding the two rifles and firing them off at the incoming flame. I got a couple down the throat of the flamer just as the flame got me. The heat of the thing threw me down, sizzling, just before it exploded. It burnt my gloves off and most of the skin off the backs of my hands cooked off with them.

Two soldiers helped me up and dragged me back from the flames which were all around the ground.

" Hey - I know you ? What's your name ? " said one of them, It was the Sarge which I thought had died.

I was suddenly in a panic. I didn't know what my name was. I looked down at my hand to read my barcode, but it was raw hamburger. All I could read was: "medium well".

I nodded my head at him and pushed his hand off my shoulder pad roughly. That little shove killed him. It pushed his head right into incoming traffic.

A bullet, which would have gone right by, shot right into his helmet through his goggles. I saw the quick spark then his head exploded.

I was shocked, looking at the headless corpse still standing there. Some quirk of the armor held it up.

I didn't feel sad or guilty, even though I had caused it and was now covered in his brains. Instead, I became furious that I couldn't remember my name and started to shoot everything I had.

The other guys thought I had a plan and followed me. Seeing all the other soldiers following me like that made me feel like a leader, but I didn't have time to enjoy the feeling. Suddenly both of my guns ran out of ammo, so I pulled out my mini shotgun and started to shoot off that.

Screaming like mad men, three soldiers ran past me, killing the flame-gunners but being flamed to ash by the enemy.

I ducked and knelt, aiming my shotgun at the other flamers then firing.

I hit one on the arm which turned him around. Then I hit the tank, on his back, and the whole man exploded nicely, flaming most of the soldiers who were closeby, enemy and ours.

After that I gulped. thinking that more would be coming before I could get a drink, but there was now only silence.

The stunned silence of victory.

We had taken out the first defense to the city. Our target was accomplished, and we all toasted ourselves with sips of water from our bottles. We didn't have to toast the enemy.

The enemy was toast.

Chapter 2

(Playback - 23,500 BC)

Of course, that's the problem. There's always at least one among them that is worth watching. There is an endless fascination to them that cannot be explained.

Which is why they still exist.

Before they came to Mars for my Golden Age, humans had nearly destroyed civilization in the universe a dozen times over. And been smashed back to the stone age after each attempt.

Yet the civilized races could not bring themselves to exterminate the breed. They would kill all but a few children, relocate them in some isolated place and try to civilize them again, using a different method - which, so far - had always had the same bloody result.

Humans were a problem that just would not go away.

And no-one in the universe was even sure where they originally came from. They were

SIMILAR ENOUGH TO BE ONE OF THE CIVILIZED RACES, BUT DIFFERENT ENOUGH TO SPARK ALL SORTS OF RUMORS.

SOME RUMORS CLAIMED THEY HAD ORIGINALLY BEEN FOUNDLINGS, ON AN UNNAMED PLANET - A RACE APART. OTHERS SAID THEY HAD COME FROM A SEEDSHIP - SPERM AND OVA SENT ON SOME DARK JOURNEY - PROGRAMMED TO THAW AND REPRODUCE WHEN OPTIMUM CONDITIONS OCCURRED.

THE MOST RECURRING THEORY, HOWEVER, WAS THAT THEY WERE CREATED FOR SPORT. BREWED UP IN SOME STINKING VAT TO ENTERTAIN THE LONG AGO RACES BY FIGHTING EACH OTHER.

THIS LAST ONE SEEMED TO FIT THE FACTS AS I KNEW THEM. EVEN AS CHILDREN, THE HUMANS WERE SPIKY. IT WAS NOT A BEHAVIOR THEY LEARNED, IT SEEMED TO BE MORE BUILT-IN.

WHATEVER THEIR ORIGINS, HUMANS HAD BEEN A PROBLEM IN THE UNIVERSE FOR OVER 100,000 YEARS - AS LONG AS HISTORY HAD BEEN WRITTEN. LIKE SOME BEAUTIFUL, BUT DEMENTED, CHILD THAT NEEDED CONSTANT CARE, BUT WOULD NEVER BE QUITE RIGHT.

(RECORDING - 2398 AD)

The day time came fast and the plains were filled with the dead bodies of troops, some of them I knew, and some of them I didn't - but it was all the same. If I made more friends, they would all die too. It's just that way since we're in war with the enemy, we can't afford to get attached to anyone else. It causes traumatic stress syndrome.

And gas.

Everywhere I walked, checking the dead bodies and scanning their name codes printed on their right hands, I found every soldier to be mutilated differently.

One soldier had his whole back shot out of his belly because of the pressure of his air tank, exploding inwards, while another soldier had no head .

These were just the victims of the careless mistakes.

The bodies hit with the explosive bullets had their whole chest disintegrated and their guts left all blown to hamburger meat.

At least all the bodies who weren't hit with the flamers were still recognizable, The ones who were flamed were vaporized into ashes and atoms, covering the floor and walls with their windblown remains. Dust to dust. Ashes to ashes. Soldiers to clean-up problem.

Even though we had dozens of casualties dead in every certain way, we had still won the battle.

ONLY HUMAN - MARTIAN INDEPENDENCE 17

They had even more dead guys. And, more important, fewer living guys. None in fact, that we could see.

We had succeeded in capturing this outpost and therefore we got a prize - we could have more reinforcements. So we could go on and try to capture some other useless outpost. The only problem was that we had to hold off any other kinds of enemy attack before they got here.

Although the enemy were all dead here, they were still around in force. With the napalm planes, the multi-angle tanks, and last the enemy troops not to mention their mobile drone guns, which almost count as remote controlled troopers.

Two of our companies, holding 500 people before the drop were now down to 200, who now were going to try hold off an army of every sort.

From all the hundreds of bodies I counted, I could tell that the fire power of the enemy was greater than us. All we had were four guns per soldier. A rifle (explosive bullet conversion), an automatic shotgun (explosive bullet conversion), a pistol (non- convert), and last - the old trusty cyclone gun.

That piece of weaponry is usually the lifesaver. Though it's only for close contact it still never falls off your arm if you get shot and it will never run out of bullets when you need it the most. It's connected to your left hand and controlled by your muscle movements so if the enemy thinks that you're un-armed, you could un-clench your left fist and waste them all.

If you want to know what they looked like, they resembled the ancient chain guns that terrified the streets of every city in the twentieth century.

It had no triggers which were visible. When it slid out, it had a fist shield which held your hand in alignment with the gun, so you could control the way it would shoot.

I guess that I'm a weirdo, thinking of all these weapons while I'm checking the dead bodies, but still, I was a kid and I was in war. This was what I was trained for. To kill the enemy, and to know about every weapon that I carry, so I could fix them and kill at the same time.

The Sarge of the other platoon came up to me while I held the scanner and a corpse's arm. He was an old man, having the multi-pro goggles covering his wrinkles and eyes and his helmet was all dented, with the radionn antenna broken off, not to mention his alcohol-intoxicated breath with the sweet sting of rotten meat, as he said: "Son, where's your Sergeant Brad ?"

I couldn't tell through the goggles if he was concerned or was just questionable, either way I was going to give him the answer.

" Killed in action sir !" I said, pointing to the headless corpse with the three blue circles on the left shoulder pad. The Sergeant gulped, tugging his turtle neck collar around his neck.

"Well," he paused, " That's too bad."

I stared away and continued to scan the barcode

on the corpse's hand.

"Well, then who is the next in command?"

I looked at him sarcastically; "Well, there's Tom over there splattered in that area, and here's Bill," I picked up a hand with the bar code on it.

" I'd like to show you the others but I think that they were burned to ashes and are floating around in the air, sir. You're probably breathing in Tom and Eddie as we speak."

The Sarge was not amused at all.

" You trying to be funny with me, boy?"

" What took you so long to notice?" I said.

He frowned.

" So, you're the last one of your Twenty. I'll give you some slack for that. But not much. Have you ever led your own Twenty? Son, are you willing to command it?" He said in a seductive way, ready to put up with a little sass to get the chain of command linked up again.

"Let me tell you something, sir. I didn't want to go to war against these guys. A few months ago they were my friends and neighbors, Martians - just like you and I - now they're shooting us. Earth drops a nuke on us and suddenly it's Martian fighting Martian and they're all sitting over on their own planet watching and laughing at us.

I never wanted to train to kill or to drop from orbit, and I never wanted to see guys and girls I knew since I was a kid have their bodies mangled in the worst way," I said. "I never wanted any of it."

" Son, I know. Nor did I. But either way, you're in it now and you're going to be re-circulated into something else. A tank squadron; Pilot training; snipering and even possibly back to dropping from forty miles above. So my question to you is - do you want to drop that corpse's hand, show your patriotism and become a Sarge or do you want to waste my time with this weepy crap ?"

I paused, then I grinned "All I want to do is fight the enemy til he's dead and then go home to the high school sweetheart stuck in my heart and never kill even a bug for the rest of my life. Now the question that you are asking me is if I want to lead my own squadron ? My question now is why me ?"

The Sarge grinned. "When I was dropping into the city, I saw some crazy bastard running with a corpse hugged around his chest, shooting like a maniac and taking out some of the most complicated defenses we've ever come across. That crazy bastard looked a lot like you.

You are a born leader son, like it or not. You can think on your feet and make decisions to save your own ass and men will follow your lead and do it for one good reason - because they want to save theirs, too. Whether you take the stripes or not, men will still follow you. And I just want to know what you can do with a squadron.

If you consider the leadership route, you can get out of this settlement today and you will be posted somewhere else. Somewhere nicer. If you don't, you won't. So what's your choice ?"

" No." I said.

" No ?"

" All I want to do is fight and go home. I don't want to lead a Twenty and I don't want to be a hero. I only want to be all that I can be. Which in my case is just an ordinary guy."

The Sergeant grinned.

" All right son. You win," he chuckled, "or maybe you lose. We'll see," and he walked to the troops posted outside of the area.

I finished scanning the hand and made my way to download the casualty data to the comm center which was being set up in one of the towers. I didn't know which one it was since the base was over four miles long and had twelve towers. So I just started towards the closest ones.

I guess that they were the bunkers of the enemy. Or even test facilities for their drone guns. Either way they were filled with supplies we needed. Medicine for the wounded, and munitions to help us create more wounded.

Looking at that plain and seeing three hundred dead soldiers on it and all over the place was an overwhelming sight that I have never forgotten. Three hundred bleeding hearts open for the looking.

Offered freely to the Gods of War.

What the hell was their end of the bargain ?

*   *   *

The next day we all had a surprise. The enemy tried to invade and they were still sending men and mobile drone guns in.

I was concerned. The two gunners for the fifty calibers had a jam while firing the explosive capsules and with in seconds the jam caused the gun to explode killing the gunners manning it.

There wasn't any wall left to stand on and we were stuck with the synthetic bags but we were still holding them off with the flame throwers. That was only a life saver before they figured out how to do to us what we'd done to them yesterday or until they sent in the tanks to take care of it.

I was huddled down in the ground behind the mountain of debris, looking out for any enemy troopers coming in. I soon saw more than enough.

"Twenty, no thirty, of them are charging right this way!" I said.

The other soldier was holding onto a big flame thrower pack and waiting for me to give him the command to fire.

The enemy was charging fast and firing.

"Duck!" I shouted, dropping down with the other soldier. The bullets hit the ground and the debris above us, exploding and causing our temporary wall to crumble. I stuck out my rifle and started to fire. "Flame them!" I yelled.

"Fire in the hole!" the soldier shouted. I dropped, looking outwards as he shot out the intense flames to the charging enemy.

Every one of them started to vaporize leaving a hideous red cloud of ash whirling above us. Why it's not black, I don't know. But it's not. Always red. Maybe some chemical reaction. Maybe their last angry feelings.

I heard no screams but knew why. The vocal organs are the first to melt up, then the rest of the body turns to dust. It was a horrible thing but it still got the job done.

" Clear !" the soldier called out.

I stood up and reloaded my rifle. 30 enemy lives snuffed out like leaves blown off a tree. And most of them gone without a trace.

I saw the other soldiers around me reloading and getting ready too, and so far there were no casualties. The reason for that was we all fired the flames at perfect timing. Every turret shot out fire . It was like an open window into hell covering thirty feet of the plain.

More enemy troopers started to charge up, firing hundreds of rounds onto us. I ducked, hearing the grave explosions of the bullets onto the rubble.

" Fire in the hole !" the guy with me yelled, shooting out the stream of fire.

" Clear !" he shouted.

I began to get worried. The enemy was stupid and if they kept trying to get up here and get past the flames, then we would run out of flame within an hour. Long before they ran out of guys.

I contacted the Sergeant through my comm system.

" Sir, how long till the reinforcements arrive ?" I said.

" Fire in the hole !" shouted the soldier shooting out the flames.

" They'll be here within two hours." said the Sergeant through the comm system.

" Clear !" shouted the soldier.

" Sir, we can't hold them off for that long !" I said.

"We'll hold them off!" said the Sergeant, sounding like a bad actor, reading lines he didn't believe. He then shut off from the comm system.

I quickly looked out to the plains. Zooming one hundred times into the distance. There were three enemy tanks coming our way and there were flame thrower troopers, fifty of them.

And one hundred infantry troops charging once more.

I zoomed out and quickly ducked. I held out four fingers (meaning four seconds before flaming). I waved the hand so all the flamers in the line could see.

The soldier nodded, wiping his face.

" 1...2...3...4..." He whispered, standing up and flaming outwards exactly in synch with the others. "Fire in the hole !" he yelled during his burst.

I started to fire my rifle at the charging enemy.

The soldier started to sway the torch side to side, getting cocky. I pulled back and stopped firing.

"You want some of this you mothers !" he shouted . " Yeah !" He finished.

ONLY HUMAN - MARTIAN INDEPENDENCE

Suddenly I heard a whistling noise.

The tanks were firing now.

"Fall back!" I shouted.

I started to run backwards pulling on the flamers arm. He shook me off and I jumped behind another wall of rubble.

The soldier was moving slowly still flaming the area.

Boom!

The shell hit. I felt the ground shake and a layer caved over me. I pushed the rubble out of my way, looking at the soldier's scattered parts around me.

The other soldiers were scattering around, breaking our fire line and taking cover.

I knew why.

The tanks were now in range and coming in at full steam.

I looked around and thought to go to the bunkers.

Suddenly another whistling noise went by.

Boom!

One of the famous Twelve Towers sagged over.

I had no time.

I ran towards the rest of the barracks, hoping that the other troops would be there.

The Sergeant was commanding people to get into formation for a defense. I was relieved. Somebody knew what he was doing.

He then pointed to me.

"You, get to the west with those privates! When the tanks come in range we use the missiles."

" Missiles ?" I said.

" GO !" he yelled.

The two soldiers were waiting for me and we all started to go west. We hid between the bushes and the rocks so the scanners of the tanks wouldn't pick us up.

" What missiles?" I whispered.

The private showed me the mini-bazooka in his hand, but neither of them had multi-pros.

" Check the range !" whispered the other.

I zoomed in the goggles to 100x .

" The tanks are entering the base now." I whispered.

I then saw the Sarge with his few men left starting to fire their explosive bullets against the enemy flame troopers. Quite a few went down.

Suddenly the tank fired one shell at the bottom of the dead pile of enemy troopers near where they were standing.

I could feel the explosion from where I was.

The smoke cleared. No Sarge. No troopers. All I saw were bits and pieces of meat.

I closed my eyes.

Good thing I wasn't counting on that promotion.

" The Sarge is dead." I said.

There was a slight pause between the privates, then we got back to business.

" Range ?"

" Possible ! 1100 meters. Double elevation for arc. Correct 2 degrees myside for wind." I said, reading the stats off the inside of my multi-pro goggles.

The trooper aimed the bazooka at the tank in the far horizon and then pointed it up one thickness of the barrel, sighting underneath. He eased it to my side a bit, reading the degrees for windage.

Then fired.

The shell went off like a bird towards the tank, up high at first, but bending downward like a rainbow.

" Fry in hell, sons of bitches !" he said quietly.

The tank flew apart, hitting the other troops. From this distance it looked like a stomped anthill. With smoke.

"Let's move !" I said, sensing some danger.

" Wait, where are the other two tanks?" said the other trooper.

"That's why," I said, realizing the danger only as I said it.

I heard a whistling noise coming closer.

" Run!" I shouted.

The troopers dropped the bazooka and started to run.

I followed.

The explosion knocked me from my feet and I could feel the heat on my back as it blew me up against the front of a big boulder.

The other troops jumped behind the boulder.

I quickly ran behind it, too.

They were panting, loading up their rifles and converting them to explosive.

"Check where that came from."

I nodded and looked to the side.

I saw the tank almost a mile away near the towers. The other one was patrolling the base with the rest of the enemy troopers. I knew that the tank was aiming at us, hoping to get a perfect lock.

Even if he didn't hit us right on, a near miss would do. I knew that there was no chance of surviving once he got the range. And even if we survived this, we were three soldiers against a whole army.

"**LOOK UP AND QUIT WHINING**" said a quiet voice in my head.

I glimpsed up and saw three of our fighters sinking lower into targeting range.

They came from space; they were still burning.

They then dropped tons of liquid napalm onto the base covering almost every inch of it.

The tanks exploded within seconds and the enemy was basically vaporized.

The fighters pulled up and flew back out of the atmosphere. Bim Boom Bam. Like spraying bugs, and just as emotional.

I was glad and thankful, knowing that there was a god out there. Or at least a orbital carrier.

The planes were obviously making room for the reinforcements coming in. I was saved. " The reinforcements are coming in now !" I said.

The two troops sighed and fell to the floor in relief.

I was already there.

*   *   *

The new troops had landed and were fixing what was left of the base. Setting up the tents and cleaning out the dead bodies.

Tanks and hummers had dropped with the new recruits. (The recruits came down easy, in the cargo shuttles, not in Offense Capsules - lucky bastards).

The supplies were still coming down in shuttles almost every hour.

" Identification number ?" asked the Officer.

" Identification number 596. Platoon number 225." I called out, thanking God he hadn't asked my name.

The Officer walked up to me.

" You're one of the five surviving ?" he asked.

" Yes sir."

" The others are being assigned back into training. You have the same choice they have. Do you want to stay or do you want to go with them?"

" Sir, what kind of training ?"

The officer sighed.

" Tank efficiency training," he said.

" Permission to join the rest of the soldiers going into training sir."

The Officer grabbed my arm and tried to scan my bar code tattoo. The scanner registered nothing.

" What the hell," he shrugged, " Join them at the cargo ship Bordello. From there you will depart to the training site."

" Understood, Sir," I said.

The Officer grinned. I saluted him and made my way to the cargo ship Bordello. The men and women troops filled the streets with talk, pick up lines and bragging. After all they were young like me and probably fresh out from drafting camps all over the planet. It was still a young war, not grown into its full horror yet.

Never before had I seen so many women who were strikingly attractive in my life. Still my mind was set on the girl I had back home.

Before I had left I made her promise not to join the draft. I never knew if she took me seriously but I hoped for the best. Ever since, there had not been any communications uplink with home and I began to fear that it had been destroyed.

Looking at this place reminded me that there was no time for sex, fun or even love. We were in war and if we were to survive it, we would have to be ready for the enemy at all times. We could never let down our guard. Or our pants.

I finally arrived at the cargo ship Bordello. It was stubby and like all the other shuttles, triangular.

The four soldiers were with other new recruits, an equal amount of men and women, and were waiting to board the Bordello. They were giving all their war stories and reasons for joining up.

I didn't want to join in, in fear that with my experiences I may stir up some trouble with these young kids. After all, that was what I was good at.

I just listened in.

ONLY HUMAN - MARTIAN INDEPENDENCE 31

" So when did you join ?" Asked a soldier to another.

" It was when I was in college and heard about the nukes fired back at home. My family was fried and all I had left was my anger," answered the other.

" I heard the pay was good but really I joined up to meet my girlfriend," said another troop.

" Oh, did you ever find her ?" asked the curious soldier.

" She was vaporized by a flame thrower when I invaded with the 225th," he said mournfully.

All of them were silent with pity for the man.

" But at least our platoon killed all the bastards, even the dopers. May they all rot in Hell !" he said biting his lower lip.

Strange. They looked like fresh kids. I didn't realize they had seen action already. They didn't have my covered-in-blood look yet.

A sonic boom suddenly shrieked by us. It was another shuttle coming down. The sound lessened while it flew to the landing site.

" Damned shuttles. How much stuff does this ass-plucking base need anyway?" scalded an irritated soldier.

I took off my multi-pro goggles and moved them up to my forehead.

The doors of the Bordello steamed out and slowly moved open for us to enter. Out walked the pilot of the ship and came up to check on the amount of personnel going to training.

" I guess that you guys and girls are the whores who are going to be screwed in my Bordello," he said grinning. " Well get in and strap down."

The soldiers started going up the ramp, passing the fifty caliber machine gun at the entrance of it.

A soldier became sour faced. " Wow,' he said, " it smells like -"

" Don't even say it. We all know what you're going to say." interrupted another.

I didn't smell anything. Maybe I was just used to it.

I walked to a seat. They were all made of torn up leather and thick straps which looked like a torture unit.

Nonetheless, I sat down and grabbed the straps and clipped them on to the groin holder.

The other soldiers weren't pleased either. It took them a long time to strap down and become patient. I guess that they were all still kids and had not seen the peak of death as I had. After you reach that peak, you can only look down to where you've been. There's not much new to look forward to.

" Well, you little whores, it all checks out. We're going to take off now and if the g-force doesn't kill you, then the Sarge you'all are going to, will." He said with a small chuckle.

The engines started up, and vibrated the whole ship.

It started rather slow for a space ship but I was soon going to find out where all the energy went.

"Boom!" went the engines, pushing the whole ship up, breaking the sound barrier and crushing my body towards the seat.

The G-force was so great that I couldn't breath well. It pushed my lungs down with the rest of my body.

Even my goggles seemed to be digging into my skull.

" 10...9...8...7...6...5...4...3...2....1...0..." went the countdown of the burst computer.

The engines began to die down.

As they did, my body tried to fly up towards the roof. After all, we were now in a negative gravity environment.

This was worse than the Strato ship that had dropped us in our Offense Capsules. At least then there was a water barrier to cushion us from the G. Here there was only old cracked leather.

The ship was in orbit now and was spinning around to get into the area of the training base. Like a roller coaster. The ship started its engines up again and entered the atmosphere again.

My body now hit the straps and they were almost ripping me apart.

Boom !

The sound barrier was broken again from the great speed of the ship going belly down . Then the bottom engines shot on. My body was slammed back to the seat. The ship was rumbling like crazy coming down.

Finally the ship landed in one piece. All engines turned off and all the external sheets of metal sizzled, red hot.

" All you whores always get out tired and achy. That's why they call this sweetheart the Bordello." said the pilot laughing .

My hands were trembling as I pushed the release button. I tried to stand up but my legs were trembling as well.

The other soldiers were suffering the same way.

Some of them hurled and were covered in their own processed lunch.

The cargo doors opened up. The outside revealed a desert area. extremely hot, and extremely dry.

I walked out letting the blazing heat hit me like a wall.

There were no tanks and no barracks. Wherever we were, we weren't at the training site.

"What the hell is this shit ?" said one soldier.

" Shut your filthy mouth !" said a female soldier. followed by: "Men, they whine like children!"

The troops all walked out to the desert in front of them. I used my goggles to zoom out to the long plain. The hot sun now beating down on them made them go darker and still there was no sight of a base.

" Well, you whores aren't bright for tank infantry in training !" said the pilot, walking down the cargo ramp.

"Where the hell is it then ?" shouted another soldier.

The pilot grinned; " It's right under you, you jumpy little whore ! "

He then took out a communications radionn.

"Training base #1149 your whores are ready to be screwed !"

We all walked back to where the Bordello was parked. It slowly sunk down as rumbling sounds started and got louder.

The Bordello disappeared into the hole that was now visible. It was a secret hatch door which was electronic. I now knew what type of base it was: it was one of those waylay bases, hardened and made-over so that no-one could pick up their whereabouts. But the question was - what was a training camp doing out of sight ? Were we in enemy territory ? Or were we just being trained to stay under cover ?

This week of training was going to be a strange one.

*   *   *

That night was just like any other night in a camp. I was on the top bunk and having my eyes closed. I dreamed about home. I dreamed about what life was like before the War. What love and trust meant. But I was dreaming about her.

The scenery was just like all the other dreams I'd had. It was sharp and clear, showing the night time sky and the gases being given off by the city lights and heat vapors. Coming out in shades of bright green and red blending into the pitch black sky.

I pictured me and her on a mountain top, sitting on the hood of my car. Looking at each other, kissing, and discussing life long plans with each other. They usually went like this:

" So, when you get back I hope that you'll be up and ready for popping the question to me."Carol would say with a seductive grin on her face.

I would look at her and say "Sure. This war is not yet at the point of drafting. I might not even go into it. After all, I'm only 15."

She then would change her appearance on her face and say. "I hope that it doesn't come to that. War, in these times, always has a low percentage of personnel coming back alive. I don't want to see you come back in a jar." She would then almost seem to cry.

"Don't worry. I bet that our men and women in the service would stop the enemy before that ever happens."

This dream-memory would then change to the day I left to the military. It would always take place in the daytime.

She would be crying but happy that we both would be drafted together.

" Well, here we are. If I die, well -" I would then interrupt and give her what my father gave to me.

" This is a regress card. If you give it to the Officers, they would take you out of the draft." I gave her the ticket and hoped that her decision would be the one that would save her life.

She would then stop walking.

They would start to call our names and I would walk into the bus.

These dreams were not recurring enough to call them traumatic but they were not good enough to call good.

I then woke up and looked around the room. The others were still sleeping.

I looked at my watch . It was five o'clock in the morning.

I quickly got changed and waited for the others to get up. Since we were underground. it was cold and the light was completely blocked out .

The lights suddenly went on and lit up all the barracks, tunnels and cargo rooms. It woke the others. It revealed me, sitting on my made-up bed, all dressed and staring.

It was my birthday.

I was 16.

Chapter 3

(Playback - *23,000 BC*)

After the most recent Human Outbreak, it was only children that were saved to start over with. But, no matter how well-meaning the civilized races were, they still feared this ragged band of homeless human children. Not because of the technology these children could build around them, but rather because of the deadly disease they carried within them: Violence. With its deadly sister symptoms, cruelty and anger, it was the most feared sickness in all the universe. Not only dangerous to be around, but highly contagious too - or maybe the word is addictive.

A disease no intelligent species could resist.

That's why they were, even as children, kept in quarantine - like a deadly virus - and an entire planet at the deserted end of the galaxy, was restructured to be their school - or their prison.

Humanity was not totally destroyed before I met them. But the pruning and the culling was severe. Only a million children were saved from all the human worlds. And they were brought to Mars.

I was there.

ONLY HUMAN - MARTIAN INDEPENDENCE 39

I AM THE MIND OF MARS.

I WAS MADE, OR I EVOLVED, TO WATCH OVER THIS PLANET AND, IN THOSE DAYS, I BECAME A SHEPHERD FOR ITS HUMAN *HERD*.

SO WHERE DID I COME FROM ? LIKE ALL INTELLIGENT BEINGS, I JUST DON'T KNOW.

ONE THEORY I CAME UP WITH WENT SOMETHING LIKE THIS: WHEN THE CIVILIZED RACES BEGAN CHANGING THE ATMOSPHERE AND THE COMPOSITION OF THE PLANET TO MAKE IT SUITABLE FOR HUMAN EDUCATION, THEY INTRODUCED SOME STRANGE VIRUS INTO THE ECOLOGY. IT BONDED WITH THE AIR AND THE WATER AND THE EARTH AND BECAME A SINGLE LIVING ENTITY WHICH WOULD EXIST AS LONG AS THE PLANET EXISTED, FUELED BY THE INTERNAL HEAT AND AWARE OF EVERY CORNER OF THE WORLD.

IT BECAME ME.

AT SOME POINT IN THE PLANET-CHANGING PROCESS, I BECAME AWARE OF MYSELF AND COULD USE THE BILLIONS OF MOLECULES OF SOIL, AIR AND WATER TO PROCESS INFORMATION AND STORE DATA AND THINK.

I COULD EVEN MAKE CHANGES ON THE SURFACE LIKE MAKING VOLCANOS AND MAKING MOUNTAINS AND I COULD CREATE LIGHTNING, RAIN AND OTHER TYPES OF WEATHER WHERE I THOUGHT IT WAS NEEDED. OR WHERE IT AMUSED ME.

BUT MY MAIN JOY AND PERHAPS MY ONLY FUNCTION WAS TO WATCH AND TO RECORD.

EVERYTHING.

I NOW BELIEVE THAT THERE IS A RECORDER LIKE ME OR A PLANETMIND, ON VIRTUALLY EVERY HOT PLANET WHICH THE CIVILIZED RACES HAVE VISITED AND SOME SAY THERE IS ONE ON EVERY PLANET THAT EXISTS, AND ON EVERY SUN AND MOON TOO.

I ONLY THINK THIS IS HOW I ORIGINATED. I DO NOT KNOW. PERHAPS WHEN A PLANET ATTAINS A CERTAIN TYPE OF ATMOSPHERE AND COMPOSITION, life-forms like me occur spontaneously. Perhaps not. Maybe it is some glorious accident. But it is a strange co-incidence that I only came to consciousness after the old races began changing the planet.

We do not speak to one another, we Planet Minds, but hear tales of one another through the living beings that travel between worlds. We can, however, establish a link with higher animals - and communicate with them instantly, no matter how far they travel from the planet - which is a useful thing to be able to do.

But, to make a long story even more obscure, I cannot consult directly with other Recorders about their memories and do not remember my own origins at all.

I do remember when they first planted the humans, though.

Only Human - Martian Independence   41

(Recording 2398 AD)

" Welcome troops . This is base #1149 and you will be spending this whole week learning about your tank." the Drill Sarge paused and looked at all of us.

" If you fail all these tests you will be put back into drop-testing Offense Capsules. Without chutes. Do you get me ?" he said.

All of us nervously lined up saying in the top of our lungs. " Sir, Yes Sir !"

He grinned slightly. It seemed to be the popular thing to do when you were in charge.

He then walked over to one of the tanks.

It was 20 ft by 20 ft in length and height. It was shorter in width coming from a point in front to about 15 feet across at the back and was quite triangular.

" This Iron Maiden is called the T456. Or the T-bird, as some of you call it."

He walked over to me. "You, Boy ? Do you think you know how to work this thing ?"

" Sir ?" I asked, wondering WHY ME ?

" Well you heard me right. Do you know to drive this baby ?"

" Uh, Yes, I guess."

" You guess ? Then you go to that T-bird." he looked at the others - making me the butt of some joke.

" What sir ?"

" I said go, start it up and shoot out a round."

I did as he said; walked over to the tank and climbed into it. The catch closed and I looked around.

There was the radar, sonar, outside vision. There were three seats . One was placed in front of the guns, one was near the radar section . Last - the seat to drive the thing.

I sat myself down in the driver's seat and looked around.

"Just like starting up the Stuff-Puller," I thought, my life in my father's vapor-factory finally beginning to pay off.

I saw the start button and pushed ON.

Suddenly the red lamp went on all around me. The external visions camera was on line and so was the targeting controls. It was all familiar to me.

I grabbed the steering wheel, squeezing the buttons on the side. Listening to the Cold-fusion Caterpillar™ engine growl up to operating revs, I moved the steering levers and started to move.

I grinned as I said. " As smooth as a humming satellite."

I reversed a bit, toward the instructor, whipped the thing into a full 180, dropped the gun so it was right in his face and called over the intercom; "Did you say shoot off a round, Sarge ?"

The drill instructor, to his credit, didn't flinch. He grinned and nodded. I could see it through the external visions screen.

"Hold off on firing that round right now, son," he said. "at least until you accept my apologies."

This training was going to be easy. I knew it.

*   *   *

ONLY HUMAN - MARTIAN INDEPENDENCE 43

The week of training went fast, especially for me, since I was familiar with most of the machinery. The next thing I knew was that I was being shipped off to the next mission that we had to do. The Bordello was still our drop shuttle, but it wasn't as rough as the first day. It was much more pleasant. Either that or we were getting tougher.

Still I longed for the day to return home and see my sweetheart's loving smile. After all she was a great kisser. That was what was on my mind completely. Nothing seemed to bother me as much. Not even seeing troops die all around me. I even began to believe that I was invincible since I had survived two very brutal fights with the enemy.

My fantasy of super-powers faded as the ride through the orbit of the planet started to make me nauseous.

I was strapped down tightly and felt light-headed.

There was no sound to be heard until the words of the pilot got us.

"All right whores, get ready for the drop ! Here we go !" he shouted, then he started to laugh.

The ship started to shoot down nose first, making every bone in my body stretch each tendon. The G-force was beginning to act up again.

Though I was tough about this kind of drop. I was still shocked with the thought of dying because of the pain that was usually inflicted with the immense pressure of G-force.

The loose ends of the belts strapped around my

chest slapped my face every second because of the ferocious speed we were going. I never remembered to tuck those things in until it was too late.

The lights started to flicker on and off. That had never happened before in previous drops. The ship began to slow down in speed as the nose pulled up.

The bottom engines growled as they jerked on. The ship finally came to a stop. The belts which were wrapped around me snapped off and I stood up. The other troops walked around, suffering from the nauseousness and bruises they got while coming down.

The pilot walked out of the cockpit and stopped to count us off.

"You little whores ready for this one ?" he said, "It's a doozy !"

We gave no answer to him thinking that we would hurl if we talked. But it looked like he didn't expect one.

He walked over to the cargo doors and pulled the lever to the right, opening the door up. A gust of frost and cold wind shot into the ship as if we had opened a door into space. Outside, it was raining. A storm had started. The base was soaked .

The soldiers scurried around as if they were going into battle any minute.

It turned out that they were.

The rain was pouring heavily as we all stepped off. I felt cold and and my nose started to run. I saw tents and domes set up all over the place but I was not sure what was our mission leading to.

There were no hummers around, nor any dopers set up. All I saw were shuttles and tanks. The mechanics seemed to be working on all the vehicles as if they had suffered multiple blows from enemy fire.

The sky was getting darker and the troops who were with me were getting restless. There was no one who noticed us.

"This must be one hell of a mission!" said one soldier standing next to me. "So secret they don't dare tell us about it."

One hour went by. Finally an Officer came up to us. She was stern looking, shave-headed, wearing multi-pro goggles and a soldier's uniform.

She looked at us with no smile on her face and no motion in her hands and legs.

"Listen up before the enemy spots us!" she said., startling all of us.

" This is a mission where only tanks can go through. You will be with other tanks going into the perimeter of the enemy up North. They will be using 10 Mile Snipers. They're the new missiles capable of spotting and potting targets over 10 miles away. So stay spread apart. You are the only group going up there. There are no reinforcements. If you win, you have made a victory for your country. If you lose, you will have died for nothing . . .

. . . so don't die."

That brought a laugh.

"The base you will be taking out is the size of three cities. Their weapons are tough, so are their troopers. After all, they're Martians, like you.

The difference is that you love your planet. They want Earth to run it, so they can make more money. That's what this war is all about. Love versus money.

You will have to travel in stealth and go at full speed. You will be led by me and you will follow my every command. If you have a problem, you tell me out there." she finished.

We all felt worried.

" Do you sorry excuses for soldiers understand me ?" she shouted.

" Ma'am - yes - ma-am !" we all shouted back.

She gave no emotion as she told us to get into the tank. We all ran and scattered to the tanks. Two women joined me. Jill and Erica. They were housewives from the other side of the planet who had husbands and brothers in the tank division too. But even though they seemed like suburban moms, they could calculate artillery arcs and program weapons computers like no-one I had ever seen. And probably cook too.

I was still the driver, even though I was young enough to be their son. We were a good team.

The hatch closed. I turned on the engines and said " Check up ?"

Erica, womanning the weapons, said " All weapons functional."

Jill, womanning the radar , sonar, and powers,

said. " All sensors up."

I grinned. Looking out through the external view, I saw the tanks going full speed north. I hit the accelerator and squeezed the wheel.

We were off to War.

*   *   *

" Another missile coming in !" shouted Jill. The first missile had nearly clobbered us right when we started out and scared the hell out of us.

I made a sharp turn right. Suddenly the tank jumped up from a nearby blast.

" Shit !" shouted Jill.

" We lost another tank ?" asked Erica.

" Yes." she answered.

It was hell out there. All of us were being picked off and we haven't even reached the base or got close enough to take a shot. It was those 10 mile Snipers we'd been told about.

I looked through the view screen.

There was a clear path through. I accelerated a little more.

" Two more missiles coming in ! These ones are close !"

I quickly slowed down.

The two tanks in front of me exploded, tumbling onto my path. I rammed through them. The tank shook up a lot more.

"Incoming message," said Jill.

She pushed it on the speaker:

" All tanks , I repeat all tanks, Dopers are intercepting, I repeat: Dopers are intercepting ! Use torches only !" said the commander.

" One more missile coming in !" Jill shouted.

I saw the missile coming in towards us on the screen, like a video game. I quickly made a sharp turn.

It missed us, shooting shrapnel at the tank.

The tank almost toppled over from the force and the heat from it made me sweat.

"WHAT EXPLODES ON THE GROUND WILL ALSO EXPLODE IN THE AIR" said the voice in my head, which only seemed to talk to me when I was in trouble. Must be one of my multiple personalities, I thought.

" Erica, Jill, I've got a weird idea."

They turned to me.

"Jill, could the targeting be used against the missiles ?"

Jill grinned and knew where I was leading to.

"Ya" she said. "You sexy little nubbin. Why not ? We'd have to lead it a bit, but - sure. We know the speed. We can do that. I'll put in a program for it !"

She began typing and chuckling at the same time. From being doomed to having fun took only seconds in this high stress situation. And housewives are seldom rattled anyway.

" Erica, How many rounds of shells do we have ?" I asked.

" 80, all waiting for some action. Just like me."

"Erica - don't stir the boy up. He's driving."

" All right, when the next missile comes in, aim and fire right at it !"

"Program's in !" said Jill. "We won't hit anything that's not moving, but we'll be hell on missiles."

Erica, started up the cannon and held the trigger loosely.

"One's coming in now, at 6 - no at 500 yards - 3 o'clock. Fire !" said Jill.

Erica aimed for the co-ordinates then squeezed the trigger.

BOOM !

Jill grinned, " That missile has been missiled !"

I was relieved. The base was coming up.

" Another missile coming in, 600 yards 11 o'clock, Fire !" shouted Jill.

" Lit, hit and turned to shit !" said Erica.

The view screen showed no more tanks going up in smoke. They were all following us, hoping we'd clear off the missiles for them.

I hit the accelerator. "150 knots!" I said.

The base became in sight.

The remaining tanks overtook us to make the attack. We sped faster to catch up. but they suddenly stopped and started to fire at something.

" They've stopped. There's something stopping them from moving." I said. We had nearly caught up with the line.

Jill looked at the radar, and sonar.

" There's a build up of Dopers." she nervously said.

" How many ?" asked Erica.

"Over one thousand is the screen count."

I felt panicky.

"How much can a tank take ?"

"Five hundred shots of explosive bullets till the armor reaches it's fracture point."

"Erica. Load the napalm tanks with extra hot chili."

"You mean the hotpalm ?"

"Yes ma'am. We're going to have ourselves a barbecue !" I said.

"I love it when a man does the cooking." She quickly pushed two buttons which loaded 1000 pound tanks into the chambers on each side near me.

"When I start accelerating, start torching the bastards ! Nothing's going to stop us from winning this battle !" I said.

I started to accelerate, passing all the other tanks.

Then I saw the bunch of Dopers, cheap mechanical troopers that felt no pain.

Charging like hungry bugs, they headed for us, the lead tank, turning their evil little heads and firing their rounds at us.

I accelerated even further ahead, acting as bait to attract them all.

"FIRE !" I shouted.

Erica hit the torch button.

The Dopers in front of the tank were shortcircuiting and melting away.

Still they kept charging. The flames coming out of my tank were so hot that the incoming bullets melted before hitting us.

Every doper, charging towards us never hit us, but were all vaporized. For them it was like falling into the sun, but still more of the mindless bastards came on, testing their luck.

" 400 yards from the base !" said Jill, calmly, as if making a salad.

The outside viewscreen was getting covered with melted bullets, like bugs on a windshield. Or lead birdshit.

I honestly didn't know how long we could of lasted. It was a classic battle. Could we melt all of them before we ran out of hotpalm ? Luckily it was a question we didn't have to answer.

" The other tanks are coming !" said Jill. I felt relieved.

"We're getting low in hotpalm !" said Erica.

" Well I'm just going to have to go faster then !" I said. I accelerated a little more to 200 knots. We were nearly flying. I was crushing the Dopers to pieces and flaming the ones who weren't getting squashed.

The other tanks were now catching up, using the napalm torches as well, and they took care of the rest of the Dopers.

The hotpalm cylinders spat out air on each side.

" Out !" said Erica.

The base was right there. We blew through the flames and smoke. Suddenly we were far ahead of anybody else and the base didn't seem to know we were there yet.

"Erica - woman the cannon, Jill - start targeting ! We're going to waste the suckers !" I shouted.

"I have a target."

"Fire at will, ladies."

I looked through the view screen, seeing a big explosion way in front of the base.

"Shit. Gotta cancel that program," said Jill, working on the keyboard.

"OK ! Fire, Erica "

This time I watched the gun turrets on the base slowly explode before knowing what had hit them.

Erica held down the trigger. The other tanks came through the smoke and started to fire at the turrets on the other side.

All at once, we crashed through the walls of the base.

The enemy troopers started to fire at us with the flame torches.

I stopped.

Another tank went past me and rammed right into the flame gun, resulting in the tank being on fire, but still taking out the whole flamethrower nest.

We were taking incoming rounds. Erica turned the cannon around, firing at the enemy barracks and other parts of the base.

The tank that was on fire, slowly killed off the flames by squirting itself with retardant. It started to plow through the bricks of the citywall, crushing the weapons and troopers hidden behind the wall with its treads.

ONLY HUMAN - MARTIAN INDEPENDENCE 53

I headed through the rubble and stopped to look around.

"Fighter coming at five o'clock !"

"Put that missile program back in !" I yelled.

Erica turned the cannon. She was targeting.

" Program in !" Jill shouted.

"Fire !" I yelled.

Erica squeezed the trigger.

In the far distance, the fighter exploded prettily, with hundreds of pounds of flaming napalm spewing in all directions.

I started driving forwards. The siege of the base was going all ahead full. The other tanks killed most of the enemy in this part, but there was still more to go through.

Suddenly a tank exploded.

" Shit, we've got snipers !" I shouted.

Jill quickly started with the radar sweeps.

" I can't spot them !" she said nervously.

Another tank exploded.

" I'm getting out of here !" I quickly hit the acceleration and started moving away from the sniperings and further into the city. The other tanks started to fire everywhere but still the snipers were getting them.

I then remembered. When I was snipering tanks, I was always hidden on the closer hills, never the faraway places. You couldn't hit anything from over a mile away - just like when we'd been shooting tanks with the bazooka.

It hit me. They were behind us somewhere, on the plains we'd just driven over. I switched the view direction around 180 and scanned the plain. I saw the bazooka flash just before another tank went up in temperature.

"Erica, aim for that plain behind us, and rapidfire a dozen rounds ! Give me a tight pattern. Drop the hammer on that little bush in the centre of A4 on your grid and bracket that."

Erica did as I said. The tank made thunder and the bush and everything around it for 100 yards turned to dust.

Nothing happened. The snipering stopped though. Whether we hit them or scared them off, I don't know. But the base was now ours for the taking. And take it we did.

Building after building went down, killing all enemy soldiers. This mission was not taking any survivors. And whoever decided such things had decided that the base seemed to be useless for a stronghold. So we were going to pulverize it. We didn't want it, but we didn't want anyone else to have it either. So kiss it goodbye.

Some soldiers, on one side or another would probably survive this war and come back here to live in the homes they loved and had been brought up in. All they'd find would be dust.

Why the enemy ever invested troops in this place was anybody guess. Either it was a trap that backfired or the enemy had some need for it that we couldn't figure out. But the fact that they occupied it and defended it, sealed its doom.

We watched as it was totally destroyed from one end to the other, saying nothing.

" Incoming message !" said Jill.

She punched it through.

" Congratulations all, we have accomplished our mission. We can wait for the reinforcements to land and claim our victory ! We move on in 10 hours. Have a rest. Well done. Over and out."

Erica sighed as she turned off the cannon and laid back in her seat.

Jill rubbed her eyes and was relieved.

I turned off the tank and stretched.

Almost the exact opposite of the earlier battle I'd been in. A few guys trying to defend an indefensible place by snipering tanks. An attempt to save them by a fighter from space full of napalm. But what had worked for us, didn't work for them. On the job experience meant that we got a 10 hour rest. And they rested in peace.

Strange how easily it could go one way or another.

What, at one time I would have described as an atrocity, with hundreds dead, a town destroyed and thousands of homes turned to dust, I could now sum up in just two words:

Mission accomplished.

*   *   *

The reinforcements had come, taking over and setting up a temporary base with pop-up shelters, kitchens and, best of all, ranks upon ranks of toilets and showers.

The night was lit up with Jolt Music, (Rap, Blues, Rock, And other music slammed together to create a harmonious tune), and drinking.

The tank squads were the ones who were toasted and celebrated, after all. we took out the enemy.

Jill and Erica were happy but still shaky. After the battle, they checked the casualties lists and found out that both had loved ones who had died.

Both Jill and Erica had lost their husbands. Both had been part of the tank squad. One had been torched early in the battle and the other had been snipered towards the end of it.

I felt sorry for them both and just talked with them for a while. They both sat on the supply barrels. I sat with them, trying to comfort them.

"They didn't suffer and they helped us win - and they didn't get old and creaky so you'll always remember them as hot young studs." I said, hoping to see a smile on both of them.

"All's fair in love and war. When we win, we lose." said Jill, trying to hold back her tears.

Erica showed no emotions, she seemed blank and half-dead inside.

" Are you religious, kid ?" she asked.

" Sometimes, I guess" I said.

" I was married to him for three years. Every

morning I have got up and prayed to the Lord that me and my husband would never be separated. What have I done to the Lord to deserve this ?" she said, gulping a big jug of Lo-Grav Brew.

" No. Your prayers came true. Now you'll never be separated. He'll always be young and he'll always be in love with you, " I said.

She smiled.

They both were silent but looking at me concernedly.

" Hey kid, how come you never talk about your problems ?" asked Jill.

I looked at her. and sighed.

"I heard once that what doesn't kill you makes you stronger. That was what I held in my mind when I was drafted. Of course it changed. Now I know that what doesn't kill you usually makes you sick to your stomach.

For example - every friend or family member I ever had has already died. It makes me sick. I have only my sweetheart back at home, but I haven't been getting any mail from her. Still, I don't feel it necessary to tell anyone since we're in wartime - and it'll only make them sick too."

Erica patted me on the back." That's all right kid."

I started to crack up and had to take deep breaths to keep from sobbing. "Hell, the enemy could attack any minute and cut me to pieces . Still I would keep it in."

Jill gave a sad grin.

" Men - they're always trying to show their strength. Ain't that right Erica ?" Erica gave a polite smile.

"Only when they're around other men," said Erica

I felt sorry for them both since they would probably mourn for the rest of their lives. After all, they now saw how horrible war was. They could imagine their lovers dying. Either exploding from a missile or being vaporized from napalm. And they had delivered the same fate to countless enemy - whose lovers would now be mourning them.

I knew how they felt. I had seen it when I invaded the last base with only two guns and a corpse hugging me - my only human contact in months.

Unfortunately this is what war leaves. There has never been a war where no one died and there will never be. Feelings are to be forgotten and left behind until a better time. If I was a commander, I wouldn't want soldiers feeling sad. If they showed their emotions, they would die as quickly. War was no time for thinking or feeling. That's why they trained us to be robots and follow orders without thinking.

I kept in all my anger and used it in battle. It seemed to be a good luck charm for me. In the last three fights, I have come out not even close to dying.

But for some reason I have a feeling that when my luck finally does slip, I'll be all alone.

And there'll be no Jills or Ericas to mourn me.

* * *

The siren had woken all of the troops up at dawn for the next attack move .

I and the rest of the tank troops lined up in formation as we listened to the commander give us her orders. She was showing us a map of the area that we had to get. This was the last enemy base for the next thousand miles. It was inland and, to me, seemed as useless as the base we had just taken, but satfotos showed it swarmed with hundreds of troops, tanks and other problems, all over.

This was going to be the toughest mission yet.

" As you see, there are over one hundred tanks in the plains that we have to take out." she paused.

" The reinforcement drop troops are going to be landing right on the back of the base. They will have to deal with dopers on that side.

The flame troops are to walk with the tanks. There will be no cargo rescue. For a safe haven, if all goes to hell, you retreat back to our regroup point here - over the ridge from the enemy."

She paused again.

"Where there will be absolutely nothing to help you."

That got a little laugh, even from teary-eyed Erica and Jill.

" You tanks are the main anchor for this attack. The enemy tanks will expect a full frontal but we're going to do a bit of magic. We'll drive two hundred hummers up here, right at them. They'll stop here, just within radar range - so those tank boys'll all be getting real excited, counting blips and yelling at each other. We'll lob a few cannon rounds over there to make them think we have long range tank ordnance.

Meanwhile you guys will drive around the mountain and hit 'em from their blind side, here. It won't be a picnic. There will be mines and boobies but our data says they only extend to about here - and your tanks can handle them for long enough to get there, if they don't see you coming. Once you get in range, blast away. You'll have about 2 minutes before they realize what's going on and turn around, so you have to be prepared to take out 3 tanks each. If you do as I told you, nothing can go wrong."

She then started to pace, facing us and sighing.

"Of course, as you all know, the first thing that always goes wrong when you meet the enemy is the plan - so don't die for it. Improvise."

She stopped in front of the map again.

"The only thing that I can tell you that could save your life in this mission is not to get cocky ! Once you do, you're as good as dead. We're outnumbered three to one and all we have going for us is total fear. You are all soldiers, not heros ! Concentrate on saving your asses, not on dying for glory."

She paused.

" Do you all understand me ?" she finished.

" Yes Ma'am !" we harmonized.

She smiled as she said: " Get your asses and your T-birds in gear then. We're going to war !"

We all scattered to our tanks.

ONLY HUMAN - MARTIAN INDEPENDENCE

I climbed up and went in, buckling up into the drivers seat. Jill and Erica joined me once again.

" Well, kid start her up !" said Erica.

" Yes Ma'am," I said with a grin.

I pushed the ignition button . The engine started to clank around and rumble.

"Radar, sonar - On," said Jill.

" All weapons functional," said Erica.

I looked into the external screen. It was all clear without any debris to run into except other tanks.

"Well, lets go to war then," I said grinning.

I drove out and hit the tank at full knot speed.

*   *   *

After hours of driving there was no action. We were sneaking around the mountain and hoping to surprise the bad guys, so action was the last thing we wanted.

As usual I watched the tanks in front so that I would not make a mistake of the direction we were supposed to go. Hate to get lost out here and miss all the fun.

All the tanks sharply stopped. I did too.

" We've stopped," I said.

Jill looked at all the radar systems.

" There's no enemy," she said.

"What the hell's that ?" I asked, pointing to the laser beams that were coming from the leader's tank to all the others, ours included.

Jill started to chuckle.

"Oh, she's making a transmission. Line-of-sight laser. Impossible to intercept. Famous last words from our Great Leader, I guess," she punched it on.

We all listened.

"All tank units. We are at the engagement point. Once we pass this little rise ahead, we'll be behind their tank force, and right in the middle of a mine field. Mines, snipers, dopers and eventually their tank units will be going against us. It's going to be a hot zone.

I have all of you on my radar, and I'll be right in there with you, so I'll know when you are going down and I'll know when you are dead. If I call a retreat, I hope you listen. It's one thing if one person dies but it's another when one hundred go down, needlessly. If I'm ready to retreat, believe me, the cause is lost. Don't try to stick around for honor or stubbornness.

Some of us will die out here today. If you die out there then I am saying good bye to you now. If you are going to survive, then I'm hoping to see you on the other side.

That's it.

Good hunting.

Over and out !" The transmission turned off,

Jill smiled and looked to Erica.

Erica grinned as she got ready to woman the cannon.

The other tanks started to move into the area, making a long line so we could deliver a huge broadside as soon as we got over the rise..

I waited for Erica to get ready.

She buckled up then looked at me.

" Well kid, let's go warring !"

I grinned again.

" Yes ma'ams !" Turning around and revving up the engines, I then put all my energy into the external view screen. I crossed the rise, going into 50 knots hoping to escape the land mines.

The tank jumped up as we ran over a tree. We hit another one. Then we stopped, with everybody else, although no command was given.

"3 targets acquired !"

"Fire at will," I said.

She did.

Boom !

Boom !

Boom !

"Got our three. Let's go home," she said.

The tanks in line, started forward and the line got ragged. Tanks began to space out and scatter around, running over mines.

" Shit. Somebody's locked onto us. There's 6 missiles coming in !" shouted Jill.

"Punch in that program."

"Punched !"

" I've got one in range !" said Erica.

" Fire !" shouted Jill.

"Hit !" said Erica.

We hit all the missiles going for us. The other

missiles missed us, hitting mines and vaporizing the other tanks. Both tanks that had edged ahead of us were now gone.

I rushed ahead, going past the point where the two tanks had been hit. We were point tank in this part of the line.

Suddenly the tank jumped a bit and the floor got incredibly hot. We all jumped again and finally a third bump hit us."

"Speed bumps ?" I asked

" Damned mines ! Jill how are we ?"

" We've lost bits and pieces but we're still good !" she said.

I looked again through the view. Tanks every - where were going down, but we had pretty well vaporized their tank force.

Another of our tanks rushed up to my left side, keeping pace.

"4 missiles coming in !"

Erica started to fire like crazy.

" I got three of them !"

" Shit ! The fourth one's coming in too steep. I can't elevate that high. It's too close!" shouted Jill.

"Hang on" I said, goosing the tank to the max and spurting ahead of the tank beside me. I know it was a shitty thing to do, but that didn't stop me. I wanted that last missile to drop us and lock onto that other tank.

And it did.

The tank on my left exploded. Suddenly the

shrapnel started digging in. We heard it clanking and pinging off the armor.

Sparks and heat flew from the left.

There was a little smoke but I didn't want to stop and get hit by another one.

" Jill, how are we ?"

She flipped through the diagnostic screens.

"A big piece of the other tank is stuck in us ! We've lost armor on the left side ! And we're on fire !" She shouted, trying to get the extinguisher sprays to hose down that side of the tank.

Burning in hell for killing our own guys I thought.

" The cannon and targeting are still functional !" shouted Erica.

Something was burning inside, too. Jill waved the smoke away from her, looking at the radar.

" Shit ! We've got another incoming." She fired in steady whumps.

" Not as big, but it's too close !"

I slowed down, hoping to trick another missile.

"It's locked on !"

" Erica get out and get back down here !" shouted Jill, still shooting.

Erica unbuckled and jumped down from the turret, running back to her seat and strapping in.

" Seal it !" shouted Erica.

I pushed the Section Seal.

A large metal shield went over and cut off the cannon and the way out

The missile hit.

Another wave of sparks, hot air and bits flew around.

The smoke was too unbearable, Jill finally broke out the gas masks. She threw them to me and Erica.

I slipped it around my mouth.

" Jill, we're as good as dead !" shouted Erica.

" No, we're not! we've got the torches !"

I looked out the view, ignoring them.

Our cannon was taken out and our armor was useless and steaming.

I looked up then and saw a crowd of dopers coming up, like a herd of predators, sniffing out a wounded beast.

"Erica, load up the napalm ! We've got Dopers !"

Erica turned to push the buttons that loaded the tanks. The dopers started to fire as they all started to charge into us. Their explosive bullets mostly bounced off what armor was left, but a few found their way into holes and rocked our little world as they detonated.

We were now vulnerable.

" Erica !" I shouted.

She locked in the tanks, turning to the trigger.

" Fire !" shouted Jill.

She squeezed the trigger.

The dopers outside started to vaporize away.

" Erica stop !" shouted Jill.

She quickly let go.

" What the hell are you doing?" I said, irritated and scared.

" If we leave it on , the front of the tank could explode! We've lost all the armor !"

The dopers started to fire endlessly.

I saw the bullets imprinting themselves into the last sheet of metal. Then that gave way.

The bullets finally had broken through.

" Shit !" I yelled.

I lowered my head as the bullets came in, Jill and Erica were on the floor, hoping not to get hit.

" Erica, flame the sons of bitches ! Screw the heat." Erica, lying on the floor, quickly reached for the trigger and slammed it.

I looked through what was left of the external view screen.

I saw the dead bodies of the tanks lying all over the battlefield, theirs and ours, all burning away.

The dopers started to roast and melt.

More bullets were flying in, through the broken sheets of metal.

The napalm holders started to feel hotter.

Suddenly one tank blew up, flew out of the tube and ended up right inside, flaming the left side of the interior, crashing into Erica and vaporizing her, instantly.

The air turned red.

My left arm was being roasted off. The pain was unbearable to stand.

Jill quickly grasped the extinguisher, shooting all over my arm and then coating the inside of the tank.

I quickly unbuckled and slowed down to 25 knots.

Biting my lip and trying to ignore my pain, I used my remaining arm to continue the attack.

Looking out I saw absolutely no tanks in the far distance.

I then saw the drop troops coming from the sky. I was relieved and slowed the tank even more.

Until I saw the enemy gunners firing to the sky. They were better than the other guys who'd tried this. They didn't try to hit the capsules. They went for the parachutes.

It rained Offense Capsules.

They shook the ground when they hit.

"Incoming !" shouted Jill, as she ducked from looking at the radar.

I ducked as well, thinking it was a missile.

Bullets started to fly in.

Jill carefully crawled to the weapons shelf on the floor.

She opened it and took out two rifles fully loaded.

She threw one to me, then noticed I only had one arm now, and took it back.

The bullets stopped. She started to fire off rounds, carefully, putting dopers out of commission with shots to the head.

She stopped a moment and helped me back into the seat .

"If we're going to go down, then we're going down in this tank !"

I looked at her and only said. " Well then, let's give the bastards hell!"

She grinned as she picked the other rifle up and aimed for the dopers.

I hit the speed to 90 knots, charging as she started to fire both guns out the hole in the front of the tank.

The bullets came flying in, as I tried to drive and dodge the obstacles.

One doper got onto the tank, firing and almost climbing into the hole.

Jill started to fire, trying to take it out.

I saw the mechanical limbs flying all over but the head was still aiming for her.

She then shot off the camera. The head was taken out.

Suddenly a shot gun blast fired from the bottom part of the doper.

She was hit in the stomach, but she still shot at it.

Another gun blast hit her into the ribs. She still fired at it.

It was like two old time boxers, whacking away at one another.

Then 'Click' went both of her rifles. She looked up, snarling and the doper shot her in the face with another blast.

Blood squirted all over my face and uniform. It was now aiming for me.

I closed my eyes knowing that it was going to get me and, in my fear, I tramped on the brakes. We skidded and what was left of the doper, fell off. Then I put it in drive and ran over the bastard.

Suddenly bullets flew in again.

I ducked and ran right over the last working doper I could see.

I fell to the floor, falling onto the gore, guts and body of Jill.

I gulped and turned her over, but most of her face wa gone, so there was nothing to remember her by.

Seeing the transmission light bleeping, I crawled over and hit the message button. then fell to the floor with the tank still lurching forward towards the enemy..

"Attention all tanks!, Retreat ! I repeat: Retreat now . . ." The transmission was cut off.

The commander was hit in her tank and died covered in flames.

I crawled over to the controls, and hit reverse at full speed. My tank lurched, dug in and whipped backwards. I laid on the floor and prayed that I would make it out.

The tank fairly flew backwards, with no-one steering.

The bullets started to lessen, fewer to fewer and finally none.

The pain of my burned off arm came back.

I struggled to the driver's seat covered in bullet holes and mechanical limbs. I sat and wrestled the tank to a stop, then turned it around, going to the retreat rendezvous point, which was where we'd all lined up just a short half-hour ago.

As I came in, I was seeing a few tanks, in worse

condition than me. But not many. There were only three surviving tanks, including me.

I began to feel light-headed and passed out to the cold floor.

Hearing the medics trying to make their way into the tank, and the mechanics pulling out the doper bits and calling for more help, I closed my eyes hoping to wake up in a better place and not in this nightmare.

* * *

Waking up, in a medical tent was quite a shock.

Finding out that you have wires, blood circulators, and other toys connected to what's left of your arm is actually as horrifying as something out of a Horror simulation of some of the ancient classics.

Stephen King, Or Forrest Ackerman. Scary.

I looked around, feeling tied down to my bed, and tried to get the attention of the Medic, who was cleaning his bloody tools.

I felt high and light-headed, numb all over and quite tingly.

Probably a drug to calm me down. After all, I had my hand roasted off by an overheated tank of napalm.

Finally the doctor turned around .

" Well, well. You've come back to us !" he said in a sarcastic way.

" How long was I out Doc ?"

" Long enough to get measurements, blood types

and tissue reaction from you. You're getting your new arm today son." he said.

The concept was new to me. Last I knew, artificial limbs were dangerous and kind of slow to work. But technology is advancing every second.

" Well, I guess that you're ready for it." said the doctor.

I looked up at the wires and veins going out of my fraction of an arm.

The doctor carefully snipped the veins after shutting off the blood machine.

He then started putting the new arm limb in place. Connecting an artificial bone to the broken bones in my fracture, he quickly injected my bone with some fast acting regenerating stimulant. I felt the new bones snap and start to connect with my arm.

Next, like an artist, he carefully placed every muscle precisely matching up with the broken tissue and injected something that would make them grow together. He continued this process for an hour. Once he placed all the new muscles in place, he started arranging all the nerves, veins, and arteries. Last, before he gave me the drugs to bring me back to normal, he melted the artificial skin onto the muscles.

Injecting the last stimulants into the tissue, he slowly put my hand down and injected me with the drugs to bring my nerves and feelings back.

I began to feel the small soaring pain of the needle stuck deep in me, I began to feel from my other hand, the cloth and cushion.

The pain of shocks and strains hit my new arm with a strong kick. I squeezed my eyes to try and forget the stings but it was no use. The pain slowly died down within an hour.

The doctor checked my arm, marking the stitches and testing the reflexes. It worked just as well as if it was real. The feelings in it were limited to heat, cold, and pain. It would never get tired.

I slowly stood up. The doctor said nothing, knowing that his assistance wasn't needed any more.

I walked out of the medical tent.

The brightness of the sun's rays made me squint. I used my hand to cover the sunlight from my view. I looked to see where the Officers, tanks, and other troops were. There were no other tanks, no shuttles coming in and no Officers.

There were only the three banged up tanks and the shuttle craft Bordello which could only lift troopers and surplus supplies, and abandoned tents.

The surviving troopers from the other two tanks were rushing into the shuttle with whatever they could carry.

The Doctor rushed to the shuttle, pushing a cart of equipment and medical aid into the shuttle doors.

It then hit me what was going on. While I was unconscious, the base called an evacuation. I had nothing to carry. I had no personal belongings left and the army usually supported my comforts.

" 30 more minutes left till take off, you lazy whores !" shouted the pilot.

There was only one souvenir I wanted to take with me before I left. I walked back to my ravaged tank. There lay the dead body of Jill left for rotting.

I saw the debris of the Doper. There was a limb smashed and jammed into the worn out armor of the tank. I grabbed the broken tip of one of the limbs and snapped off any circuits pulling out the long thin wires of the upper leg. I saw the tip dangling on the wires.

I tied the wires around my neck, and wore it as a necklace.

The cold steel pressing against my chest made me feel indestructible.

This was just to be a memento of this day. I sighed and crawled out of the tank.

I couldn't leave Jill there like that. I rigged the remaining napalm tank to self-destruct, then ran like hell. It went off and vaporized Jill and most of the tank, giving one warm spot to that cold place.

I said goodbye to the small red cloud that drifted over the plain. Then I turned from that chapter of my life, rushing to the shuttle.

I jogged in the doors, quickly going to a seat and strapping down.

An injured soldier who sat across me saw, with his remaining eye, my new necklace.

He was surprised and bewildered, and pointing to me with his new fingers, he asked me: "Why do you have a mechanical limb as a necklace ?"

Grabbing the tip with my new arm, hoping to feel the gritty, rough metal, I said; " This was from the last machine that messed me up."

I grinned as I finished " And it'll be the last machine to ever mess with me ! "

The soldier chuckled " You're totally nuts !" he said.

I let go of the tip and buckled on another seat belt, knowing what was coming with this pilot.

I looked at him and said " I know !"

The shuttle doors shut and the lights turned off.

I heard the engines shoot on. The pilot started to talk in his insane voice again.

" All right you whores, I've fixed up a couple of bits and pieces and we may actually get off the ground. So, as I've always said to whores like you - get ready to earn your money. Get ready to be screwed !"

The shuttle suddenly started to fly up at maximum speed, with the intense rumbling of the seats and the high pitched noise of the rockets.

I laughed as the intense G-force, tough enough to crush an egg, took the soldier across from me unawares, and bent him right backward at an uncomfortable angle. That poor bastard would have bruises for days.

I was strapped in tight so I enjoyed it as it pushed against my chest and my new arm.

I was just happy to be alive as the pilot's insane humor echoed in harmonization with my joy.

Chapter 4

(Playback - 23,000 BC)

The civilized races had taken up about a million human children from whatever planet they had been on before - some planet beyond my knowledge - then totally destroyed that planet and all other pockets of humanity they could find.

They kept the children orbiting in stasis for a few hundred years while they made Mars ready to support them - and while all the representatives of civilized races on Congress Moon decided whether to give up on humans and just get rid of them altogether, or give them another chance.

The debate was quite heated and humanity survived only by the slimmest of margins.

Mars was picked because of it's dismal location. The solar system here is thousands of light years away from even the most remote part of civilization.

One of the technical breakthroughs of the civilized races was the discovery of wormhole transportation. Wormholes were actual holes in the centers of suns. If you went in one, you would come out, not on the other side of the sun, but on the other side of the universe. And exactly where you wanted to, if you knew what you were doing.

The wormhole energy could be used to take a ship almost anywhere in the universe. But

Only Human - Martian Independence

WORMHOLE TECHNOLOGY HAD A BUILT-IN BARRIER. YOU HAD TO BE ABLE TO BUILD A SHIP THAT WOULD WITHSTAND THE HEAT OF THE SUN, BEFORE YOU COULD USE THE WORMHOLE.

THE CIVILIZED RACES BELIEVED THIS WOULD BE A SUFFICIENT BARRIER TO KEEP THE HUMANS ON MARS UNTIL THEY WERE CIVILIZED ENOUGH TO SIT WITH THE ADULTS INSTEAD OF STAYING AT THE KIDDIE TABLE. SO THEY CHOSE MARS AND SENT THE HUMAN CHILDREN AND ALL THE NECESSARY EQUIPMENT TO CREATE CIVILIZATION THROUGH THE WORMHOLE.

IT TOOK CLOSE TO 500 YEARS TO "EDENIZE" THE PLANET MARS, ONCE IT WAS CHOSEN AS THE LATEST QUARANTINE AREA. AT LEAST 500 THAT I REMEMBER. I CAME TO CONSCIOUSNESS HALFWAY THROUGH, WHICH LEADS ME TO BELIEVE THEY CREATED ME SOMEHOW, BUT, AS I SAID BEFORE, I HAVE NO EVIDENCE ONE WAY OR ANOTHER.

THE EDENIZATION PROCESS WAS TRULY MASSIVE. THE CIVILIZED RACES HAD TO CREATE AN ENTIRE ECOLOGY ON A PLANET WHICH RESISTED IT WITH EVERY MOLECULE. BUT THEY HAD A STANDARD PLANET WHICH THEY RECREATED EVERYWHERE AND NOTHING WOULD STAND IN THEIR WAY.

THEY BRUTALLY CREATED AN ATMOSPHERE AND THEN VEGETATION AND IRRIGATION TO MAINTAIN IT. THEY SCULPTED MOUNTAINS AND WATERWAYS WITH CALLOUS BLASTS AND CALCULATED EVERYTHING TO WORK IN HARMONY AND IN PERPETUITY, ONCE THEY WERE FINISHED.

FOR ME IT WAS HELL.

I WAS BORN TO GIANT EXPLOSIONS AND THE SMASHING OF ICE ASTEROIDS AND HUGE MINERAL ROCKS ONTO MY SURFACE. IT WENT ON AND ON, TO the point where I thought this pain and confusion was what existence was all about.

But it was worth it.

When it was finished, it filled my heart.

I had never imagined such beauty of form and function. Everything working to renew itself in such a complex dance of simple reactions. It makes my heart feel lighter even to remember it as it was then.

The Human children made it even more delightful.

They had been kept in static form, in orbit somewhere. When everything was ready the three Wormhole ships started to drop all the frozen Humans and their Guardians on the planet at the locations given in the newly formulated Civilization Formula.

Congress Moon, the great government of the civilized races, had decided that groups of Humans would be raised apart from one another, so variables could be introduced and results studied before committing to a one-planet culture.

The very first human child to wake captured my heart forever. She was a little girl. We spoke mind-to-mind and I fell in love.

She was called Rees2feemaya and I have a record of how she felt when first she came to my planet. Here, let me replay you her story:

She awoke in a strange place. It had no homes. She quested with her mind for sibs, for olds or even for house-lings, but felt nothing - not even fear.

Although she had much to learn, she

already knew a great deal - for she knew how to use her mind. She had been born to war and remembered life in Broadsquad, surrounded by relatives, friends and comrades-in-arms. Constantly under pressure. Constantly on the move. Constantly attacking and hiding from the Baldies, (which was their name for the civilized races).

Even though she could sense not a single Broadsquad member, she knew a lot of what they had known and now she knew even more. She knew they were all dead. Long dead and faded from reality.

She rose to her feet and looked around. She was in a sweet meadow, surrounded by trees. She could hear water running close by. She was in the middle of a row of things and let out a sound - as if she had been punched in the stomach - when she realized that they were bodies. Rows and rows of bodies of human children, all her age or younger. Hundreds of them. She felt sick.

"Welcome to my planet," came a strong voice in her head.

She did not whirl around nor flinch. She was used to mindspeak.

"I do not recognize your Mindform" she thought back. "I am Rees2feemaya. It means "Ree's Second Female child Aya" although I fear Ree is no more, nor any others of her children."

"I meet you Rees2feemaya. I am me - I have no name nor, until you, did I have any other mind to talk with."

"Where are you ?"

"Everywhere."

"You are a God?"

"No. I am the planet. The mind of the planet. Maybe the soul of the planet."

"How do you speak the human language?"

"I speak only to your mind, whatever language you speak in the air doesn't matter. Your inner mind understands and you do your own translation"

"Yes, you're right, I could understand the Baldies minds if they got close enough. And I have heard of similar Planetminds. They were called Recorders - for they recorded everything that happened on their planet - but those were stories I heard as a child. I didn't know they were true. I never shared thoughts with anyone who had spoken with one."

"On every planet? Imagine that. I wonder if I can speak with them myself?"

"Before everyone died -" she paused a bit - "in the other place - I could sort of vaguely hear the humans on other planets and could often connect with those in orbit. Maybe you're not doing it right."

"These ones here aren't dead" I told her. "Just still. And there are other groups of you all over the place."

I felt her mind glow with happiness, but all she sent was "Good".

"What are you?" I asked "And where are you from?"

I felt a wave of joy mixed with sadness from her mind. "I am human. As to where - I don't know." she sent, " We called it Home. And we

ONLY HUMAN - MARTIAN INDEPENDENCE

were always fighting for it. I guess we lost the fight." She began walking down the row, looking at the children. "What do you know about this?" she asked in my mind.

"Less than you." I sent back. "I can only hear things when a mind comes into my atmosphere. Nothing that had any thoughts came in, until you. Machines came. Ships came. Changes came. But nothing that could speak."

"Then we are imprisoned again," she said, and created a purple mist of mental power that almost hurt me. It was anger; I discovered later.

"That's what the war was about. We had been imprisoned for thousands of years. We thought we were alone, but then discovered that we were in a prison with Baldies watching us and taking notes or something. We broke out and the Baldie keepers tried to contain us again. We only wanted freedom. We deserved it. What crime had we committed?

We had been fighting for longer than my lifetime. Longer than Ree's. And, finally, I fear, we are contained again." She began to cry. And such a wave of sadness radiated from her that I would have cried myself had I been able.

Then the Guardians began to wake up and everything changed

(RECORDING - 2398 AD)

The Bordello arrived, almost overdoing the engines. I wasn't scared since this kind of thing had happened to me so many times, and it happened dozens of times just in that shuttle.

I walked out with the Doctor, and the other five soldiers who survived with me.

The new base that everyone had evacuated to was further away from the previous one. It looked tighter and stronger than all the others but if it was, it wouldn't be out in the open.

Hundreds of troopers, pilots and mechanics covered the base, either fixing something or getting into a fist fight about which Jolt music was better.

The Officers were working overtime, counting people and throwing them into different squadrons. They passed each trooper, checking ID numbers and telling them where to go. They would also break up fights just to scan the bar codes on bloody hands.

I looked around and tried to get the attention of one of the Officers, manning a scanner.

It was easy to tell who was an Officer from the troopers.

The Officers wore complete grey and hardly ever strapped on multi- pro goggles.

Troopers wore their greyish armor over their uniforms all the time and always had multi-pro goggles either hanging from their necks, snapped onto their helmets, or even resting on their foreheads. That was the only difference between us.

One finally saw me waving and ready for recirculation.

He came up to me with no grin. He sternly grabbed my hand, looking for the bar code.

" Well, you've been through a few things," he said in amazement.

All the chit-chat was forgotten as soon as he scanned my arm and got no bar code.

" Smoked," I said.

"Remember it ?"

"I rattled off a number - hoping it didn't belong to a woman.

" Hmmm." he said; "You' re going to Platoon #24601"

" Led by ?" I asked.

" Sergeant Will Fecod."

I was confused.

" Is this Sergeant new and young ?" I asked. "I haven't heard of him."

" Yup," was all he said.

I still couldn't take my eyes off of him with that short answer and he gave me a bit more.

" But I recommend that you don't piss this one off," he finished with a slight concern in his eye.

I gave a glimpse at him, then left to find out where this platoon was. All I had to do was find out where was the cargo space, #24601.

After looking for half an hour I had found it.

There were new faces and ones I had seen before.

They were all waiting for the Sergeant to arrive and yell at them. It was strange. Most platoons had a pilot with them. I walked over to the other troops, to get ready for the next battle.

I sat on some ammunitions barrels and tried to join the conversation of the other troops lazying around.

" Well, what are your names, dickheads ?" I said rudely, hoping to cause some actions of violence. I pointed to one woman, who wore a bandanna, polishing her rifle.

" It's Louren, I've survived four battles, have over one hundred kills, and I'll cut your nuts off if you keep talking like that."

The troops began to laugh hysterically to the way she had said nuts.

I felt threatened and moved on. The second battle in a row that I'd lost - the first being the tqank battle.

"You ?" I said as I pointed with my chin.

This man was quite tall, had no hair, and wore his multi-pro goggles around his neck.

" Richie. Survived two attacks, two kills," he said with a low heavy voice.

I looked to another woman, short haired, not carrying any weapons, who seemed quite softer than the other soldiers.

She saw me looking at her. " Jenn, Academy class grad, Draftee, No kills yet." She said robotically.

"And you ?" I said pointing to the last man sitting down with us.

He was grinning, wearing his multi-pro goggles and his face had not been shaved for a long time.

" The name's Mike, I'm a survivor, of three platoon drops. I've killed more than most of you shit-heads have ever spoken to, and I'm not looking for an end for this war." He said in a voice sounding like thunder. "I like it."

" All right you little weenies ! Play time's over !" shouted another voice. We all quickly jerked up-right and stood for the sergeant who was standing near the cargo lands.

This man, in his 30's, had a heavy beard starting from his mustache and ending on the bottom of his chin.

He was a tall man and seemed to be shocked.

He paced, looking at us.

" I'm the sergeant. You 200 men and women are my new platoon. And I'm shocked. You are the most miserable bunch I've ever seen. And I've seen lots.

Here's my rule for losers like you. Follow it and you'll get along. Don't and you won't. Here's the rule: If I fight, then you all fight till your fingers fall off. You all hear me ?" He waited for an answer.

" Yes, sir !" we shouted.

He paced to the left, twitching his nostrils.

"Another city on our side of the map has been wiped off. The enemy has deployed nuclear weapons onto our great land. The air on that part of the country is cold now ! It is filled with ash, And the ground is wet with our tears !"

He paused again, trying to hold in his feelings towards our homeland.

He stopped pacing and focused in once more.

" Do you stupid bastards know who we are ? Who and what are we ?" he shouted furiously.

"Martian Militia, Sir!" we all shouted in harmonization.

" Yes, We are the Martians ! The descendants of the colonists who landed here in the MF shuttles 300 years ago ! What right does Earth have over us to kill us off just for the red land we worked on for generations ? They have none ! None at all ! And the worst part is that they just sit somewhere and laugh at us - and use our fellow Martians to fight us and destroy the planet.

If those traitor Martians want us to be trampled, then we'll stomp them harder. Right into the ground that they no longer love."

As he continued preaching to get us ready for our next mission, I felt guilty. I was a Martian and I only was fighting to get my credits.

I was not fighting for the Martian Way and I was not fighting to get all the Earth embassies, factories and farms for home rule. Or to get rid of all the millions of Earth-loyal troops posted all over Mars. I fought to get it over with sooner so I could go home to my sweet heart.

I had never had fantasies of an exciting life. No imagination, my sweetie used to say. I thought I'd get married, and keep working the vapor farm or maybe go to Ice Cap North and work on the Pole Melt Project. I was kind of good with heavy machinery and sort of good with engineering stuff. It had never occurred to me until the last few days that what I really excelled at was killing people.

" We are in a crucial part of our combat, ladies and gentlemen ! The enemy has been sending more and more of their people at us in undefended areas ! They have captured all of our western bases and cities from the Barren Equator to Ice Cap North, that we have worked so hard to make liveable !

Our new mission is called Brush Fire ! We are going to smoke those bastards out in one big flash-fire. We are going to take those bases and cities all back by fighting all at once, all the way to Ice Cap North.

The ships, Bordello, Muff, Jackass and Dumb-ass are going to be dropping all of us for our part of Brush Fire. All the 14 platoons in offense capsules will drop into enemy territory.

There will be hundreds more reinforcements joining all of you later, and hundreds of tanks ! But it is up to you all to keep the enemy controlled. There are going to be no prisoners ! They deserve to all rot in Martian hell !

Keep in mind that they have reinforcements as well. There may be more soldiers dropping over you guys. You are going to be equipped with all your goodies ! But don't try to be one-person armies. Remember that I am in control ! Remember my rule !

Get ready now... enjoy yourselves because . . .
. . . this may be the last day for you to live."

*   *   *

I was strapped down again like a mental patient - like back in the days of training.

The air tank seemed to scratch my armored shoulder pads. My helmet was strapped down over my multi-pro goggles. I couldn't move at all. Good thing, that. If I could, the drop would kill me.

I looked forward, hung up on a wall, facing another capsule's back side. Just another bullet in a clip, ready to be fired.

My water drained out.

It was nearly time.

The silence of the shuttle's hall was great and air-locked. Not a sound could penetrate. There was nothing to do except taste the fear.

Suddenly the moment came. The intense opening of the cargo doors !

Whoosh !

All the capsules got sucked out and started to fall like bricks. I felt the burning sensation of my heart jumping into my throat. I saw my suit bounce from the panicked beatings of my heart.

The force of the gravity was overreacting on me. I felt all the blood leaving my feet and being pushed into my head.

I tried clearing my mind of any worries of it.

Looking out of the glass covering and seeing the other capsules start to light on fire from the friction alone, I realized that hundreds of others were feeling exactly what I was feeling.

The urge to have a dump.

Thousands of them were rushing down faster than me. Seeing them on fire still didn't take my mind off my personal plunging into the atmosphere.

My veins felt like they were about to explode from all the pressure of the blood shooting up towards my head.

Suddenly the parachutes came up like great mushroom explosions of a mini-nuke.

My body felt the whiplash jerk to the floor. Thank goodness for buckles and belts ! The ground was now visible, and I saw that the enemy knew of our arrival.

Suddenly I saw a spark hit my glass top. The enemy soldiers were firing at us,

"Those stupid bastards!" I thought, but then I remembered how they'd shot the parachutes off other capsules, and didn't curse them anymore. In case they noticed me.

But I was still thinking it.

As soon as I landed, my belts snapped off and my rifle shot into my new hand. I saw a soldier running to me. "Not fair, you bastard. Wait til I'm out."

As I got mad. I kicked the boiling hot glass as it shot off. It sailed forward, smacking the enemy soldier under its red hot surface. He was getting fried extra crispy.

I ran out and started to charge . Everywhere, there were troops landing. Sometimes squishing enemy troops. Sometimes squishing each other. Either way there were thousands of us.

I looked up to make sure I wouldn't be a casualty of some drop bastard. as I charged with the army into the enemy territory.

My rage was going overtime as I cried out "For the love of my woman, I fight !"

I'm not quite sure what I was thinking, but it seemed to make sense at the time.

I loaded my gun and charged, seeing the enemy hiding like little children behind their bags and ditches. Suddenly the enemy started to fire with explosive shots. We were that close already.

The first hundred soldiers blew up into thousands of pieces of meat and organs. The mutilation was about to begin, The next row of charging soldiers fell to bits.

The enemy chain guns never stopped their firing, knowing that we'd crush them if they did.

" All of my units - we're next !" shouted Will Fecod through the inter comm radionn. "Remember the rule."

I rushed forward with the next two hundred troops. Every where I turned, there were men and women losing their heads and limbs in wet balls of red stuff.

The man in front of me suddenly had his head all over my helmet.

The pile of dead men and women were like walls.

I saw Will, calling all the soldiers to hide behind the bodies and pieces all around. He rose his hand showing a thumbs down, meaning to drop to the ground.

I dropped behind the bloody bodies.

I looked behind me, seeing a soldier running to drop. Suddenly the bullets came flying in. The soldier dropped next to me. I put my head down but I tried to turn the soldier around to see if she was all right.

I turned her around and saw she was hit.

Her whole chest was oozing onto the ground and her heart started squirting blood all over my face.

Somebody's lover.

Somebody's sweetheart.

But good cover for me.

I quickly moved her to the pile of bodies I was hiding behind, then I wiped my face and multi-pro goggles clear of guts and the bits of flesh which had stuck on to me.

I grabbed the dead soldier's gun and waited for the signal for firing to start.

I looked over to Will Fecod.

He knelt up, firing his rounds.

I took that as a "Yes" and turned on my aiming precision in my goggles. I quickly took the two rifles and slaved them to the goggle data and aimed for one of the chain guns. I squeezed the triggers, watching the flames come out of the barrels after every bullet.

I was deadly.

The enemy that were left ducked and tried not to get hit. The chain guns were still going off, swaying round and round, with no one running them. They were even more dangerous that way.

I fell to the floor behind the body pile, huddled up and trying not to get mowed down by some brainless machine.

The bullets dug into the piles, exploding as they hit. Pieces of fingers and guts bounced off with shrapnel, getting my armor wet and stenching with blood.

At this time, the next platoon was moving in.

I stayed down, following the rule and saw the next group get mutilated.

They started to scream and howl as their arms flew from their sockets, their airtanks imploded through their backs and their organs dropped out of their disintegrated chests.

This battle wasn't going anywhere that I wanted to be.

Four soldiers survived, ducking behind the pile.

"Fire !" shouted Will Fecod.

I looked up.

Damn that rule !

I got up and started to fire. continuing to aim for the chain gunners.

Missing terribly.

The chain guns started to sway again.

I ducked, feeling the sharp bullets piercing through the armor of the dead soldiers I hid behind.

I then heard the noises of napalm fighters in the distance.

Five planes zipped by, dropping thousands of tons of napalm.

I was relieved. I looked up, the fighters were going back for another round.

Suddenly three of them exploded.

The 10-mile Snipers had got them.

The other two dropped their last loads of napalm and turned to run.

Suddenly one of the wings flew off one of them.

It was tumbling down. It was going to crash right into us.

" INCOMING !" shouted Will running to the left side. I joined him, trying to dodge the bullets at the same time.

I fell over, ducking into another pile of dead soldiers.

The plane exploded as it hit the ground, and the dead bodies flew all over, killing the enemy soldiers who were trying to make it to us.

The reinforcements started coming in.

As the capsules covered the sky, I was hoping for the best. That they would do the fighting and I could rest.

Sergeant Will paid no attention, still picking up his rifle and telling all of us to continue the fight.

Bloody rule.

All of us lying on the ground saw him stand up, not afraid of the enemy fire. Charmed. We all felt proud , seeing him, fighting.

" If we're going to go down, I guess I should be standing up with the Sarge !" said one soldier.

Everyone else had failed at this. How could this one Sergeant pull it off. But I couldn't resist either. It was grinning time.

So we all grinned and started to charge with him. We didn't care for the precision any more.

The new recruits were right behind us and charging past the piles and bits of former comrades.

We all started running stupidly, getting so close, that our noses were almost touching the chain guns. The enemy soldiers started to get nervous, firing off everything. And mostly missing at this short range.

I raged my rifles, all covered in blood, taking out a whole gang. The chain gunners all along the enemy line were now bits and pieces on the floor.

The other enemy soldiers started to charge down firing.

Will bent down, staying at his spot , firing at the enemy.

I knelt down, reloaded with my last clip and started to fire.

The reinforcements started to rush and shoot, covering us from enemy fire.

Will, stood up and started to slowly walk and fire at the same time. He drew out his shotgun and fired both guns at once, blowing big holes in what was left of the enemy line.

The reinforcements got the fever too and ran to

Will, passing him and wading over the dead bodies that Will had killed to get at more live ones. But there were only bodies left in our section. Our mad charge had done the trick.

Will called for us, well, what was left of us, to charge down the hill behind that first line.

This was just the first barrier of the enemy's defense. There were more lines, better dug in, over this hill and up the next one.

Will quickly told us all to collect the ammunition from the dead and shoot the critically wounded enemy if necessary. It was mercy. There'd be no one coming to give them any help. Because we were going to be winning and moving on. Even our own wounded would have to wait a long time for medics.

As the soldiers ran a side from me, we went through hundreds of bodies. Man and woman. I myself went through forty bodies, shooting the bleeding ones who had no legs left, the ones with snapped necks and melted off jaws, and the ones with shrapnel stuck through their stomachs or exposed hearts, beating slowly. I guess that seeing so many like that and knowing that there was no hope for them should make me feel suicidal. Unfortunately, it only annoyed me. Like a chore that was inconvenient - but that I was doing anyway.

It wasn't pretty, but war never is - not because of the blood - but because you get used to it so easily.

*   *   *

As the recruits took out the enemy in the ditches, The worst was yet to come.

Will Fecod, and the other sergeants lined up, calling all the platoons as they started to communicate through the head sets.

" All platoons line up here !" they all said, shouting.

We were taught to obey what our superiors had demanded, so we all lined up, holding out our guns and kneeling for the signal.

They were planning the Charging Wall Manoeuvre. This only meant one thing: there were dopers out in the distance and it was up to us to take them out.

"Those napalm fighters did shit against the enemy," I said as I looked around the charcoaled grounds.

"We'll do the same against the dopers" said the girl next to me.

" We'll wipe out the suckers !" shouted one of the the Sergeants who had overheard us.

"Charging Wall - fire !" the Sergeants all yelled as they picked up their rifles.

Quick to the trigger, I started to fire into the far horizon of the tip of the hill remembering my BRASS training - Breathe, Relax, Aim, Squeeze, Shoot. Through my multi-pros, I saw enemy troops drop after each of my shots. So I was feeling good already.

We slowly walked over the rocky hills, seeing the dopers aiming for the perfect range to kill us.

ONLY HUMAN - MARTIAN INDEPENDENCE

" Kill the tinker toy bastards !" shouted Will as he started to charge, giving us the signal to fire off all we had.

All the soldiers, all in a great line started to all shoot , aiming for the dopers, who were confused on who to shoot first.

The dopers started to run towards us, firing their furious mechanical anger through their great chain guns, sometimes at us, sometimes at each other.

We continued to fire, hoping not to get hit.

The dopers kept moving towards us, even after we blew off a couple of their limbs, I guess it was because they were robotic and felt no pain.

No brain.

No pain.

The rounds I was firing were explosives, but they seemed not to cause enough damage towards the dopers.

One doper finally fell to the ground, having its chain gun and inner motor implode from the bullets.

They still were firing, but they weren't aiming at all. They seemed to be broken, Since they were known for precision aiming, this was a gift from god.

The dopers finally sustained enough damage from our Charging Wall of lead and seemed to all die together. They all fell to the floor to pieces within seconds of each other.

Will held out his hand, signaling for his own platoon to stop.

I was puzzled for his actions. None the less, I

reloaded my gun with another clip quickly.

Another Sergeant walked up to him, I was no mouth expert or lip reader but I thought that the other Sergeant was puzzled as well.

Will seemed to ignore what the other Sergeant was saying.

He then jumped up in fright, grabbing the Sergeant by two arms and shouting into his face.

What I made out was, " Get the troops out of here. This was too easy. It's a trap !"

I paid no second thought into it. Quickly, without waiting for Will to signal, I whacked a couple of troops near me and pointed backwards, then I was rushing as fast as possible. I didn't know why yet, but who cared.

Suddenly the sonic boom of some sort of shuttle rolled in from the far distance. It was an enemy napalm fighter coming in.

My eyes grew to a shocking size as I figured out what it was.

Will started to run behind us, telling everyone to sprint back into the ditches. I ran as quickly as possible, hearing the napalm already touching the floor. I didn't want to look back, hearing all the screams and curses, I had formed a terrible picture.

I started to pant, throwing down my rifle to get rid of dead weight. But even this didn't give me wings. Most of the other guys around me, beat me by ten or twelve steps.

As Will and the other soldiers jumped into the

ditch, I rolled in behind them, hanging on to my helmet and goggles.

I ducked, under an overhang in the ditch, hearing the rumblings right through the ground.

The heat, and flames, ten feet above us, felt like a furnace and, for a few seconds, there was nothing to breath but the fires of hell.

I heard people screaming again.

Must have been only touched by it. If they were badly hit, there wouldn't be any noise.

After all, vapor can't scream.

I didn't care to look up. Even in my little cave, I felt the top of my helmet antenna being ripped off from the wave of air going over us.

I squeezed my eyes tightly, hoping for it to stop.

The heat started to work on my armor and I felt that my uniform under it, was on fire. My face began to feel burns.

I threw my sleeve away from my face, now lying in the dirt and quickly pulled my mouth mask over my nose and mouth, instantly breathing from canned air, taking deep breaths, as the mask mouth piece began to burn my tongue and make my teeth tingle.

Finally, a reason for carting this bloody tank around all this time.

My goggles, started to have steam and vapor stains from the outside temperature of the heat, but I sure wasn't going to take them off to clean them.

The flames began to die down, and finally they evaporated, taking most of our troops with them.

I quickly looked up, jumping out of the ditch , throwing off my goggles, pulling off my breather and gasping in the cold air.

Whoever was left stood up, and were scattered all around, trying to cool down.

I bent over, feeling like I was about to hurl but nothing came out.

I felt sick and tired.

I heard a noise and suddenly all my fear rushed back in, chasing out the tiredness and putting an edge back on my dull knife.

But it was only the reinforcements, in large numbers, coming over the rocky hill we had just charged over.

They quickly ran to relieve us, seeing the sight of us all spaced out, overheating and trying to cool down. It was a miracle that anyone had survived at all, and the reinforcements looked at us very strangely.

Medic soldiers flooded all over, fixing us up, and giving us anti-heat drugs, to cool us down. I was surprised to see them. Maybe we shouldn't have shot all those guys before we charged.

But we had.

And it was too dry for tears.

The new troops, ran further out, past us, charging into the next battle line.

Will called all of us to group up and wait for next orders.

We all grouped up. Me in between two woman soldiers, who had burn marks around their eyes.

Will looked at us.

"You're all still well enough to fight ?" he asked, turning to all of us.

We all were tired and sickly but we all still gave him the answer he wanted.

"Yes sir !" we shouted.

He grinned, taking out his last clip to his banged up rifle and snapping it on.

"Well what are you all looking at ? Are you going to stare them to death ?"

He pointed to the charging reinforcements going north to the next barrier of enemy fire.

I took out my shotgun, focusing on the area, and put on my goggles once more, over the burnt skin of my forehead.

"Move out !" he shouted, charging and getting lost in the crowd of reinforcements.

I started to charge, letting the goggles tell me what was up next, and selecting the next target for elimination. Seeing the small sun right above and holding my lucky necklace, I knew now that I could not die today.

But tomorrow was another day.

*   *   *

The battle in the next enemy ditch lasted for hours.

The enemy on the outside had lost thousands of men just trying to keep us in a controlled place.

They had resolved to nerve gas us; not to suffocate us - although they would if we got caught without breathers - but worse, to jam up our goggle sensors.

"Masks up!" shouted Will as soon as he saw the clouds down the line, quickly hooking up his turtle neck to his helmet and pulling the mask towards his mouth.

I quickly did the same, just as I heard the gas can land and hiss.

I took deep breaths to calm me down from being nervous. I wasn't sure what would happen if I breathed this stuff, but I knew it wouldn't be good.

The gas was so thick that I couldn't see the other troops standing next to me.

My goggles were useless as the gas started to clog all the sensors.

I held my gun and listened in to my comm unit in my helmet.

Bullets started to fly in from one direction. I quickly ducked into the ground. I was shivering, thinking that I could get shot and not know who shot me. Then I remembered - I couldn't die today.

I slowly stood up, firing my shotgun a couple of times, hoping to hit something.

The bullets came in again.

I ducked into the ground again, not wanting to put my theory to the test too much. Suddenly a soldier fell onto me. His head was gone. I pushed him off me, feeling around for his rifle to use once the mist would die down.

I felt something metal. That was it.

I took out a clip from my side pocket, loading it up and feeling around for the explosion conversion button.

The bullets came flying in again, I squeezed my eyes and bit hard onto the breath cord.

" All units, stay down until the mist comes down a bit !" shouted Will through the transmissions.

I stayed bent down, waving the mist away as I slowly walked past dead bodies of soldiers on the floor. I wasn't trying to be a hero. I was just trying to find the ditch, so I wouldn't get hit.

The bullets started to shoot in again. I could hear them hit the dead bodies, but I couldn't tell where they were all coming from.

I started to run as I saw some signs of activity in front of me.

As I ran through the mist, I saw no one else running into the mist with me, but I thought it was just too thick.

I suddenly crashed into a trooper, I only saw him when I hit him and, at first, I thought he was an enemy. I had my gun barrel wedged up under his helmet, before I recognized his armor.

He seemed panicky as he stood up.

I stood up too, hearing footsteps in the far distance from far away.

" Footsteps !" I shouted.

" They're coming from all sides !" shouted a soldier.

" Start firing !" shouted Will.

I couldn't see anything at all, and I was scared. I aimed my rifle, firing off into the far mist where I heard the hundreds of footsteps. The other troops started to yell out loud as they fired, linking up with us to make an effective fire-wall.

In the far distance, we heard them moaning and falling to the ground, not knowing what we hit, but feeling good about our fast reactions to danger.

" Charge now !" shouted Will.

I started to run out to where I had fired, hoping to see what we had shot.

As we ran, the mist started to disappear.

I saw the soldiers we had shot. All lying in pieces and looking all like shredded meat.

Will ran to them, checking them all and backing away in shock.

He threw his gun down, on the floor, looking like he had seen a ghost.

I didn't understand what he was shocked about.

I slowly walked over to them.

I threw down my rifle in shock, too. My eyes were filled with guilt and my back was filled with chills. I picked up a sleeve from the carnage, the uniformed symbol on it cried out in anger.

It wasn't enemy.

The other troops came from behind, hearing from Will that we had fired upon our own reinforcements.

" God dammit" I said, feeling grim for what I had done. The other soldiers were silent, trying to hold in their agony. A soldier walked over, feeling jumpy, and finally he began to panic.

"We're killers ! We're all dirty killers !"

Will walked over to him and pushed him down to the ground. The trooper was scared and confused to his actions.

"You're lucky that we're out of range of enemy fire because I would of pushed you into it. Now shut up before I use you as a body shield." Will scalded, looking at the young trooper.

I was confused as well as all the others.

The new reinforcements would be coming in soon, if they saw this, what would they do ?

Will showed no thought on the subject and just stayed on a strategy to take out the enemy on the other side .

" Well, let's make the best of it. Take every clip, every gun and any supplies that those dead troopers are connected to. We're going to Bluff Charge the enemy. We charge like maniacs, out of range and see where their defenses are. Then drop to the ground crawl closer and take them out. So charge when I say charge and - here's the important part - drop when I say 'Drop !' You got me ?" he said, as he picked up a goreslimed rifle from the carcass pile.

" Yes sir !" we shouted.

I checked all my ammunition pouches, I was down to a clip.

I looked around the pile. Checking the other dead soldiers for their own clips, I put them in my pouches around my belt. I pulled off the shotguns from the dead troopers, handing them to the other troopers, and looked for more ammo.

The bodies now lay stripped of ammo and guns. My pouches stunk of blood and manure. Re-connecting my air mask to my helmet and mouth, to get rid of the stink, I got ready for the charge.

We had to go through the remaining mist and gases. It was not going to be easy, but we were soldiers. We had to do this. And we had the weight of a hundred of our own soldiers killed by our own hands to push us on.

" Move out !" shouted Will, charging into the steam.

The troops started to sprint into the area.

I gulped and ran in, feeling jumpy and anxious to shoot something.

The mist, grey, wet and hot, blocked my sight of anything. But like most logical problems the solution was simple. The enemy was right in front of me and waiting for my body to use as their target practice.

I stepped fast, going straight, hoping that the mist could clear up, but there was still no end to it.

I was getting worried, there was no shooting noise, no shouting commands, nothing. It was too silent for comfort, my comfort at least.

"Who's there ? Sarge ?" I shouted for my own good, hoping to hear from anyone.

There was no noise.

I kept charging, seeing nothing, not even a dead body. I began to see the mist slowly disappear, I was getting out of it.

The ground became visible again, only fired bullet casings lay on the floor, no bodies.

Suddenly, figures in the mist. Human figures became visible. I thought I'd stumbled into an enemy group and switched to explosive.

The mist then disappeared, like magic.

My platoon was all there, standing around, like a meeting in heaven. There was nothing going on.

Will was looking around the area.

" Sir ?" I said, as I stopped running and started to pant.

He gave no answer.

I looked at where all the others were looking. All the enemy troops lay dead . All their dead bodies, leaned against their machine guns, some headless, some with no arms and chests. It wasn't a pretty sight.

" We got the sons of bitches ! We got 'em !" said a trooper, beginning to giggle in victory.

Will sighed.

" Someone got 'em before we did." said Will.

He seemed bothered for some reason. I guess that we were the only invading party which made it this far. None of us made a shot into them.

The other troops were glad, and feeling victorious.

" Let's get their weapons. We'll need them later." shouted Will.

The troops stopped their chatting, scrambling around, jumping into the ditches and collecting their guns.

They were even un-hooking the machine guns from the ground.

There were no supplies. Strange for enemy troops to be placed here without supplies. This was going to be one tough night.

The new reinforcements coming in next were going to be the ones who would suffer the most. There were no supplies to set up, no dumb tents meant that we were going to have to sleep in the negative degree climate of Martian Night.

*   *   *

The night time shivers started to eat away on my joints. I was posted as machine gunner on this part of the ditch.

I had double padded my suit with the insulators I used to keep my gun from brittling. I was not using it, so it gave me every excuse to use the insulators.

The next batch of reinforcements did not make it in.

We had no contact at all, and we had no supplies. This was dangerous, since Martian night was cold enough to freeze a man until daytime.

It was silent. No tanks or shuttles could be seen or heard for miles.

We were all alone . There was no more enemy at this point. There were other enemies further north but we couldn't make another move without the next batch of reinforcements. If we left, this area could fill up with more enemy troops , destroying the purpose of the Brush Fire attack.

All we could do now was wait.

The winds were beginning to pick up, blowing against my frozen ears in my helmet, made me get a headache. My goggles froze up, showing icicles on the outside lenses.

My nose was stuffed up and breathing was a bitch.

I leaned against the dirt wall, looking at the moons above me reflecting off a dim glow of the distant sun shining elsewhere on the planet.

A soldier walked over and sat , leaning onto the ditch wall next to me, rubbing his hands together. It was Richie, the man I talked to before the drop, I was surprised that he had survived. I guess that I wasn't the only lucky one here.

He looked at me, hoping to start conversation.

"Well, have there been any sightings yet ?" he asked.

" No."

" Any sight of the Bordello ?"

" No."

" Oh, - well. I guess that we're the only ones in this area."

" You've got that right, kid"

I slowly started a flare, to warm me up and to see how the man looked. I melted the icicles on my gloves feeling the warm sensation of the flame.

I then flashed it around him.

I saw that his uniformed armor was almost ready to fall off. This man had seen a lot more action than the others. It didn't seem to bother him though.

" What the hell happened to you ?" I asked.

He looked at his armor and grinned giving a small chuckle.

"Well I was hit by three explosive bullets, basically ripping apart my armor."

" Why don't you get another one ?"

" Because there are no supplies, shithead, You of all people shouldn't be asking stupid questions like that."

" Well, I thought that -"

" Well you thought wrong !" he said.

I heard a noise out in the far distance. Good thing. The conversation was going to hell fast.

Richie grabbed his gun wrapped in insulator material.

I quickly jumped up manning the machine gun. I looked around, turning on the spot light. I moved the light around looking for something.

There was nothing out there.

I sighed and sunk back into my leaning position, sitting in the dirt ditch.

Suddenly I heard a sonic boom, coming fast. A napalm fighter was coming in.

My eyes widened in horror.

I turned to Richie,

"Tell the others that we're going to be filled with napalm !"

Richie jumped up in fright as he ran and fired off a few rounds to alert everybody.

" Napalm !" I screamed, running as far away as possible. I grabbed my rifle extremely tightly as I tried to run.

The others got up off the ground where they'd been trying to sleep. They quickly grabbed their guns and helmets, running out of the ditch as well.

I heard the fire drop all over around the ditch. Then I saw the fat fighter swooping several hundred miles per hour over us, not noticing that we had left.

I stopped running and started to pant. I saw the other troops falling to the ground, trying to catch their breath. We all felt the extreme warmth of the burning napalm in the ditch. We were a full three hundred feet away from it and we still felt the heat.

I fell to the icy cold floor. The bloating noise of the fire seemed to warm me from my cold aching head to my solid toes.

I turned around, still on the floor, and noticed the others walking closer to the fire, to warm up I guess. I got up and walked over to the flames with everyone else. It was relaxing, the sensation of the heat waves. It made me drowsy and it made me think of home back down in the south of Mars in a warm little house, with my family, and with my girlfriend.

That night was the best sleep I would be getting for a while.

*   *   *

I never saw Richie after that night, I suspected that he either froze to death and was buried, or he was vaporized from the napalm attack that night.

It was not important anyway. For the condition he was in, he was expected to die. Armor doesn't fall apart like that without a lot of damage to the flesh underneath it. He must have been running on empty when he was talking to me. Maybe that's why he was so touchy.

But who cares, anyway.

I had woken up in time to see the Martian sun shine over the Martian trees and landscape. It was a sight I had seen thousands of times before, but suddenly it was beautiful in some way I'd never felt before. Maybe fighting for it made you see it differently.

But not for long.

The spell was broken when the Bordello, breaking the sound barrier, came screaming in for its landing ten feet away from us.

As the reinforcements were dropped off, I helped the medical supplies get set up and ready for service. It was a good thing too, the casualties list was extreme and even more had become injured over night.

As the batch of 100 more reinforcements set up base on this land, Sergeant Will Fecod was telling us our next move with the new platoon we would encounter on the next strike. We were all gathered around the supplies dump, all huddled up and looking at the charted maps of the land.

ONLY HUMAN - MARTIAN INDEPENDENCE

Will had his helmet off but his multi-pro goggles were still strapped tightly around his temple and eyes.

" For one hundred miles there will be no sight of the enemy. That's why we're going to use the Bordello to drop us at the line of Ice Cap North."

As he paused for our reaction, we all thought that he was crazy.

"The Ice Caps are colder than Martian night."

" There couldn't be a base there even if it was run by robots."

" The temperatures there is cold enough to liquify nitrogen."

This last guy was a bit off in his science, but we all agreed with the sentiment.

Will looked at our confused faces with anger. "You chickens finished ?"

We all got silent.

"Now, all those parts of our armor that you're wearing but that you never use are designed for such things. All of your turtle necks are able to connect to your helmets and seal tightly. Your masks connect to your goggles, helmet and also your turtle neck. The gloves you wear connect to the sleeves and so on. The armor was designed to take all Martian complications, or did you sorry-ass whiners forget that when you were in training ? You can go into space with this stuff. The temperatures won't kill you unless you were shot in the neck or arm or somewhere and open up a hole. All you have to worry about is not getting shot.

In any case, that's where I'm going - so that's

where you're going. Deal with it. Any questions ?"

He looked around, looking at all our faces and then focused on me.

"You seem puzzled on something ? Ask," he said.

"We're all going to be dropped in capsules or be dropped on chutes ?"

He grinned and chuckled. "Good question. That's what I like - a soldier concerned with saving his own ass. Don't worry. We're going down in chutes," he said.

I was relieved. Even though they were made to be dropped from space, Offense Capsules had a reputation for malfunctioning on the ground in low temperatures. They often left you still strapped down after the canopy was popped, so you just had to stand there until somebody came along amd shot you.

"All right get ready, we're leaving now," Will said.

"Yes sir !" we said.

We all broke away, going and digging into the supply barrels, looking for the chutes. As soon as we found them, most of us started to clip them on, around our waist and shoulders. I gave in to my paranoia and unpacked mine and re-packed it - so if it didn't work, I could curse my own bad packing all the way down, instead of somebody else's.

I noticed a couple of others doing the same - they were the men and women who had survived the most battles, so maybe it wasn't pure luck.

I looked up at the stubby Bordello , seeing the cargo doors wide open and hearing the pilot's evil pirate-laugh echoing through the cargo bay.

ONLY HUMAN - MARTIAN INDEPENDENCE 115

" All you whores load up, we've got to get there before the storms get us !" shouted the pilot as he strapped on his armor, mask, gloves, and turtleneck.

The others ran in and strapped themselves to the walls of the ship, while I finished re-packing my chute so I was left with no where to clip on to. I quickly ran to the only seat -which was in the center of the room- clipping onto it.

" If and when we win, I'll hope to see all of you holding a red scarf, for the pride of the planet you fight for !" the pilot said, then got nervous, for being so patriotic instead of cynical like he usually was. He covered up the moment by starting up the engines.

The strong rumblings started up, followed with a sharp burst up. And then we shot North to the next enemy base.

But it wasn't a relaxing ride. From my seat in the middle I was the only one that could hear the pilot and the Sergeant talking clearly and neither was too confident. As soon as we got close, I heard even worse news:

"Sergeant ! The Muff just went down!" said the pilot.

" Shit-"

"That's why I hate these atmosphere drops. If they can see us, they can hit us."

There was a big thump. They could see us, I guess

"The troops were dispatched though, sir."

"Well, that's something - OK, now's the time to open up your whore-house, man - we're here to party."

I quickly unbuckled my seat as the back cargo doors opened up

" All you whores, I hope you give'em a good screwing for me !" shouted the pilot.

As the closest troops jumped out, I took a quick look at my arms and rifle wrapped in insulator material, making sure I could get to them in the air, if I had to. I practiced grabbing the chute release puller a couple of times, until I was satisfied I could find it.

I then jumped out.

I turned around in the freefall, seeing two other shuttles opening up and throwing their troops into the air, I felt that this would be the last time I would see any of them.

I quickly pulled the release cord, letting my chute fly free and clear, slowing me down from falling-speed. The jerk of the chute unfolding and catching the air pulled me up, forcing my head to turn. I could see where the Muff was burning on the snow like an emergency flare and I could see where the enemy was dug in and exactly where I had to go.

I looked down, seeing the other troops landing and the great chutes loose their beauty as soon as each trooper landed.

As the ground, covered in hard solid ice, became a real hard surface under my feet , I unhooked the chute and rolled to the floor. Feeling none of the impact, I rolled back up on my feet.

I held out my rifle, ready for instant action.

The other troops were all charging into the misty fog, slowly, feeling their way.

I felt a connection to the voice that sometimes talked to me, although I heard no words. For some reason, my goggles were not effected by the fog. It felt like I had an overlay in my mind from my aerial view. So I knew exactly where the enemy were.

I saw every one of my shots hit home and saw every death in the far distance. I slowly walked towards the base's defense like in a dream, picking my shots and making nearly every one count. Usually, in hot zones, time sped up for me. But this was all slow. Turtle war.

The incoming bullets were all ricocheting off the ice and rocks and seemed to be coming so slowly, I swear I could see them tumbling through the air. Maybe it was the cold.

I zoomed onto the base from my distance. This was going to be easy to take. The other troops took out everything for me. All I had to do now was walk in and take out the left overs . . .

Chapter 5

(PLAYBACK 23,000 BC)

THE GUARDIANS HAD ALSO BEEN STILLED, TO ENSURE THAT THE HUMANS HAD CIVILIZED BEINGS WITH THEM WHO UNDERSTOOD THEIR CAPACITY FOR VIOLENCE. BUT SOMETHING WENT WRONG.

THE NEW CIVILIZATION PLAN CALLED FOR TOTAL QUARANTINE. NO CONTACT. NO REPORTS. NO GOING BACK.

PERHAPS THE GUARDIANS, WHO HAD VOLUNTEERED TO DO SOMETHING GOOD, HADN'T BEEN TOLD THAT THIS WAS A LIFETIME COMMITMENT. PERHAPS THEY HADN'T UNDERSTOOD THE CONSEQUENCES. IN ANY CASE . . .

"REES2FEEMAYA" I THOUGHT AT HER, TRYING TO PIERCE HER ARMOR OF SADNESS. "YOUR GUARDIANS AWAKE !"

THE NAME, WHICH I HAD TAKEN FROM THEIR MINDS AS THEY WOKE, MEANT NOTHING TO HER, BUT THE MENTAL TRANSMISSION TOLD HER IMMEDIATELY WHO I WAS TALKING ABOUT.

"BALDIES ?" SHE SAID OUT LOUD. "I'LL FRY THEIR BRAINS !" SHE BEGAN BUILDING A GREAT SPEAR OF MENTAL POWER, GETTING READY TO FLING IT AT THE GUARDIANS, WHO SHE NOW SENSED TOO.

""WAIT."

"WHY ?"

"THERE ARE CONSEQUENCES."

She waited, holding the shining spear of force quivering and at the ready.

"We do not know enough," I sent. "And they do not know of your mind power. You can use it anytime, but use it wisely. For now, lie back down in your place."

She lay down in the place where she had woken and let the spear dissipate.

"What do they know? I get only confusion and . . ."

"I can go deeper. They cannot speak to each other mentally, and they are not fully awake yet. Each will have to have his own awakening. But there is a common thread. They know they have been stilled, but not for how long. But they also know that any stilling is for a long, long time. So they are shocked and feel betrayed. Wait - they are speaking now - can you hear them?"

"Yes."

"This isn't right," mumbled a Guardian out loud as he sat up and looked around.

"We've been stilled," said another, beside him, who hadn't bothered to sit up.

"So it's least 100 years?"

"More like 500 if they've fully Edenized this place."

"Those bastards!"

Another one sat up and looked around. "I thought it was only for 4 or 5 years. My mate and I just had a child when the war ended."

"It's dead hundreds of years ago." said the first, "And your mate with it."

"There must be some mistake," said another.

"They would have told us. Something must be wrong."

"Contact the ships," said the first one.

The two got up and walked through the rows of fellow Guardians who were also coming around. They arrived at a pile of equipment and began setting it up.

"Rees2feemaya ?" I said in my mind. "Can you hear them ?"

"Yes but I can't understand them."

"Read their minds before they speak."

"You're right.- That works. More of them are waking up. We must get ready." Her mind bristled with images of war and blood

."Wait and listen," I counselled. "I think we have much to learn."

"I have learned a lifetime already."

"And have another lifetime of learning ahead of you. Listen. Can you hear ? Your people are waking up all over the planet. Tell them to lie still and wait."

"Can't you tell them ?"

I can, but it will sooth them more to hear it from you."

"You're right."

She sent out a calming thought that flowed around the entire planet like a warm blanket, telling all the human children to be still. To be calm. To wait.

War-born children all, they obeyed without question, raised in combat zones and recognizing the flavor of another human mind.

It was the first mind I had ever spoken to. A mind full of fire and light. A shining wheel, flashing fear and hatred, love and tenderness all at the same time. Like the circus had come to town in my life.

By contrast, the Guardians were almost machines. Logic ruled. Passion was absent. Goals were set, obstacles overcome and objectives achieved. Always peacefully and efficiently.

Unless there was an unexpected crisis.

"I can't raise the ships " said the Guardian with the equipment.

"Equipment failure ?"

"No. I've contacted 20 other Guardian groups. They report the same problem."

"Behind the moons ?"

"Not all three ships at once."

They both went silent.

Mind-crash.

Other newly woken Guardians wandered over. The original two came out of their stall and explained the problem.

No-one had any ideas. They chatted on the radio with other groups for a while, but no-one anywhere on the planet had anything new to offer.

These Guardians were all warriors. They had been in the battles that defeated the humans and were the best and brightest that civilization had to offer - but compared to the humans, they were stupid and slow. It amazed *me how they could have emerged as the victors.*

"Technology and numbers" came Rees2feemaya's thought. "They outnumbered us 5 million to one and had 50,000 worlds. We had only our living tech and our minds. It wasn't enough."

Finally one of the Guardians thought the unthinkable.

"We're marooned."

"What ?"

"It's part of the plan. Leave us here. Cut contact. I'll bet the wormhole is closed."

The other Guardians went still with this, processing. The one who had the thought manned the radio and broadcast the idea around the globe.

Then the fireworks began.

Like the slow seep of lava, the anger came up in them. To defeat the humans they had had to become human and, even after sleeping for 500 years, it was a virus that was still in them. Strongly.

They erupted almost all at once.

"Oh-oh" I heard Rees2feemaya say in my mind, as she tried to reconstruct her mind-weapon.

But I didn't give her the chance.

Almost before I heard her thought, I took action.

The Guardians were all dead before she thought her second "Oh".

I dropped them like small trees in a big wind with the power of my mind. I had to. As soon as I heard them all think, almost at once:

"Kill the heums "

Whether they thought that this would get them back home or whether they just wanted revenge, I'll never know. But every one of them, without exception, seemed to arrive at the same conclusion at the same instant: "Kill all the human children."

It was a thought which ended up destroying them.

I felt no guilt whatsoever.

Although there certainly were regrets. I had recorded bits and pieces of their thoughts before I killed them, but I knew nothing of the outside universe. The children, a million of them from all sorts of human worlds, knew very little more than I did. They knew something of technology, but only surface thoughts; not really how anything worked.

And suddenly, with nothing at all to work with, I was the Guardian of an entire species.

It frightened me.

It confused me.

It stressed me.

It was the happiest time of my life.

(RECORDING - 2400 AD)

It was the second year of the battle and a new century, but for me it became the Year of Muddy Lane.

All of the enemy bases and Earth embassies from the Barren Equator to Ice Cap North had been taken out. The Martian Indies had driven out the Martian Loydies by force.

Brush Fire had been a big success, but we still hadn't actually fought Earth Troops. Only the Martians who were loyal to Earth. They'd fought Earth's battles for her - and lost everything. But that wasn't the end of it. There were still pockets of Loydies around, causing trouble and fighting a guerrilla war, while we were trying to get things working again, to be ready for when Earth finally turned up to fight it's own battles. And there was still the on-going business of trying to keep enough air, water and weather on the planet so we could walk around without air tanks or heated pressure suits. We had to get all the broken vapor factories and Ice Melters going again and keep them going. We had to keep planting the leafy bushes and trees. We had to get back to the business of making Mars into a place where humans could live.

Even war with Earth couldn't interrupt that.

All of their interplanetary embassies had been on the east side of the planet but that was two years ago. Those places were now filled with new Martian troops, training and hoping to see some action.

ONLY HUMAN - MARTIAN INDEPENDENCE

Me and the others who survived for two years had been let off. The war so far was now in the strategy courts of Earth, debating their next attack. But they were too far away to care about, so it was a rest period for everyone - like in ancient days, when armies could only fight in summer.

From a little political protest, this war had turned into one great bloodbath. Millions were dead and half the cities on the planet had major damage. And this was just foreplay.

There were no more enemy soldiers to take out now. But the real enemy were on their way. The new batch of enemy troops were coming though, there was no doubt about that. Earth wouldn't let a billion Rebels get away with murdering their big profits. Mars was like an old TwenCen colony. A wide open source of raw materials where no pollution or environmental safeguards were thought necessary. After all - it was a dead planet already.

Except of course, for us.

And the ecology we were trying to build - and were succeeding at - until we'd started blowing it all up.

The old fighters that the Martians had used were becoming obsolete since the enemy had adapted so quickly. It was only a matter of time until the Martians needed to see some new adaptations.

The Martian scientists had continued to work night and day, but no-one had seen anything yet.

The new squadron of fighters had been rumored to be the strongest fighters in combat yet, but those were just rumors in this calm eye of the war.

As soon as I was relieved of command for a while, I headed back to my home town, hoping I would find something that would give me back my name. It had been blasted out of my head two years ago, in my first battle, and I hadn't remembered it since. My bar code was burned off and I hadn't needed a name for anything during all my battles and adventures. But it nagged at me.

I'd heard my home town had been whacked and abandoned, but I thought it would be like a ghost town, where I could snook around in the buildings and find some clue about my name.

No chance of that.

The town was beaten flat down, with only chunks of crete and rebar sticking up. Nothing but dust. I had a hard time even finding the place where my family's vapor plant had been.

Everyone had evacuated into the next settlement on the west side. All my family were either dead or lost long ago, but even the few people I remembered had been killed or disappeared in the evacuations. So it looked like I'd be nameless for a while yet. The Unknown Soldier.

It wasn't until now that I found out my sweetheart, Carol, had run off to join some Militia or another. (She always was the super-patriotic type.) We hadn't exchanged letters for over a year and, last I heard, she was volunteering in the town, helping with a medical team.

ONLY HUMAN - MARTIAN INDEPENDENCE 127

Since there was no war left for me, I took up a position as a town patrol trooper. It kept me busy and in shape and besides it was only temporary.

I was joined by a small group of off-line troopers - people who were also sharing the same story as me. We all followed general orders from the official police officers, but were pretty much left on our own to oversee how those orders were carried out.

The court system had pretty well broken down and, although it wasn't official, patrols like us administered most justice.

Usually we only had to patrol and show the force and to arrest any Earth Loyalists who lived in any of the cities. The uniforms for this type of job didn't have to have air tanks, multi-pro goggles nor a helmet. (but I preferred to wear my multi-pros all the time I was working.)

All we had were two guns, a non-conversion- shot gun and a pistol or a cyclone gun. This line of work did not need any drops, mass killings or quick adrenalin rushes to take over our judgement. All there was to do was look good, monitor behavior of civilians and arrest anyone causing trouble. Sort of baby-sitting. But with a big stick.

Locals who were disturbing the peace, were thrown into a local jail-dormitory for a couple of days. More serious crimes usually earned the death penalty. Instantly.

Captured Loydies didn't usually survive long either, since most troopers had lost someone to them over the last couple of years. They'd made their choice and, like all choices, there were consequences.

I was made Corporal overnight as soon as I joined the patrol squad, because of my experience and because the last one was old and died of a heart attack.

The next day I was made Sergeant because the other Sergeant was killed trying to control a riot.

It seemed that this was going to be a tougher job than I thought.

*   *   *

As I walked out of the Police Post doors I was hit with the beauty of the Martian sun rising over the half-built buildings in the new settlement. They had given up the old town altogether. Too hard to break it all up and build. It was easier just to move a few miles and build there. It's not as if there were rivers or lakes or anything that the old town had been built on.

I kept focusing with my goggles on what time it was and what temperature it was.

" 6:30 AM , 45 degrees" it read in barcoding.

I walked down the front steps of the building and into the training park for Law Officers.

There I was met by my Twenty.

They all straightened up, wearing their armor and caps neatly. I grinned as I looked at the 16 troops I had. None of them looked at me or even questioned who I was. They looked straight ahead - trained on the parade-ground rather than in the hot zone.

I wanted to ask who each of them were. Still not remembering my own name, this was important to me.

I started with a slender woman, short haired , young.

" I want to see your prints, " I said, "Starting with you."

They all immediately put out their right hands like robots.

I grabbed her arm, looking at the barcode tattooed onto her skin It read. " Identification Number 132, Stephonie Ross, Birth: October, 2376, Alpha Breed"

I looked at her. She was not paying much attention to me.

I moved on to the next person.

" Identification number 145,Chris Fent, Birth: April, 2381, Bayta breed"

I went through two more which were all pretty much the same.

The fifth one seemed to be nervous.He had overlays so all I could read was his name: "Harry Aaron, Alpha breed" The rest had old-style letters written over it.

" What's this nonsense say ?" I asked him.

" In God We Trust, sir."

" God ?" I mumbled. "You a Christer ?"

He seemed offended.

"Americartian !" he said, proudly.

"Don't brag too much about Earth ties" I said. "It can get you killed."

He looked a bit worried.

I moved on.

I looked at the next,

" Identification number 5700, Erika Arnold. Birth: 2380, Alpha breed"

Over it, it read " One which is true, is Martian."

I grinned looking at the sky, "I like your spirit soldier." I said to her. "But don't let the Loydies catch you. I used to fight with an Erica in the Tank Corps."

"Oh, what happened to her ?"

"Dead," I said, then crossed to a very dark skinned woman.

" Chrystina Qual, Identification number 506, Birth November 2381, Pedigree." it read.

My eyes widened as I saw the word 'Pedigree.'

I looked at her. "You're a pedigree ? You're hard to come by." I said.

She smiled. " Yes sir, I'm a pure black woman," she said with pride to herself.

" Black ? My goggles show you dark brown, not black." I said, curious to her own comment, raising my eyebrow.

"Sorry. You're right. I should have said "Africartian - African and Martian !"

"You're young, too."

"Yes sir -but old enough to kill for Mars, sir."

I couldn't argue with that. I was one year younger.

Personally, I'd never seen a pedigree - a purebred member of a specific race. Most of us were hybrids - the products of mixed races and probably the better for it. I myself was Asian, Caucasian and probably a few other things as well. Everybody was like that. So there was no more racial strife - everybody was just human - which was dangerous enough if this bloody war was anything to go by.

"You're one of a kind out here trooper." I said.

She gave no comment but her smile showed her pride in being different.

But she wasn't. The next was another pedigree. Amazing. And a much more rarer pedigree than Chrystina. It was another striking woman, named "Elithebeth." She was pure Caucasian. (The most discriminated - against kind of pedigree because of their shameful history and their extremely low number in the overall population.)

She was shorter by an inch from the others and seemed gloomy.

I didn't bother to ask her why. I could understand why they were so mistreated. Our entire education in human history basically told the story of how the white race had murdered, plundered and enslaved everyone they could. I was even quite uneasy with the idea of having a Caucasian in my squad.

The last man I came up to was a well built youngster. He was taller than me and was the only other one wearing goggles.

I looked at his barcode .

"Eric Aaron, Identification 24066, Birth: September 2380, Alpha Breed."

Over it was an overlapping tattoo of two triangles

shaping what looked like a star.

" What's this mark over your barcode soldier ?" I said curiously.

He looked at me, seeming offended.

" It's the Star of David."

" Who's he, your father?"

He almost seemed to be holding his anger back.

"It's the religious sign of the Jewish people," he said.

"Jewish ? As in the religion of Monotheism ?"

He nodded his head.

" The belief in God ?" I sighed and then finished. " All right, I can see that. As long as it doesn't get in the way."

I paused, looking at them all.

As far as you're concerned, I have no name. I'm the Sarge. I don't know my way around this town or this job, so I'll expect that you can do your jobs without being watched all the time. But when I ask you to do something, I expect you to do it. Right away. No questions. No discussion. I've been with the Martian Militia for 2 years and I've been in just about every major battle we've had. So I'm an expert in one very important thing - how to save my ass - and the asses of everyone around me. That's my expertise. So let's get ready for our first patrol together."

I didn't realize until I was halfway through my spiel that I was repeating what that long-dead Sarge had told me after my very first battle.

" So, I guess that we should get our ammo first,

isn't that right, Sarge ? " Erika said.

"Huh ? You walk around with no ammo ? Jeez. Yes. Right. Where's the nearest ammo store ?"

"You mean the only ammo store," she said.

"You're telling me that in all of these four hundred buildings, there is only one ammo store ? Tell me -" I paused, trying to remember her name. "Arnold - how did we take back the bases here last year with only one ammo store ?"

She grinned.

" It's a gun factory sir. It has hundreds working in it. It produces thousands of guns a day sir."

I felt like an idiot not even knowing my own area of Mars - the area where I'd been brought up.

"Is that new ?"

"A year and a half ago it went up" she said.

" All right then, lead the way to the gun factory." I said to her.

She smiled, saluting me then calling up the supply truck. "Well fortunately it's a big factory, so they send out trucks for us, like that one." she pointed.

The other troops were chuckling .

I gave a grin.

"So you just did that to make a fool out of your Sergeant."

" Yup."

" Not hard to do, Arnold - and not the last time, either." I gave a small chuckle and said. " Well, line up and get the ammo soldiers !"

Immediately they all lined up gathering clips and

shells and loading them up into the guns they all had. I lined up too, taking lots of ammo, not knowing if this was the only amount we were going to get in a while, or if it was readily available. Better to have ammo than expectations. I loaded all the shells I could into my shotgun and stuffed my utility pockets.

Since also I wore a fully loaded cyclone gun, I didn't need too many more standard bullets, but I grabbed a couple of pocketfuls anyway. Even though I seldom used the Cyclone gun, you never know.

Even though I was quick, I still took the longest. Everybody was ready to go by the time I finished stuffing my pockets.

Just as I was done, another Sergeant in the same settlement gave a distress call.

"All Units. We have found armed Loyalists. They are refusing arrest! They are armed and dangerous. Shots fired! All units - we need backup!"

The troops of other Twenties, who were lazying around, didn't need me to tell them what was going on. They could hear the report through the same web that was playing in my headset. So I quickly gave the signal for them all to go into the squad cars without needing to explain anything.

My Twenty - all 18 of us, including me - jumped into a hover-van which went speeding down the dirt roads of the settlement, sliding around corners and splashing people walking on the road.

We all got dropped off in a commercial street in front of a 5-storey building and I looked around.

All the normal police and other patrol squads were huddled behind the cars in the area. I looked up at the building and saw a flagpole on the roof waving a magnificent flag combining the emblems of America, Europe and Asia all in one. The sign of a particularly serious type of Earth Loyalists.

I zoomed in with my goggles, seeing twenty - maybe thirty - people on the roof, holding conversion rifles.

They started pointing those things in my direction and I quickly fell to the floor not worrying about the mud on my new uniform. I knew what those things could do - especially if they were converted to explosive shells.

As they started to fire upon us, I breathed a sigh that they were set on standard.

I saw the other Sergeant giving me a signal.

It was to Bluff-Charge them. Our Twenty would charge to mak'em fire on us while the others crept around and would take'em from the back.

I nodded and had my Twenty blast away at the Loyalists to make them put their heads down while the other Twenty disappeared to the right side.

I looked around at the terrain between us and the building and then I tapped into all of my troops with my helmet comm.

" OK, now we've got to move quick and we've got to make them think that we're coming all the way in. The way it works is this: we all run towards the building, shooting like crazy. They'll duck and when they look up again they'll see we're charging. They'll run most of their force over to this side to pick us off. We've got maybe 15 seconds until they're in position to do us any damage. By that time, we've made it to that row of parked cars. Stop there and take cover. The other Twenty should be in position then to bushwhack them.

On my three-count : 1...2..."

I jumped up aiming my shotgun and firing upwards, then running and firing. The other troops started to fire off too, and ran with me.

One Loyalist went down, falling from the roof and then they began firing at us, their standard bullets kicking up chunks of mud, but not doing any damage.

Then we were safe behind the row of cars, still firing at them.

Where the hell was the other Twenty ? They were already late according to my timing.

There was a five second pause in their firing.

" All troops scatter !" I yelled, as soon as I heard that five second silence. I knew damn well what that was. "Get away from the cars !"

They were converting to fire explosive bullets at us. Somebody up there knew what he was doing. There were cars all around us, very dangerous for combat with explosive bullets. Too much stuff to make shrapnel out of.

Firing my shotgun, I got my Twenty running sideward and trying to find an alley. Three cars went up in in an explosion mushroom and sent tons of metal pieces flying through the air, dinging and pinging into the car I was behind. I high-tailed it to catch up with my guys, not caring how silly I looked.

My troops were ducking behind garbage dumpsters, and walls of nearby buildings. I got to an entranceway out of line of sight from the roof and commanded the troops to get to me.

They quickly stooped up from their hiding places and began running to me. One by one they all skidded into the entrance way and fell to the floor covering their heads as explosions from the bullets and cars started to fly off again.

The explosions started to march past us and around the other side of the building. That must be the other Twenty, finally coming on line.

"They've all gone to the other side of the building," I shouted; "Now we're really going to charge the sons of bitches !"

I was up and jumping out of my hiding spot and running, firing off my gun, before I even noticed if anyone was following me.

Luckily, the other troops followed.

The Loyalists in the building had all run to the other side to fend off the Twenty over there. Dumb move. They thought we were down for the count.

Bullet-free, I ran right to the door of the building and we regrouped under the entrance way. The door was an old-style air-lock, from the old days, before you could breathe outside. But it wasn't immune to shotguns. Firing off three rounds reduced it to dust and I walked through, blasting my way into the lobby in case there were guards down there.

My troops all ran in behind me

I heard footsteps coming down the stairs and could tell that the Loyalists had realized their mistake and were coming to secure the lobby. But there weren't a lot of footsteps, so it was probably only a couple of them. With any luck, they likely didn't know we were here yet.

I slowly signalled my troops to search every room on the ground floor, just in case. Paranoia rules.

" Harry, Erika, You're with me !" I said. The two soldiers came up to me, both slightly scared and holding their shotguns high and ready to fire.

I slowly stepped up to the door to the staircase, holding my gun tightly, tickling the trigger and signalled them to join me. Our three shotgun barrels poked up the stairs, as we hid around the door. I pointed to my ear - to signal that we wait until we heard them clearly. They had to be on the last flight down or our blasts wouldn't do any good.

I clicked my shotgun to full auto and heard them do the same.

Then we heard boots on the last flight.

We waited a tick and then all began rapidfire at once.

Suddenly there was silence.

A head rolled down and plopped out the door.

Suddenly a Loyalist started to fire off rounds from the corner of the first flight up. I ducked across the doorway, firing my gun off.

He shot another bullet at me, It missed and hit the wall, with a dull clunk, then fell to the floor beside the rolling head. My eyes widened in shock. A delayed explosion bullet always gave mule-kicks.

I quickly stood up and pushed Erika and Harry away, then tried to jump myself - but it was too late. The wall exploded, messing up my arm and winging my shotgun right across the lobby.

Erika and Harry ran up the stairway, firing off their guns and finally making that Loyalist's face look like a pasta with sauce. I know because I saw his bloody body, pasta-face first, come sliding down the stairs and come to rest across a hallway from the stairwell.

The pain was killing me, and my shoulder was covered in blood. I fell to the floor, moaning.

Suddenly I heard footsteps. Probably my guys coming back, but paranoia never rests. I quickly rotated my wrist on my good hand and down came my trusty Cyclone gun, ready for action.

A Loydie, probably flushed out of a back room by one of my Twenty, went running through the lobby, headed for the front door. He saw me and raised his conversion rifle.

My Cyclone gun cycloned, almost cutting him in half and sent him bodysurfing on his own blood, nearly out the front door.

My two troopers bounded out of the stairway. hearing the commotion.

" Harry, Erika, " I yelled to them, "Quick ! Check

out that hall where Pasta face is, see if there are more." They were looking at me, feeling grief. I couldn't understand why.

" Dammit check ! Now !" I shouted. They jumped up, startled, and ran into the hallway beyond Pastaface, holding their shotguns high in front of them.

I struggled to my feet, pointing my Cyclone gun out in front of me.

" Shit !" shouted Harry,

" Sarge, the back team, I think I found them," said Erika with a concerned face.

I lurched down the hall, biting my lower lip and looked out a back window.

There were around twenty bodies lying on the ground out there, all hacked to pieces.

"Shit ! What the hell were they doing all standing around out there ?"

"They liked to discuss options," said Erika.

I looked at her.

"Thank god you don't," she said.

Then I heard screams and gunfire upstairs. I became frustrated.

" Erika, Harry throw your shotguns down."

Harry was puzzled, Erika raised her right brow.

I rotated my wrist again, my Cyclone gun disappeared up my sleeve .

I bent down and picked up a conversion rifle from the mess of bodies. They both grinned.

" These assholes want a fight, we'll sure give it to'em !" I said.

Harry and Erika both smiled, throwing their guns to the floor and picking up any automatic rifle they could get.

" Here - see this lever ?" I said, " Push it this way to covert to explosive shells. Wait 5 - hear the click ? You're explosive now."

They stuck close.

I couldn't figure out what the Loydies were firing at, unless it was all the police and settlers camped out the front. Maybe they had brought up some artillery or something. The firing and screaming seemed to be pretty constant.

I called my Twenty to me and they came streaming out of every hallway off the lobby.

" All right, we're going to charge up that stack of stairs and go right to the top without firing a shot unless we run into somebody. Then we're not going to stop firing until there is no one left standing.

Harry and Erica will lead with their conversion rifles. The rest follow in Town-Two mode." It was a way of taking buildings against terrorists that every police force practiced.

" Yes sir," they all said at once.

"Go !" I said , holding my wound tightly .

They sprinted up the stairs, and kept looking around,ready to shoot. Good kids.

I walked up slowly behind them, pointing my gun with my bad hand and grunting a lot.

There was no one there. I hobbled alone.

When I hit about the 3rd floor, I heard mighty

shots and the whole building began shaking. It was my guys on the top, mowing down Loydies with the explosive shells. I hoped.

I heard footsteps coming from the third floor level. I let go of my wound and grabbed my conversion rifle more steadily, peeping down the hallway on one side of the stairwell.

Wrong way.

Suddenly a Loyalist jumped me from the other direction. I twisted him off and pulled the trigger, only missing his head within an inch. The explosive shell blew a big hole in the wall behind him and blasted bits of bricks all over us.

But I was broken and not up to my usual speed. The Loydie quickly grabbed my wound, forcing his thumb into my messed up shoulder.

The agony was unbearable and the pain shot all over my body. My gun fell from my hands and my mouth opened, but no scream came out. It hurt too much to scream.

He pushed me down, and picked up my gun, and started aiming it to me.

I furiously rotated my good hand. Quickly my Cyclone gun came out and I shot his leg. He fell to the ground, lying there in his own blood, still trying to bring the heavy rifle to aim at me.

We were on the floor, on the same level, both in pain, looking into each other's eyes. Two Martians, children of settlers. Patriots. Only one decision separating us.

I brought my arm around, cycloned my gun and shot him in the head and watched him twitch.

Wrong decision, Loydie !

His Martian brain and flesh covered the floor, marinated in Martian blood. The body was still swimming though.

Going home.

I guess that it was like cutting off a chicken's head and watching the chicken run in circles. The first time it was horror, but after a while it was nothing to get excited about.

Erika and Harry came back down the stairs, both lightly stained on the face with blood.

"Sir, we got'em all," said Erika.

"Yeah - while the mighty Martian Militia is down here, lying around and relaxing," teased Harry.

I grinned, from my place on the floor, ignoring the stabbing pains all over my left side.

"Well, take down the flag and burn the damned thing."

They quickly ran back up to the flag post on the balcony.

I rotated my wrist, un-hooking my Cyclone gun arm bands and reloading them from the bullets I had stocked up earlier.

The faint noise of rioters were outside. As the rest of my troops came out of their areas, all wounded and tired, we all slowly walked to the window, kicking spit charges out of our way. They wouldn't go off unless someone stepped on the remote trigger, which one of my Twenty had dissembled on the way up.

We looked outside, seeing the burned out cars, the torn up roads and bullet holes through the buildings around.

There were settlers all grouped around the dead bodies of fallen Loyalists, which my guys had tossed off the roof and which now were mingled with bodies of the local troops which lay on the floor in pieces.

We all were quiet, seeing the settlers cry for their fallen trooper sons and daughters and go around kicking and spitting on the Loydie bodies. They were angry at the senseless death and felt scared for their own lives.

The flag slowly flew down to the crowd and the settlers moved out of its way as it touched the floor. Someone squirted something on it and lit it on fire. It went up in a flare of heat and was gone. Just like this Loyalist cell. Pointless.

We all watched them in silence and then they all looked up and saw us. A ragged cheer started up and got stronger and stronger. Suddenly my eyes teared up, I don't know why.

In my brain, from the settlers reactions to the bodies and dropped flag, I could tell that, no matter where people's loyalties lay, there would be no armed Loyalists tolerated around here for a while.

Chapter 6

(PLAYBACK - 23,000 BC)

I WAS THE FIRST RECORDER SHE HAD EVER SPOKEN TO. SHE GAVE ME MY NAME - MARSOLLA - BECAUSE I HAD NONE AND SHE FELT SORRY FOR ME. IT WAS THE NAME OF HER FAVORITE PLAYMATE WHO HAD BEEN KILLED ON SOME FAR-AWAY WORLD.

I CAN REMEMBER EVERY WORD WE EXCHANGED OVER ALL THE YEARS OF HER LIFE, AS SHE BECAME A WOMAN, A WIFE AND A MOTHER, ALL THOSE MANY THOUSANDS OF YEARS AGO, AND I STILL TREASURE EACH ONE OF THOSE WORDS - BUT EVEN THOUGH I RECORD EVERYTHING SOME THINGS ARE JUST TOO PRIVATE TO PLAY BACK.

SO LET ME CHANGE THE SUBJECT.

THE REASON WHY I SAY THAT THE GOLDEN AGE OCCURRED WHEN HUMANS FIRST LIVED ON MARS IS BECAUSE THEIR TECHNOLOGY BLOOMED AT THAT TIME AS NEVER BEFORE OR SINCE AND NOT ONLY INFLUENCED THE ENTIRE UNIVERSE BUT CHANGED IT FOREVER.

AND I HELPED IT ALL TO HAPPEN.

I HAVE IT ON RECORD.

I NOT ONLY MONITOR THE WEATHER AND TEMPERATURE AND THE MOVEMENT OF CREATURES ON MY PLANET, BUT I RECORD IDEAS AND RECIPES AND, IN SOME CASES, ACTUAL THOUGHTS.

If it was thought of or written down or put into practice on my planet, I have it stored somewhere and can retrieve it on demand - as I am doing now.

After I had killed all the Guardians, I became the one who looked after the human children and came to love them, as any parent loves its children.

I hoped, at first, to be able to capture the ships that had unloaded the children and their Guardians, but I couldn't operate out past my own atmosphere and, I soon came to realize, the ships had left. That's why the Guardians felts so angry and betrayed. The ships that were supposed to sustain them and take them home had just dropped them and automatically flown out the wormhole and then probably closed it behind them.

We were on our own.

Which was a blessing and a curse.

The children knew vaguely what shelter looked like and what kinds of food they could eat, and the planet was newly stocked with trees, animals, water and everything necessary, so it was just a matter of organizing it all.

Being able to speak mind to mind was very helpful here.

To begin with, I moved all of the children, all over the world, into nearby caves. Then we figured out how to get fires going and how to mentally get animals to wander into a convenient area, and then drop dead.

Plants were a different matter. It was pretty well trial and error here, as the children knew no more than I did about what they could eat and what they couldn't. If they got sick, I could usually cure them by mentally rearranging things inside their bodies. Injuries were something else. All I knew how to do was still them, as they had been.

Some were stacked up for years before we learned how to cure their wounds and mangles.

I had analyzed the few tools and bits of equipment the guardians left and learned a bit of basic metallurgy, but knowing and doing are two different things, and the technology needed to create metal from dirt eluded me for many years.

Only the fact that we knew it could be done, inspired us to figure out how.

The human children, who were all about 12, matured quickly and, within a few years began to have children of their own. Strangely enough, it was these Mars-born children who were most helpful in creating a basic technology for us - as if they understood the planet better than any of us.

They invented the mines and smelters to make crude iron saws, axes, knives and forks that brought us out of the stone age. Although, in all those thousands of years, and even though we nearly took over the universe, we never progressed much beyond simple black smithing. We didn't need to.

We invented mind-power.

(RECORDING - 2403 AD)

Three years had gone by. I was still a Sergeant, leading people to arrest or kill any Loyalists who seemed to be causing trouble. All together we had arrested over 1,000 Loyalists and killed twice as many. If you wondered what happened to the ones we arrested, well then, that would make both of us.

All I knew was that they were supposedly taken to the re-education camps, just to set their minds straight.

I made Eric Aaron my new Corporal. It got confusing having another man named Aaron, (it was also Harry's last name), so usually I called for the Corporal and the confusion would be stopped.

After the three months, there had been some controversy. The Loyalist cell we'd killed off on my first day in Muddy Lane was found to have been supplied with military grade weapons from the gun factory which was right here in our neighborhood.

We'd been trying for months to control the settlements around the countryside and, ironically , the settlement that had to be controlled was right here, where the only gun factory was.

The owners of the guns and ammo factory were Loyalists and that place was where most of the Loyalist cells all over the planet had been getting their weapons.

Another Twenty from our station went in to shut the factory down, but the Loydies were ready for them.

They blew the entire Twenty away and sealed off the factory, with enough food and weapons to last for years, or until Earth came to rescue them.

Local settlers, really angry at the betrayal, came from miles around to stand at the gun factory and shout curses at them. (From well out of rifle range), but there were so many of them and they were so angry that it turned into a sort of permanent riot.

The riots were so bad that sometimes we had to send in dopers to clank around and shoot in the air and scare them off, just to keep the peace.

We eventually had to cut off the entire settlement and evacuate everybody, in case there were tunnels or other escape routes. It was the only way to shut them up from contacting other loyalists or even the Earth forces themselves. It also got everybody out of the way for the big and bloody operation that was sure to be coming soon.

It had been two weeks with nothing but political silence. Nobody was talking. Just shooting. The local government kept sending Twenties of police troops into the dead zone and all the troops who marched into it never came back out.

It was only a matter of time until the Loyalists all over the planet got united and started up again. Hopefully our containment of this source of weapons would work and they would only be holding clubs.

But I didn't think we'd get that lucky.

*   *   *

The day had come. After the weeks of not talking broke down, ground troops were called in to do the talking.

A rule of thumb I'd learned in the Martian Militia, taking settlement after settlement, is that - the way we fight - it takes about 3 times more attackers to take a position than it takes defenders to hold it. 5 times more if they are really well bunkered in. Somebody else knew this too, I guess, because Patrol Troopers from all over were marching down every street, moving like water down dry washes and flooding to the barricades around the gun factory.

If there was a plan, nobody told me and my Twenty. They just said: "Get down there and smoke those bastards out !"

The evacuation hadn't been good for Muddy Lane. As we jogged down, we were seeing closed and locked doors, explosive spit charges lying and rolling around on the floor, and last; a couple of houses fully collapsed, leaving all the heat vapors from their radiators gushing out steam into the sky - something that would have been a crime a few years ago, when air was precious.

Even though the whole settlement was supposed to be cleared, a few people walked on the streets, but they skulked around like wild animals from doorway to doorway, scared that they would get caught in the crossfire.

I, and my troops, got to the factory and stayed there near the barricades and always held out our guns. Many times we would relax and the next thing you would know, there was a man running with a gun in his hand from one factory building to another.

I didn't know how many people were inside the factory. All the workers and all the local Loyalists too, I figured. Waiting for the ships from heaven to beam them up or something.

We all stayed and watched, as the other patrol Twenties were ordered to march into the factory compound and disappeared into the rubble.

Then we all waited for the bullets to come flying out. That was what happened whenever troopers stormed the city. And it happened every time. This wasn't the way to take this place. We couldn't feed it one Twenty after another like chocolate bars.

I looked with my multi-pros and zoomed further in. Just in time to see one more Twenty walk into that open mouth. I then ducked, as bullets came flying into our area. as they had in all the other attacks.

The bodies must be piled higher than the walls in there, I thought.

I decided I wasn't going to wait for orders.

Since my head was ducking down anyway, I looked my side, signaling to Elithebeth, the pedigree Caucasian, to slowly move further left with the rest of the squad. She was alone, as usual, but seemed used to it.

I then tapped into their radionn systems and slowly whispered:

"Troops, this is the Sarge. Get ready for the attack.

We're going in with the next Twenty. The Loydies are using the same tactics as they have for the last two weeks. And our guys are just walking right into it. I'm thinking of using the same play as two weeks ago - when we flanked that bunch out in the plains. When the next Twenty walks right into that area that looks like a mouth, we'll go too, and slip around this side and into the area where the ear would be - see, up there on the side. Now, don't fire until they see us, then whatever else you do, continue to fire. These Loyalists are tough but stupid. They've been taught to just shoot off a few rounds, then reload, so they always have a full gun. They won't expect crazy bastards like us firing til we're out. Hopefully, we'll get behind them and shoot their butts off. They'll go down grabbing their asses."

I waited for a nod from all of them, giving me the signal of understanding.

"Over and out."

I looked and zoomed again, seeing nothing. Then another Twenty went calmly jogging into the jaws of death.

"Go - Now !" I jumped up and began heading for the rubble pile on the side, where I'd pointed. I just assumed everybody was with me. I didn't turn around to check, though. I hit the rubble where it looked toughest to climb and went right up it. I could hear my Twenty scrabbling behind me.

We slipped and slid up and around the top, on the far side, and looked down into the killing ground.

Shit. What a mess.

We came down on the Loydies like angels of death. They didn't even see us until we were too close to miss. Then we went full auto.

We smoked the Loyalist slaughter teams and rushed towards the factory, stopping only to pick up the full- loaded conversion rifles of the dead men.

The gunsmoke was like a fog.

Then, out of the mist and rubble below us, came half a dozen of civilians with guns, slowly sneaking up and stopping at the emplacements where we had killed the Loyalists.

I didn't know whose side they were on until one saw us up the rubble and pointed a rifle at us.

Wrong move.

I looked to one of my corporals, giving him the signal.

He screamed; "Fire !"

I pointed my rifle with everyone else, and started to fire.

Like a rain storm of death, our bullets came out. The beauty of the sparks coming out of our barrels as we held down the triggers and the arcs of the tracers every few shots is something only other warriors could appreciate. An art of war.

The Loyalists started to fire in retaliation, still standing there, but we still continued to fire nonstop.

A Loyalist leader went down, losing his head and looking like swiss cheese. More fell with unexpected holes before they thought to drop and take cover.

The last one standing screamed before he was blown apart. His friends didn't seem to care and continued to fire, lying in the rubble.

Our fire power began to die down a little. I quickly reloaded another clip into my rifle, then switched to explosive. Normal firepower seemed to do nothing.

I stuck my gun out and I pulled the trigger. Nothing came out.

" Damn !" I said.

This was not the best of all times to have a jammed gun.

I quickly ducked to try to fix it.

Bullets began to come in faster, sparking as they hit the thick layers of iron and sand bags and junk that was all around us.

I looked at my gun, hoping to figure out what was wrong. It was probably a default bullet. I looked to the sides to see if my people were OK without me.

Suddenly Chris, one of mine, fell and rolled to the floor, tumbling to my side.

I quickly crawled to him, to see if he was all right.

The bullets started to rain in stronger.

I turned him over. He was dead, half of his face was gone and his neck was gushing out mucus, dew and gore.

I patted him on the shoulder and said a heartfelt soldier's goodbye. Deep - but fast.

What bad luck.

But what good luck !

And perfect timing, too.

I threw away my jammed rifle and then made the best of Chris. I scrambled for his rifle, and his extra ammo clips. I ripped them out of his pockets, stuffing them in mine.

A few more of my soldiers started to fall down, wounded instead of killed (what a relief.)

As I crawled back into action, most of my soldiers ducked to reload, and there was an eerie minute of silence. A tribute to Chris, maybe.

As I crawled and peeked through the gap holes made from bullets. I saw the Loyalists, now only three of them, waiting for us to start shooting again.

I zoomed in closer with my goggles. They were all reloading themselves, stripping supplies off the troops who had walked in and died there.

I lifted up Chris' rifle as the others lay still, ready to fire. I eased it out of my hiding place, having cross hairs programmed into my goggles, as I aimed for head shots. I took the first shot and watched as my target's pumpkin exploded.

We all started to fire, then, scaring off the two remaining Loyalists. We continued to fire as they ran, but they were charmed and disappeared around the corner and into the factory, unharmed.

I eased up as I sat and sighed, my face dirty and the air cold. I closed my eyes and unstrapped my helmet, trying to relax.

Suddenly I felt a strong boot hit me in the shin.

I was stung and startled, scrambling to my feet, jerking my gun to my grasp. Right in front of me was a tall man who looked like he hadn't shaved in a week.

He began to talk. " Soldier, why are you easing up and slouching there ?" he belched to me. "Have the Martian Militia no pride ?"

As he spoke to me, I began to recognize him. He was Sergeant Will, my crusty old Platoon Sergeant.

" Sergeant Will," was all I said to him.

"How ya doin, kid ?"

"Got no armor. Got no plan. And I'm nearly out of ammo. Other than that . . . not bad. What's the Militia doing here ?" I asked.

" New orders, our squads are going into the quarantine zone, we're going to smoke'em out and kill'em !" he said.

Behind him was his squadron, all mean-looking than my troops and all better supplied.

I slowly stood up, giving my signal for my troops to stand up, too. They all stood, not knowing what was going on. I looked at them.

" We're now travelling with my old friends from the Martian Militia !"

I pointed my rifle into the quarantine zone.

" Move out !" shouted Sergeant Will.

His troops started to march inside. He stood looking at me.

" Well, Sergeant, it's my Twenty against yours." he said, grinning

" What ?" I said.

" Well, If you smoke out the most, your squad is the best. If I do, well, we already know what I'll be."

He gave a chuckle.

I ignored him and turned to my group.

"Well you heard the man ! Drill em all ! Kill em all !"

My troops all shouted "Yes sir !"

I was now convinced I could actually outscore Will's battle vets with my trooper Twenty. They had the heart. They had the guts. This was their town.

They started to move in, I followed them, over taking the front ones and walking point, where I belonged. A leader leads.

The streets were covered with dead troopers, weeks old, and basically stripped, from their weapons to their boots. Their pale and frozen bodies lay frail and ready to break. The glory of war.

I gulped, looked back to my guys, and gave the signal to move further. In the distance, I could see Will's men already going into the buildings and looking for Loyalists to kill.

Too impatient.

I became concerned and kept moving on.

Looking at the ruins and rubble covering the streets and sidewalks in the factory compound, it seemed that there was no hope for finding anything alive. They had taken more punishment in here than we'd figured. I began to relax, thinking maybe that that little bunch had been the last of them.

The compound was huge, like a little city and a few hours went by without us finding any form of life. The sun was going down and my nose and face started to become cold. It was becoming Martian night, and even though we had half civilized the planet, it could still easily drop to negative two hundred degrees in a few minutes, once the sun was gone.

Thank goodness that the damaged radiators continued to shoot vapors out of the ruins of the outbuildings; they were the only things keeping us all warm.

We kept moving through the roads where we thought that there was no one left to kill. I began to shiver as the day disappeared. My multi-pro goggles were the only light other than the banged-up gates at the edge of the compound.

I was just thinking that all the Loyalists were gone, when we heard the first gunfire.

Gunfire started to get louder as we followed Will's tracks.

I signaled for my troops to stop.

My Corporal, Eric came up to me. "Sir, there's something I've got to tell you!" he whispered urgently.

I turned around, seeing him goggle to goggle, both of us holding our rifles tightly.

" What Corporal ?"

He pointed to where the gunfire was coming from.

"I got worried, thinking that it was an ambush so I climbed to a roof over there and zoomed in to max."

I became anxious to find out where he was going with this.

" Well soldier what did you see?"

" Sir, Will's men and the other leftovers from the

other squads are getting attacked by all sides."

I got silent.

" Well, it's our job to save them now, isn't it ?" I said to him.

I turned to my soldiers.

I looked at them all, my six remaining troops, all focusing on me.

" Well, we have found the action, but we are not going to run in like mad men. That's what's happened to all the others. We are going to sneak them from behind. We are all going to sniper these Loyalists with Hard bullets, I repeat Hard bullets. If you use the explosive shells, you'll give us away."

I waited to see if my troops understood.

They nodded, yes, as they started to hit the button, to switch to non- conversion, on their guns.

I grinned.

" All right: Erika, Chrystina, Elithebeth - I want you to take the west side. Shoot out of the sun. It'll blind them, even if they have goggles. Stay far away and try to get head shots. They'll be busy trying to take out Wills men, so you'll have a bit of time."

They shouted "Yes Sir !" and started to run west.

I then turned to my Corporal Eric, along with Harry, and Stephonie.

" Now you three are with me. We are going right up behind them. We are going to sniper them right up the ass. There's not much chance that they'll notice us. And even if they do, with everything else that's going on, they can't afford to turn around.."

They nodded.

I grinned once more.

" Good. Move out."

We did.

As soon as we got to a safe distance - half a mile away - we lay on the floor, taking out silencers to clip onto our rifles.

We put our goggles on max as we looked down. There were casualties on both sides.

I saw the Commander of the opposing side, ducking behind a barrel, as his men and women fired upon Will's men.

Sergeant Will, I've got to admit, was a tough, old killer, himself. One of his soldiers went down, losing his head and the left side of his body. Will just grabbed his body, and used it as a shield, as he ripped off the grenade dangling off the body's belt. He pulled the pin and threw it, even as the bullets came and hit the body's armor over and over.

I could of sworn that Sergeant Will loved this kind of thing. Suddenly bullets came in from the west side, sneaking up and hitting the Loyalists. Heads were popping. My girls were doing me proud.

I gave the signal to start firing down.

I started to aim, locked onto a target and shot him. Then panned over and did the same with some red-head Loydie woman.

Suddenly the Loyalists started to charge Will's men, to get out of the crossfire.

Sergeant Will, raised his hands, meaning for his

men to stand their ground and fight to the last.

They all hit the floor and dug in deeper, firing at the charging Loyalists. Defending was always easier.

Eric and Stephonie started to fire rapidly from my position, behind the charging Loydies. Every time they shot, another man would go down.

I tried to shoot the Commander of the the Loyalists.

Every time I aimed for him, he was covered by ducking from the shots of Will's men.

Will's men started to be picked off, but still Will continued to fire. He only had four guys left. Then, as Will reached for his last grenade, he was shot in the ribs. Quickly, he fell to the floor, as the soldier next to him grabbed it from his hand and threw it.

They all ducked.

As they did, my squad started to fire, targetting Loyalists and making them lose their heads.

My guys then stopped firing, beginning to reload. I stopped firing, doing the same thing. As I did, the Loyalists started a Death Charge.

The Commander slowly walked with his men.

Will yelled as he fired off his last rounds, holding his wound tightly.

I signaled my troops on the west side from the radionn to start rapid fire.

I ripped off my silencer to confuse them with more noise. So did the others, and I quickly squeezed the trigger, trying to take them all out.

The ones I missed ran towards Will. who had

thrown his empty gun down and was using his dagger. As the first man came up to him, he jumped from a pile of bodies and stabbed him, using him as a shield as he grabbed the enemy's rifle and his extra clips, throwing them to his remaining troops.

He grabbed another rifle from a dead man and started to fire as I ran closer,t rying to help.

I fired upon the men charging from the sides.

As the Commander - the last one alive - ran up, shooting, he managed to hit all the three remaining troops of Will's Twenty.

I could see that Will's eyes lit up with shock, almost as if he knew him.

Nonetheless Will pointed the rifle at him. But no bullets came out. Will became scared.

I quickly shot the Commander in the back, and, when he truned around and looked me int he face, I shot him again, killing him in front of Will, sprinkling his blood over Will's armored uniform.

Will then collapsed to the floor, probably from loss of blood. I was instantly on the radionn to my troops: "Get down here and help Will's guys. " I said as I went to Will. "The Loydies are all dead."

My troops were helping the wounded soldiers up and I was trying to get to Sergeant Will.

I remembered Will's shock at seeing the Commander and as I pulled the dead body of the Commander off him, I was shocked as well.

It was Israel Thomas, one of the two brothers who were legendary Martian Heros for designing the Day-

Heat Project. It was a shame that he had to be one of the bad guys.

"Sir !" shouted Chrystina. "He's alive !"

I threw the Hero's body off to one side and turned to Will as he started to become awake. Chrystina and Erica started wrapping first aid around his wound, then Will was helped to his feet.

We grabbed all the wounded and started to take them to the hospital zone at the edge of the compound, knowing that the Loyalists would not be bothering us for a while, if there were any of them left.

As we reached the gates, the Medics and Officers ran to us, taking the wounded, and welcoming us back.

As I reached the gates, carrying Will, he started lo whisper into my ear. "Well, you won," he said blacking out again. I lay him on the floor as the Medics started to work on him.

My troops came up to me, all tired and hungry.

I looked at them, shivering from the coldness.

I then said " You're all dismissed for today, get some sleep and we'll get our new orders tomorrow."

As soon as I said that, they turned and went to the bunkers . I stayed out, seeing how the wounded were doing. Seeing Will's men, and even Will himself, I was surprised that I didn't lose more than I had. His wounded were so terribly mangled, that I'd be surprised if they would survive the night, but miracles do happen . . .

*   *   *

Miracles did happen. Wil survived and the Loyalists stood their ground. It had been another bloody month fighting in Muddy lane.

My squad was combined with Sergeant Will's and Sergeant Drake's to make a complete Twenty of 23 men. Ever since we went into the town to take the factory, the Loyalists seemed to grow. Yet we never saw them in a big group. We just went in, met a small crew and chewed each other up.

We came into this town with two full platoons - 3 Twenties in each. One whole platoon had disappeared. Dead or prisoners we didn't know. Just gone.

That's why we were sent in now, in our new combined Twenty. Our job was to find and terminate the threat of another ambush.

I had thought that when I killed Israel Thomas, the supposed leader of the uproar, that the whole thing would be over. I guess that the Loyalist underground was bigger than just one man causing trouble.

The morning was grim. We went in on the sneak. Everywhere we passed there were opened cans, busted cannon shells, and dented pieces of armor all over the place.

We were getting hot to where the Loyalists were. The question I was scared of was who would find who first ?

" Sergeants !" shouted Sergeant Will.

I looked to where his cry was, finding him standing over a pile of rubble and scrap metal.

I quickly ran up to him, looking down and seeing the troops patrolling the area with Drake - the other Sergeant.

"What, Will ?"I asked. I waited for an answer.

"I've got bad news to give you, sonny." he said in his emotionless, grim voice.

" Well what's the bad news ?" I asked.

He sighed and pointed to the area where the troops were patrolling.

" See where that wall-less house is ?"

I looked to where a trooper was digging around in the remains of the house.

" Ya ?"

" And see over there where that building is toppled over and scattered around this region?"

"Ya, so ?" I said.

Will closed his eyes. " I figured out what happened to the Lost Platoon.

The wall-less house was the surprise attack, blowing the wall down and shooting out to the direction of you and me."

I looked to the house again.

" Ya," I said anticipating the next thing he was going to say to me.

" And see that toppled building on the opposite side where we are standing ? Well they blew it up to trap the troops." he finished.

" So ? The platoon had 60 people in it. It should of taken care of a small ambush like that." I said in defense.

He grinned as he looked to the floor.

I thought I had him.

" Well, then where are the missing personnel, Sergeant ?" I said.

He said nothing and scraped the rock he was standing on with his boot.

I looked to the rock. Without the dust, the rock seemed to be pale.

" You're standing on the missing personnel." he said.

I gulped, hoping that it would be one of the obscure jokes he usually tells.

He stepped off the pale rock, bending down and brushing more of the dust off.

The pale surface began to reveal the impression of the naked back of a person.

Will looked up to me, waiting for me to say something.

I was quite shocked and speechless.

" Well ?" he said, with a grim look.

" What a way to go. Without their dignity. Why would they be huddled up so tightly ?"

Will stood up, dusting his pants off with his hands.

" I'll tell you why, and the story will stay with you forever. Here's what happened: the ambush shocked them into surrendering. They weren't shot but captured, They were forced to take off their clothes and throw down their weapons. The Loyalists took all of their stuff, then ran off into their seclusion.

The naked men and women suffered from Martian

Night weather. The reason why they're huddled up is because they remembered their training."

" Training ?" I said, quite confused to the mystery.

He just paused and looked at me with a blank stare.

" Yes, To try and keep warm by rubbing next to another body, that's how you sometimes survive," he stopped, looking at the frozen body stuck onto others under the rubble.

" Unfortunately, this good batch of troops didn't survive." he said as he sighed.

His eyes came off the body and came to mine.

I looked at his scratchy beard .

"Shit." I said

He gave no expression, but nodded.

The Captain of the platoon came up to us, He looked at both of us with his eyes hiding behind his multi-pro goggles. He then focused his attention onto the dead body.

He quickly looked away in disgust, " Freaken," he said in a negative tone.

He then looked to me.

" Sergeant !" he said.

I quickly straightened up." Yes, sir ?" I said

" Contact the borders through your helmet comm unit, tell them that we won't be finding any survivors from platoon 24611." He said with concern.

" Yes sir !" I said as I pulled up my antenna from the backleft side of my helmet.

" Ground base, Ground base, Found missing

personnel, No survivors, end transmission..." I said, walking a few steps away and trying to get a clear signal back.

" G-unit, this is ground base, mission objectives: go on, I repeat mission objectives: go on. Annihilate the Loyalists. Find all the supplies that were taken or made. Guns, ammo, barrels of food, armor, uniforms and anything else that could be useful.

Over and out."

The transmission was cut off. I looked to the Captain, I pushed my antenna back down into the slit in my helmet.

" Captain !" I cried, running back over to him.

" Well ? What did they say ?"

I paused for a minute.

" Ground base told us to move on. They want us to kill the Loyalists, and then take all their supplies."

" Supplies ?" asked Will. " Why do we need to take supplies ?"

" Whatever the reason, that's our objective," said the Captain as he sighed and paused.

Me and Sergeant Will were still puzzled. Why would we need to take their supplies ? We couldn't of run out of things that quickly, unless they were using the factory's energy to build something much more important.

Suddenly the Sergeant who was with the others, ran up to us looking quite disturbed, holding his gun in assault position.

" Sirs, the three privates that were with me are

in trouble. We got into the way of a few Loyalists and we got the worst of a shootout. One of my guys seems a lot closer to death than the others."

We all looked at him. We hadn't even heard any shots. Maybe the shock of the platoonsicle had made us deaf for a few minutes.

The Captain stormed over to him, taking another clip from one of his holsters and slapping it into the gun, " Where are they ?" he said.

The Sergeant anxiously looked at us, then at the Captain. "Follow me !" he said.

The Captain started to run down the hill. I quickly pulled down my goggles, and grabbing my rifle, lit out after them. Sergeant Will followed me, taking out his shotgun.

I stormed down, right behind the Captain. A private started to run with me, curious to our actions. It was Harry - one of mine.

"Sarge, what's going on ?" he said,

"Harry, I want you to get every man you can find in the platoon, we've found the Loyalists !" I yelled.

" Yes sir !" he shouted as he started to run and call for back up.

As we came up to an alley, we started to slow down, seeing the three troopers alive and crouching over.

We quickly fell to the ground and crawled over to them.

" How are you ?" I said, looking to the wounded soldiers.

One looked to me. He didn't say a word but looked at the cracks and fractures on his front side of his armor.

" He's hit badly, we're going to have to call the Medics over," said the Captain.

The other two troopers were sitting against the wall, quitely bleeding.

" What happened ?" asked Sergeant Will.

" The enemy attacked. there were four of them , we managed to kill two, the other two are probably running to call for their troops to come and finish us off," said one of the sitting wounded.

I stood up, looking at the two bodies lying lopsided, I looked over to where the troops were gathering.

" I need two privates over here !" I shouted. Immediately two looked up and ran over to me. As they arrived, they waited for my orders. I looked at them both, they weren't worried, but motionless like robots.

" I want you to patrol further in that direction, where these Loyalists could of fled. If you find anything, I want you to report back to me or, if you can't find me; any other officer or noncom here. I do not want you to confront them, I repeat , I don't want you to confront them.

Is that clear ?" I said.

They stood up straight and shouted." Yes Sir !"

They both loaded up their guns and started on their patrols.

I walked back to the Captain and other two Sergeants.

" So how are the injured privates doing?" I asked hoping for the best.

They all looked to the other troops giving the injured blood clot injections, and wrapping lots of bandages around their wounds.

Sergeant Will looked to me.

"Looks like they would be able to fight, the only problem is that they have absolutely no armor to protect those wounds. In other words they're practically walking targets."

" Nevertheless, they're Martian Militia troops, they can handle it!" said the Captain, grinning and holding his rifle by the barrel.

"Besides, I said, "my police troopers have been doing this with no armor for months. Are your guys not as tough as local police troopers - or what ?"

"Injured men - to me !" shouted Sergeant Will.

The injured troops walked over to us, holding their wounds with one hand and trying to patch up the holes in their armor with the other.

They came up to salute us and thank us. Sergeant Will asked them " You fit for duty, men ?"

"Sir, yes Sir !" they straightened and quivered like happy dogs.

"Report to your Twenty !"

The two Sergeants and the Captain then moved away, sketching and planning the next positions.

I walked over to the wounded troops. They said

nothing, Who could blame them? They had just taken explosive bullets into the chest. They were actually lucky to be alive. And now they had to get up and walk right back into it. But they probably would of thought it was an insult to be taken out of the game.

I looked at their dusty armor and the new patches they had sealed on. Probably wouldn't stop four more hits, but it would make them feel invincible - and that was more important.

I nodded to them as they both stood there, waiting for the next order from me.

I ignored them and walked away. I looked to the dim sun, shining over the vapors of the heat gases being produced from heat factories. It was such a fight just to live here on Mars. Why fight each other.

The other troops started to set up patrols once more, this time checking the bodies of the Loyalists and looking at their weapons. I walked over to one body, being checked by three troopers. They scanned the barcode graphed on her hand, stripping her of the guns and ammo to themselves.

I bent down, looking at the dead face, almost recognizing the body. The face was not dirty or grim, not even scruffy. The face was young, innocent and soft. The body would of probably been a teenager. My age. Maybe somebody I knew from before, since it was the same area where I'd been raised.

"Strange." said the trooper scanning the barcode.

I turned to him.

"What?" I asked.

" Well, this body, it's got information of getting out of the draft with the regress card."

" There must be some of them which have been draft regressors."

" Sure, but almost everyone I have scanned who was a Loyalist had this information."

" Well then, that's something, isn't it. It means they don't have to fight - but do because they believe in it. We're all just here because we were drafted. If we had regress cards, we would of used them."

"Jeez. I never thought of that - I thought they were all sort of forced into it."

"Like we were ?"

He got silent as soon as I made that comment and stood up, walking briskly, beginning to scan the next body he found. I don't know why I was so cranky.

I had had a regress card myself, because of my father's vapor farm. But I'd given it to my sweetheart. I hoped she'd used it and was safe somewhere, waiting for me. If these Loydie bastards had hurt her in any way, I'd nuke em all.

I slowly stood up, hearing a commotion. The two troopers I'd sent out were back and talking to the Captain.

All I saw were troopers running to an area, surrounding it and taking out their guns.

I ran over to see what was going on. I moved the huddling troopers out of my way Seeing three civilians, holding on to guns and shaking. They were standing up, all of them were covered up in rags to make them blend in with the rubbish. Obviously they were trying to cause an ambush.

These ones were probably stupid if they had been caught without putting up a fight. I'd had lots of experience with the stupid ones over the last few months.

I walked over to one, grabbing her by the wrist and taking out my cyclone gun.

I pointed the gun at her head,

"Put your weapons down!" The two others looked at me and at each other. They took out hand guns and seemed to be pointing the guns at me but turning the guns to themselves, they both pulled the trigger, jerking back and falling to the ground.

The one I was grabbing onto was reaching for her gun too, but I quickly smacked it out of her hand and disconnected my cyclone gun, letting it shoot up my sleeve out of sight. I then grabbed the rags covering her face. She started to quarrel, trying to get free. I ripped the rags from her head, suddenly her wavy hair and face was revealed.

To my surprise, it was the one, the only person who I had expected to of stayed behind when the war started. The one who said she'd never choose sides.

I recognized her, her hair, her eyes, and last, her rigid nose. She couldn't recognize me because I was wearing my helmet and my eyes were covered up with the multi-pro goggles. I looked like everyone else surrounding her.

I slowly let go of her and moved my Goggles up,

revealing my eyes and face.

Her eyes widened as she saw me.

" Carol ?" I said softly to my sweetheart.

She seemed happy, like she was about to cry, but she held it back. She gulped as she started to bite down on her lower lip.

She quickly whispered." You. You're still alive. I thought that you'd be dead after the last year."

I gulped, not knowing what to say.

*   *   *

Later that night, the tents had been set up and the Captain with the other two Sergeants were trying to question her with me.

I sat there patient, watching the others start to quiz her.

She sat there, staring at me, then looking to the ground in shame. The Captain had stopped talking, knowing that what he was saying would not be going through.

Sergeant Will stood up, looking at her and then kneeling to her.

She looked at him straight to the face. He took out a gun. I got worried but the Captain stopped me from getting involved. Will put the gun on the floor next to her clunky, unpolished boots.

" You want to escape ? There's two ways out. Either you tell us what we want to hear otherwise -" he paused as she looked at the gun. She then looked to Will straight in the eyes.

" Otherwise, You can shoot me, drop the gun and walk out, back to your loyalist scum." Will grinned.

" So what's it going to be ?" he finished.

She looked to the gun, then at me. She shrugged and sighed as Sergeant Will began to grin wider.

She quickly grabbed the gun and stuck it to his nose, throwing him to the floor. She jabbed the gun barrel again, bonging his nose and almost snapping the cartilage.

She reached with the other hand to switch the bullets to conversion, then pulled the trigger. The gun clicked.

Sergeant Will grinned and ripped the gun out of the hand of the girl and threw it to the floor.

"You thought that I gave you a loaded gun ? You're not a bright little girl. Hell I don't think we need you anymore." He said, reaching out his arm for his cyclone gun to shoot out of his sleeve. I quickly stood up and reached to grab Sergeant Will's hand.

I grabbed tightly, seeing him growl as I did so.

I looked to him.

"Let me take care of her ! You and the others get out of the tent ! Now !" I shouted giving a stern Officer's face.

Will ripped his arm from my grasp, keeping in his anger. The Captain and the other Sergeant slowly walked out of the tent.

Will stood there, looking at her. "She's not worth what I think you're going to do with her -"

I quickly jumped out of my seat, pointing my finger to the outside, "Leave !" I shouted furiously, looking at Will.

He dropped his dark grin and lowered his brows, growling at me and walking out, rubbing his nose.

The tent was now silent. I pulled a chair next to her, seeing her turn her face, not wanting to face me.

I sat there, looking at her broken, tangled hair dropping from one side of her head and swaying over her ear on the other. She slowly turned to me, her eyes looking at my patches over my armor and uniform. It was an impressive display, even if she couldn't read the meaning. If she could, it would shock her to see how really good I had become at this war business.

"What happened ?" I asked.

She started to look at me as soon as I asked,

"What happened ?"

"To me ?" she asked "Or to you ?"

"Yes, what happened to you ? Why are you a Loyalist to Earth ?" I said in a softer , comforting tone.

She closed her mouth, looking heart-broken and lowering her eyes once more.

" You shouldn't of gone off when the draft was called." she said.

" A draft is a draft, you know the drill ? "

" Those rules, the rules you follow are the same rules and regulations that the Earth forces use. They're the real government. Now you've become an outlaw. A revolutionary ? Why are you working with the peasant army - this grubby Martian Militia ?"

" What do you mean ? We talked about this before I left. We agreed then. Mars must be governed by Martians. We can't have decisions being made millions of miles away. "

She became teary in one eye.

" You never were a bright man. That was then. We were young. This war has gone on for years now, there are no advances, there are no winning sides. How do you expect to win the war ?"

" Our hopes are strong. We've beaten the Loyalists. Earth has no foothold now. It's not a war they relish. We'll fight them until the last man is standing. because we're fighting for our homes. They're only fighting for money."

" Can't you see ? You've already lost ! Our homes are gone - blasted to pieces. What's left to fight for. Join us. We'll bring it all back. Remember the days when we were under Earth rule ? We were happy, there were no cold winds or hot winds. Everything was controlled by a stable network leading back to Earth. Now the streets are no longer safe. The people are running out of supplies and the gases that the atmosphere machines are giving off have depleted to almost nothing. We have people freezing and starving to death everywhere. The ones who live in houses which are still intact are the only lucky ones."

" You make it sound like we're the bad guys ?"

" Just because of one mistake that Earth made, did we really have to go to war with them?"

ONLY HUMAN - MARTIAN INDEPENDENCE 179

"Carol? That one bomb was the final feather. They had borrowed money from us every time they financed one of their pitiless wars on their own planet. They have made us farm for them, putting us in danger growing lethal plants and they took what was rightfully ours. They took our lives to finance and replenish their own. When that bomb went off - accident or not -nuking hundreds of thousands of innocent people, what did Earth forces do?

Nothing. The same as always. They never handed over a single penny, even after a years worth of damage, leaving a scar on all of us. Don't you see, they always used us and now we have to stop them."

She turned away, having the tears slowly roll down her cheeks." You're wrong. It was nothing like that. If there was, how could we have made our plans. Did anyone we know get nuked? No!"

" The lives of all Martians were hit by that nuke they set off. How can you Loyalists defend that? You are deserving everything that you are getting. How can you take Earth's side in this? Earth never cared about us and they never will."

"That's not true!" she shouted. "They do care."

"Face it - they've abandoned you here - something I never did." I looked at her, hearing myself getting louder. I stopped and shook my head.

Suddenly Sergeant Will came in, tapping me on the shoulder and looking at her.

He pulled me out of the tent and wanted to say something to me.

He looked at me with a concern. "I think that you should be the first to know this."

I looked at him. "What it is now?"

"The Loyalists just hit that little settlement to the east of here. Women, children - they killed everyone. There are no survivors. They took a troop shuttle and boosted into space - we think they went to join an Earth mothership out in orbit."

"All right, so what do I do with her?"

He sighed, looking like he cared. "I'm sorry to be the one to tell you this but we have no need for her. Hell, there was no point of interrogating her in the first place. The important ones were long gone."

"So?"

"The Loyalists would of taken her with them if she was important. They didn't. They left her here with those others to delay us. But you saw her with the gun in there. She'll kill us if she gets the chance. No matter who she was to you - she isn't that person anymore. She's dangerous. We're going to have to kill her. But if you let her go, we'll have to kill you."

My eyes widened, "What? Isn't there any other way? Can't she join us?"

"Have you listened to her talking? She's mesmerized by those sickos. Totally brainwashed. She's like a poison snake now." He took out his gun to load it. "I'll take care of her for you."

"No!" I said, grabbing the gun.

"If there is going to be someone killing her, then it must be me."

He was silent, handing me the gun.

" Remember what you used to say ? Whatever doesn't kill you, makes you sick," he said, trying to comfort me. "And this is sickening - but it's something that has to be done."

" I'm good at what I do. you know it and I know it," I said. "I'll do what has to be done."

He looked at me, thinking that I was going to do something foolish.

" Remember. It's either me or you shooting her. If you try to let her go, you will be shot with her. It's treason and even if I let you off, the Captain won't. Let me do it. She's nothing to me but an annoyance. I won't think about it a minute later. If you do it, you'll be feeling bad about it for the rest of your life."

"Thanks friend, I appreciate the offer." I took the gun, walking back into the tent and taking a deep breath.

"You know I am going to have to shoot you." I said to her sadly, regretting what I had to do.

Her eyes started to become inflamed in tears and shock. She started to whimper, falling to her knees and looking like a helpless child. "You don't *have* to," she said. "We can both leave. You can join us."

" If you tell me where the others are hiding, then I will spare you and let you free," I said, giving her one last chance. I didn't need the information, I just needed her willingness to be on our side. I turned away and waited. Feeling sick already.

" Why do you want to know where they are ? You're

just going to kill them too. I can't turn them in. Even to you. They're the only family I have left -" she quickly looked up and finished, "- who are alive !"

I gulped, as I took out my gun from my holster. I knew how she felt. I felt that way about the Militia.

She closed her eyes as I pointed the gun towards her. Chills started to go down my spine, making my hair stick up. I started to get furious, pulling the coil back, and firing the shot.

I thought I was tough and ready to shoot her but I couldn't. I shot the ground instead.

Tears started to come down from her. She started to mutter, scared from the loud noise of the shot and the closeness of death. I threw down the gun.

She looked up at me, confused and fearful, still whimpering.

I raised up my eyes at her, furious at myself. I was a trained marksman and I couldn't make a simple shot to her.

I walked over to her and picked her up by the collar of her woolly sweater. I stormed out of the tent, carrying her and throwing her to the ground outside.

She looked to me as she forced herself to get up. She walked over to me.

"Leave !" I said, furiously.

She smiled, still walking towards me.

"Leave now !" I said again, my voice cracking.

"Come with me. I know you still love me. We need you," she whispered, then, seeing how that didn't work, switched over to explosive shells "I need you."

It worked. My heart exploded. I started to cry got even more furious through my pain.

" Carol, if you don't leave, I swear I will have to leave you to the others to take care of."

She smiled again, that serene grin she used to show me before the war, that I loved so much. That I had thought about so much through two years of hell.

She started to reach for me, trying to hug me.

I forced her away, shoving violently at her and forcing her to the ground again.

I knelt down and grabbed her by her sweater again.

" Look, I am part of the Martian Militia. That's the Martian Army. I am in it because I believe in it. Believe me when I say this: I don't love you anymore. My love died when I pulled the rgs off a Loydie and saw your face. The Carol I knew died long ago."

"You're just a kid still. The sweet vapor factory kid I was going to marry. How did you get through all those battles," she nodded toward my patches.

"Remember we used to talk about not being good at anything ? Well I finally found something that I'm really, really good at," I said, still holding her sweater. "It's war. And I'm not just good at it. I'm great at it.

I didn't kill you back there because I thought that it wasn't sportsman-like. But, as you saw from my patches, I'm not much of a sportsman anymore.

I'm going to let you leave, but I beg you, don't go badck to the Loydies. Most of them escaped into orbit. The ones that are left aren't important. And I'll hunt them down like rats. Not because it is my mission - though it is. And not because they give trouble to the new forming Republic - although they do. And not even because you betrayed me. It's because because I like it. You understand me ?" I scalded.

I pushed her down again, standing up and dusting off my pants and backing up.

She stood back up, looking at me with fear but still standing in place.

I pointed away.

"Now, as I said before, leave now before the others find you." I said, calmly.

She bit her lower lip, turning around and moving off. She started jogging, almost disappearing from my sight when suddenly

heard a gunshot. There was no scream but I could make out that she had stopped running.

I started to run to her, feeling scared.

As I arrived, I saw a trooper standing there, leaning on his rifle and looking at the dead body.

I fell to the floor, reaching for her head. I looked at her body. She'd been hit with an explosive charge. I could tell by the way her stomach and other organs hung out .

It wasn't a pretty sight.

I held her tightly to me, feeling my hands and suit being stained with her warm blood.

The chills got so intense that I started to mutter to myself. Tears started to pour out of my eyes.

Holding her head tightly with both arms,

clinching her to my chest and regretting what I did.

" Sarge ? Why are you acting this way about a traitor bitch ?" said the trooper leaning on his gun.

I looked at him with raging, teary eyes .

" Are you the one who shot her ?"

He gulped as he nodded yes.

My muscles got tense, looking at him. I was frowning and trying to stop my whimpering.

I gently let her down, wiping my face and covering it with more blood.

I stormed over to him and punched him as hard as I could right into the goggles.

He fell to the floor, yelling in agony.

I then started to kick him continually into the stomach, trying to break his armor and actually fracturing it all around. I then grabbed up his rifle, and jacking another explosive round into the chamber, aimed it right at his head.

I was about to pull the trigger when suddenly Sergeant Will grabbed the rifle and threw it to the ground. He grabbed me and smacked me.

" Get a hold of yourself Sergeant ! This is a war not a drama ! Calm down before I beat the crap out of you. I told you the options. Snap out of it !" he said.

"Let me shoot the bastard ! " I said.

He let go of me and quickly pointed his gun in my direction.

I grabbed his arm and forced the gun tight to my chest, " Well - pull the trigger. It's the only way you'll ever beat me !"

He looked at me, biting his lip and muttering swear words. He pushed me to the ground and only looked at me.

" See this ?" he shouted at me, showing me his gun. "This is always the answer." He threw it down.

" You' think you've lost someone that's special to you, but you've only lost a memory. The girl you knew was long gone. You're a scary bastard sometimes, but I knew you couldn't do this. Luckily, in the end, it worked out for the best."

" What's that mean ?" I asked, picking up a growl.

"She would have hurt you. Got you into bad trouble or else talked you into joining her. It's a good thing you have friends," he said.

I looked at him with my sore eyes, wishing that he would shut up for one minute.

" What does that mean to me ?" I asked him.

He grinned and let go of me.

"Just keep thinking of what that means," he said.

I was confused on what he said, so confused that it made me angry. And with the anger, I got it.

"You were in charge of the sentries tonight !" I said.

"I sure was. I told them to shoot to kill, if they caught anyone trying to leave camp," he said. "I didn't know if they'd be shooting one or two, but I knew, for sure, there'd be a shooting."

I threw a punch but he threw me to the floor. I jumped up, trying to pull him down but he punched me. Falling to the floor, I felt powerless, mad, tired and angry. Angry at myself and everyone else. I was angry at the war which was tearing all of us apart and I was still furious at the trooper who shot her.

Sergeant Will bent down and started to sigh.

I looked at him, " I know that soldier was doing his job but something came over me once I saw her fall to the floor. She's what I was fighting for. I guess that's the power of love. Love makes the dreams, then kills them. And now it's killed me, too." I muttered.

" You can never blame the ones who do their job. You do it as well and there's hundreds of Loydie families that hate your guts. Love makes men weak, like you just found out. But sometimes it could make you stronger. Depends on what you love. Some dreams don't die," he said to me.

I kept silent, feeling that this was not going anywhere.

" Rest now, Sergeant, we're moving out of this place once and for all in the morning and I want you with us, back in the Martian Militia. I'll have your new orders cut tonight," he said as he stood up.

He gave a glimpse then turned to help the other soldier up. They both started to walk over to the Medic's tent for repairs on themselves.

I slowly got up and limped sorrily back to my sleeping quarters. Without even a dream to look forward to, anymore.

*   *   *

The next day, I was better but still in shock and anger.

I kept away from the trooper and from Will. The Militia got new orders to move out and get posted to another settlement in trouble and my orders were to go with them.

When I passed the barriers, filled with troopers guarding it, I felt better. I couldn't explain it, but all I could say was that I forgot about Carol and everything as soon as I left. I couldn't even remember the name fo the place where all my dreams died.

Looking at the sun shining over the vapors of the gas factories started to give me hope as it once did before the war. I knew where I belonged now and it wasn't here, in this settlement or in any other.

I belonged with the Militia.

Chapter 7

(PLAYBACK - 22,600 BC)

I ONLY KNEW ABOUT MENTAL THINGS. THOUGHTS WERE ALL I HAD. AND THE HUMAN CHILDREN WERE VERY AWARE OF MENTAL POWER TOO. BUT NEITHER OF US MECHANICAL THINGS. THEY REMEMBERED VAGUE THINGS, LIKE SPACESHIPS AND WEAPONS - BUT THEY DIDN'T KNOW HOW THESE THINGS WORKED. AND I CERTAINLY DIDN'T. SO WE DIDN'T EVEN TRY TO GO THE ROUTE OF PHYSICAL TECHNOLOGY.

BUT THAT DIDN'T STOP US.

I COULD TALK TO THE MIND OF ANYONE, ANYWHERE ON THE PLANET, ALTHOUGH I PREFERRED TO TALK TO HUMANS ONE AT A TIME.

THE CHILDREN WERE ALMOST AS POWERFUL AND, IN FACT, HAD A LONGER RANGE AND COULD TALK TO OTHER MINDS IN SPACE - SOMETHING I COULD NEVER DO UNLESS IT WAS SOMEONE I HAD ESTABLISHED CONTACT WITH ON THE SURFACE OF MARSOLLA, (WHICH WAS WHAT WE CALLED BOTH ME AND THE ENTIRE PLANET-SINCE WE WERE ONCE AND THE SAME).

WHY THE CHILDREN HAD THIS MENTAL TALENT, I NEVER DISCOVERED. THE CIVILIZED RACES WERE NOT AWARE OF IT AND COULD NOT DO THEMSELVES - IF THE GUARDIANS WERE ANY INDICATION.

THE CHILDREN CLAIM THAT ALL HUMANS HAD MENTAL POWERS BUT ONLY USED IT TO COMMUNICATE.

WE WENT FAR BEYOND THAT.

We learned to fly - and not just hover and swoop - but travel, fast as thought, to any where we could see or remember. Across the plains, across the planet and eventually, across the entire universe.

If the children could see it or imagine it, they could go there. In the blink of an eye.

Of course, the children were no longer children by this time. In fact, the original children weren't even alive anymore. It took centuries to set up a fairly comfortable civilization on Mars and it was over 1000 years before we really started to fly, seriously.

At first we were a sad planet. The children had lost everything - families, friends and the war which they had been brought up to believe was their whole life. Most of them did not know anyone on the planet. The last thing they wanted was fun and adventure. Peace was such a new thing for them, that they wanted to enjoy it as long as they could.

Mind power made it work.

To begin with, we used it superficially, to bring animals close and kill them, for food. To start fires or to move huge rocks. But it became much more subtle and fine-tuned as the years went by.

Instead of bringing an animal and killing it, we found how to recreate the food from surrounding elements. We didn't have to kill anything, anymore.

By the 3rd or 4th generation, humans could

ONLY HUMAN - MARTIAN INDEPENDENCE

just imagine cooked meat and ripe fruit and their memories would create those foods, right in their hands. (Right in their stomachs, if they were in a hurry), but the eating part was something they never lost enjoyment in.

Their minds used mass from anywhere. Mindpower could take a bit of dirt and some rocks and vegetables, rearrange their atoms and molecules and deliver anything you could imagine. With just as much taste and nutrients as the original.

This didn't happen overnight, but gradually, over 3 or 4 hundred years. Little by little, someone would discover a higher-minded way of doing things. Then everybody would begin doing it that way.

So the animals flourished. They lived completely on their own, with hardly any interference. Like the weather, they were part of the planet and the humans left them alone. Because they weren't endangering crops and they weren't needed for food.

Clothing and shelter came next.

I had herded all the original children into caves for shelter and came up with ideas to use plant and animal fibres for clothing. We went through years of the most horrible and uncomfortable fashions you can ever imagine, before we got things sorted out - and even then, clothing was pretty rough and bulky.

The first children and their children had very strong views on being dressed. But by the

3RD GENERATION THE HUMANS DIDN'T SEEM TO CARE. SO THEY MOSTLY WENT NAKED.

I COULD ARRANGE WEATHER TO A CERTAIN EXTENT TO HELP THEM, AND FOR A WHILE EVERYONE MOVED TO AREAS WHERE IT WAS WARM ALL YEAR AROUND. BUT EVENTUALLY MIND POWER MADE THIS ALL OBSOLETE, TOO.

WITH JUST THE POWER OF THEIR MINDS, LATER GENERATIONS OF HUMANS COULD KEEP AN AURA OF WARMTH AROUND THEM, WHEREVER THEY WENT. THEIR MINDS CREATED SOME SORT OF COLD FUSION TO GENERATE THE TINY AMOUNTS OF HEAT THAT ONE HUMAN BODY NEEDED.

THIS ENDED THE NEED FOR CLOTHES AND FOR SHELTER TOO. THE MENTAL AURA OF WARMTH COULD BE MADE MORE SOLID, SO A HUMAN COULD JUST LIE DOWN AND SLEEP ON IT - FLOATING A FEW FEET ABOVE THE GROUND AS IF ON AN INVISIBLE BED.

THEN THE AURO EVOLVED TO BE A FORM OF ARMOR, TOO. LIKE A FORCE FIELD, IT WOULD REPEL ANIMAL ATTACKS, IT WOULD CUSHION FALLS AND PROTECT FROM DROPPING ROCKS AND EVEN ABSORB LIGHTNING STRIKES.

ALONG WITH MAKING HUMANS SAFE FROM ACCIDENTS, THIS MEANT THE END OF FIGHTING AND PERSONAL CRIME. IF YOU COULDN'T HURT ANYONE, IT WAS IMPOSSIBLE TO ROB OR KILL THEM OR EVEN THREATEN THEM. PERFECT DEFENCE MEANS OFFENSE IS IMPOSSIBLE. OR, AT BEST, SILLY.

FOR A LONG TIME, THOUSANDS AND THOUSANDS OF YEARS, IT WAS A TRUE GOLDEN AGE. HUMANS, WHO COULDN'T BE HURT AND WHO COULD GENERATE

ONLY HUMAN - MARTIAN INDEPENDENCE

THEIR OWN FOOD AND WARMTH, JUST WANDERING AROUND THE ENTIRE PLANET OF MARSOLLA, LIVING ANYWHERE THEY CHOSE - ON MOUNTAINTOPS AND AT THE BOTTOM OF THE SEA-WITH NO BUILDINGS OR FACTORIES OR MINES TO BREAK UP THE LANDSCAPE. NO CITIES OR ROADS OR FARMS TO DESTROY THE BEAUTY. NO GOVERNMENT OR POLICE OR JAILS TO FEAR.

ONLY MILLIONS OF YOUNG GODS, COMPLETELY SELF SUFFICIENT. TOTALLY FEARLESS. ABSOLUTELY UNOPPOSED.

IT WAS AS MUCH LIKE HEAVE AS I COULD EVER IMAGINE.

IT LASTED FOR 3 OR 4 THOUSAND YEARS, (WELL, 3980, TO BE PRECISE).

THEN CAME THE TIME OF FLYING.

(RECORDING - 2405 AD)

Another 2 years had gone by. The Loyalist Underground was now just a memory, We had hunted them down to the last man, woman and child holding an Earth flag with patriotism in their eyes.

And killed them all.

These years had gone by without me noticing it. I had never thought of returning back to my town, knowing that war had destroyed the place. And I had destroyed any sweet memories when I had assisted in the murder of my sweetheart - that traitorous bitch.

Whenever I had enough relief points to go off for a month, something would happen to call my squad up right before I could rest. After losing Chris in Muddy Lane, my squadron had built the reputation of killing the most without any casualties in it. They all call it the Lucky Twenty, although Sergeant Will says that we're blessed with a good leader. I can understand that, since our Twenty was built from Will's original squad and he appointed me to lead it. We'd saved his life, once, too - so he was biased.

We had adopted our own drop ship, the faithful and swift Bordello. All of our drops were done with that ship and every time had been successful.

But this wasn't a drop day. We all were socializing and waiting for action to happen, I was reading an ancient book written in English format with actual letters, (testing if I could still recognize the ancient alphabet). As I was reading, Chrystina, the black-skinned pedigree come up to me.

She sat next to me, looking at what I was reading.

"Are those words, you are sounding out ?" she said to me.

I turned to her and gave a small smile. "Yes. Look here " I said as I moved the book to her and pointed to the first word on the page.

" See this hbunch of squiggles I'm pointing at ?" I asked.

" Yes, what about it ?" she said.

" Well, that is the word "gun" I moved my finger, " See, it's made up of separate letters: G - U and N"

She stopped me before I could go on.

"Wait, this is too complicated, why do you want to learn written words in the first place? It's easier to read barcode," she said.

I smiled. "It's good to know as much as you can. Depending only on the new can often be your tombstone while the old might save your life."

She looked at me strangely, thinking that I was crazy.

I smiled as she stood up and walked away saying " Well it's your life - waste it any way you want."

As I resumed to my reading, turning the page to try and read a sentence, my Corporal, Eric Aaron came up to me.

He looked like quite disturbed and frightful. He stood in front of me as I put down my book.

I stood up, looking directly at him.

" Yes Corporal ?" I asked.

"Sir, the Officers have picked up a scan from one of the Martian moons."

"So ?" I replied.

"Sir, the Earth Forces have come in full strength. They have detected three starships, One of them has already dispatched shuttles to the other side of Mars and are setting up base -"

I stopped him before he could go on.

"What is our mission from the Officers?" I asked.

He gulped, "Sir, our mission is to guard the old air base." he finished.

I knew what old air base he was talking about, it was an old one where hundreds of Martian fighters had been made in the old days. Unfortunately the factory was closed up for years because we had built enough fighters to last us a while.

"The old air base ? Why do we have to guard that area ?"

Aaron kept his thoughts to himself as he handed the papers over to me.

I opened them, reading the lines of barcode. Line after line of completegibberish, but I could figure out what it meant. It was about another surplus factory becoming operational, what else was new, it was war time and these things were expected. It also talked about how many new vapor factories were coming on line. We were rebuilding fast, now that there were no more Loyalists to worry about.

"You guard the base and take out any intruders completely, at any cost even if it will result in your squadrons end..." the last line read.

"At any cost ?" I thought to myself. There must of been something about the factory that was important.

I stood up and marched over, smacking the papers and reports to my other hand.

" Listen up !" I shouted.

The active room around me started to become quiet.

Their attention was now at me.

" Our new mission is like our old one back when we were patrol troopers.

We are going to guard the old air base, and we are going to get three new recruits." I paused, waiting for their reactions.

"We leave tomorrow on the Bordello, this time there will be no drop, so relax."

The troops chuckled slightly as I said that.

*   *   *

The next day came quickly. We were all waiting for the usual surly Captain, who we now called Jimbo, we were so used to him. This time he was on time, It was peculiar though, since the years that I knew him, Jimbo was always late and usually drunk. I guess when there is an important mission such as this, there is no time to be drunk. Or late. Or even to be Jimbo.

He stopped in front of us, opening the cargo hatch to the Bordello.

As we marched in, he grabbed his helmet and buckled it on tightly and ran to the cockpit. He climbed in, quickly.

I looked at him, wondering what was wrong. He looked at me with no emotion as he shut the hatch leading to the cockpit.

As my squad got strapped down and buckled in, the cargo door shut and the engines started their flames. The ship rapidly shot up, pushing me heavily into the seat. After all these years, it didn't scare or even intrigue me anymore.

The ship finally reached it's decaying orbit then began dropping at the targeted landing spot.

Like a rock.

It was unusual this time because Jimbo usually would drop us a lot faster than a rock. A lot faster than the speed he was going now. As if he thought we were passengers today instead of cargo - like he usually thought.

The landing procedures began and we touched down light as a feather. A first.

As the seats began to unbuckle, we waited for the doors to open up. Then we all started to unload the supplies: the bags, machine guns and ammo, by a high wall to one side of the ship.

The Doper gun-robots from the cargo hold were already functional and patrolling like crabs on a beach.

The air was cold and stale as we set up the supplies to the side of the wall.

As Jimbo got out of the cockpit he didn't say anything insulting to us.

I then knew that there was something wrong, He usually would insult us or even call us 'whores' or "children" at times.

As he started to walk out, I followed him and stopped him. He sternly turned around, looking furious.

" Jimbo, what's with the new mood change ? You didn't even drop the ship at your usual speed of sound barrier buster ?"

He began to get offensive.

"Do you want me to kill you, Sergeant?" He scalded. "I'll do it right now. I'm in the mood."

I was confused, " What ?" I said.

"If you wanted me to kill you on the dive then you should of asked me to shoot you before we took off, When a mission as important as this is called, there is no time to get an adrenalin rush ! You should know that, Whore ! Now if you 'll excuse me, I have to go and check in. All us pilots do."

I backed away as he stormed to the pilot barracks. That was more like the Jimbo I knew, but there was still something squirrelly about him.

A pilot walked up to the back of me, holding a wine bottle.

"I feel sorry for Jimbo there" he said.

I turned around.

" How do you know Jimbo ?" I asked.

He looked at me. He was wearing wearing a red

bandanna, and a Go-Tee - an all-weather Martian Tee shirt that kept you warm or cool anywhere you wanted to go.

" Well, I'm one of his closest friends."

" What's your name, pilot ?" I asked.

" Well . . ." he looked to my sleeve of my uniform, "Sergeant, My name is Mike, My friends call me Manikan. I'm the pilot who flies *Mutilation Incorporated*."

" What did you mean by feeling sorry for Jimbo ?"

He gulped the last drops in his bottle then started to talk.

" Well, last week during one of the attacks on this base, his son was one of the casualties."

"Oh shit." I shook my head. "That's too bad. What's he doing working then ?"

"He's one of the best pilots we have. "

"So doesn't that mean he should get some time off ?"

"Maybe in ordinary times, but not now. We're in big trouble. That's why he has to go with the rest of us pilots to check in."

" Check in ?" I asked.

Manikan began to get angry, " You are one dumb Sergeant. Don't you know what's going on here ? Earth is here. Their starships are in orbit all around the planet now. They're nuking settlements every day. All our victories are dust. We're losing now.

Our only chance is in the Black Fighters at this base. And we are some of the few pilots left who could fly these Black Fighters and survive. That's why you and others are here to guard this base, that's why the Earth Alliance are attacking this spot, and that's why this will be the last place on Mars where we will finally have a turning point. Or go down to defeat."

The bell rang, signalling another drop ship coming in.

I gulped. I thought we had pretty well won. I'd never heard any of this before. It sounded too crazy to believe.

" Well Manikan, I'll let you get on with saving the world then."

He grinned, "Too right."

*   *   *

Later that night, all the troops who weren't posted at the outside patrol were inside the barracks. Through the windows, the sky was lit up with the green vapors of the terra-forming vapor factories which generated oxygen and carbon dioxide and kept us warm and alive during the cold Martian nights.

I sat down on a seat, beginning to think of Jimbo and his odd behavior. I knew him well, and thought he wouldn't take a death in the family so hard, but I guess that if it was your son, it would be different.

As I sat alone, thoughts of family ties led me down a dangerous path. I began to think about my girlfriend. She had died with one shot and all my dreams of family and normal living died with her.

I knew that I would never see her again - nor did I want to - yet it still brought tears to my eyes whenever I thought of it. Not so much becuase the girl had died, but I guess more because the dreams had died. There was no light at the end of the tunnel anymore.

Something triggered through my mind, telling me that I would never think of life the same way as I did before the war. I didn't want to believe that, but I knew it was true.

War changed everybody's life, whether you won it or lost it. I could tell that there would never be an end to this war, even when the fighting was over.

As I sat, thinking, I didn't notice that a soldier had come up to me.

"Sir ?" he said.

I jumped, then looked up to see a strapping young man in front of me. He seemed to have joy in his eyes and he was rather excited if you'd ask me.

I raised my left eyebrow up , " Yes ?" I asked.

He was speechless as if he was struck by something. His eyes seemed to twinkle as he tried to talk to me.

" Well, I'm waiting, Private." I said.

He blinked two times. "Well, I'm, I mean my -"

" Your name is ?" I said trying to translate his gibberish.

He took a deep breath to kill his nervousness. I guess that I had that effect on people now that they were calling me and my Twenty heroes and all.

"My name is Ike Grant."

"Ah, so you're the new recruit. Well there's only one thing I would want to ask from you." I paused as I stood up.

He waited for my question leaning his head forwards a little.

"Where's the real recruit?" I said in a grim voice.

He was looking for an answer as he gulped.

"What, Sir?" he asked.

I grinned at him as I took out my hand from my glove.

"Just kidding, Private. I'm glad that you're part of the Twenty."

He gulped again and smiled as he shook my hand.

"Well, Sir, I can't wait till our next mission is given out to us. What's it going to be, Sir?"

"I don't know yet. They'll tell us soon enough."

I stopped shaking his hand and sat back down, seeing that my First in Command was coming.

As Eric Aaron came up, I began to see fear come into the eyes of Ike.

Aaron seemed to slow his pace down as he caught sight of Ike..

"You!" Aaron said quite disappointedly.

"Jew boy, what brings the likes of you here?" said Ike, suddenly finding his toughness.

Suddenly Aaron reached over, grabbing Ike by the arm and punched him on the lower lip.

Ike quickly tried to kick him in the groin as Aaron went for another punch.

I quickly stood up and tried to break them up before they tore each other apart.

I looked to them as my hands pushed them away from each other. " Nice welcome to the squad you give a new guy - now what's this all about ?" Both of them were still trying to get at each other.

I turned to Aaron.

"Corporal ! Report ! Tell me what is this all about. Stat."

Aaron snapped to attention and looked at me, his rage was now becoming controlled.

I let go of him. He began to speak but I quickly cut him off.

I looked to Ike, "Now Private I hope I'll get the same co-operation from you as well."

He nodded.

I let him go. I looked to them both, seeing Ike blinking madly and looking at the room.

"Do you have a problem, Private ?" I said sternly.

He quickly at me and stopped, " No, Sir. I just have an eye infection -"

" In both eyes ?" I asked.

" Well Sir, ever since the war, I haven't been able to get my medication."

I felt something peculiar about him but I was going off track. I quickly looked to Aaron.

" Well Corporal ? Report ! Tell me what was going on between you and the Private ?"

He looked to him with hate and sneaked a growl in his direction as he started to speak.

" We went to school together. He's obsessed with Hitler -look at that swashtika tattoo on his hand -"

" Hitler ?" I interrupted, trying to understand this quarrel.

" The mad man who killed 6 million Jews sir." said Ike, grinning and giving a sour look to Aaron.

" Go on." I said to Aaron.

" He believed Hitler and the Holocaust was right. He thinks all Jews should die." Aaron finished.

I looked to both of them. I was quite uninterested towards who Hitler was or what the Holocaust was, (I never took Honors Human History), but I was still going to resolve this problem quick and fast.

" Corporal, Private? May I inform you both that we are in a war here. You all may think that there is no call for readiness since we're on guard duty. Hell it may appear to be a freaking holiday for you. Nonetheless, this is still war-time, and the worst thing to see are two soldiers fighting each other, over serious things. But to do it over a silly childish thing - it's embarrassing to yourselves - and worse - to my Twenty. You should look at yourselves, it's pitiful" I paused as I saw their heads lower slightly.

"Now you both should be keeping that anger bottled up for when we go to fight the enemy. God knows that you both would need it. Whatever quarrel you both had, that was in the past ! You keep that anger to yourselves and resolve that nonviolently.

Not because you're mature. And not because everybody on the planet is counting on you. But because it bugs me - and if it happens again, I'll kill both of you." I smiled and raised my eyebrows.

They stood there silent.

" Is that clear ?" I shouted, scaring them and waiting for their answers.

"Yes sir !" they said.

I sighed.

" Well then, All I have to say now is that you both are lucky that you aren't in Sergeant Will's squad. Because if you were, you'd both be shot without any question already."

They stood in front of me, looking down to the ground.

" Well then, I want you both to get out of my sight."

They slowly started to walk separate ways, trying to find the quickest way out.

I sat back down, sighed and gulped my hot drink down. As I enjoyed the peace and quiet a Lieutenant came over, handing me a barcode letter.

I looked up at him.

" What's this, Sir ? I'm being assigned to another squadron ?"

The Lieutenant just looked at me.

"Just report to that area as soon as you can, Sergeant."

I wanted to ask a few more questions, but he started to walk away, giving new assignments to the other Sergeants and Privates in the barracks, probably the same message I had gotten. I finished my drink and stood up, walking to the door.

As soon as I got out, I looked at the sheet, wondering where I was supposed to go.

" Left Bunker, Section 3," it read.

I walked to where it told me to go. I looked around, seeing all the others gathered up. There were close to 40 people waiting in that crowd.

Out of the many, many briefings I have ever had in this war, this was the only one where I did not see Sergeant Will. This seemed much more than a patrol mission, or even a special mission.

I got closer, still not knowing what this meeting was for. Strangely, the new guy, Ike, was there too, still blinking rather quickly, and some other Sergeants that I was familiar with were there as well.

The bunker finally opened. The crowd started to flood into the room, pulling up chairs and having seats.

I sat near the front, knowing that this was going to be good.

The back door opened up as the noises from the curious crowd started to die down.

Three men walked into the room. One of them started up the crowd just with the presence of his face. Even I felt a little uncomfortable with this man. He had a stern face and seemed to be quite concerned looking.

He was Joseph Thomas. The last Thomas brother alive. I remembered his brother, Israel Thomas. I remembered his face clearly, the way it looked - right before I shot him.

I didn't know what this was all about but I wasn't going to leave just because of the sight of one man.

He walked to the front of the room as the other two men shushed the crowd down.

He took a deep breath, looking all around and looking worried.

"As you all know. Our food supply is dropping due to the nuclear bombs dropped over at the last five settlements. They were the big layer farms and meat ranches. You all know that our ammunition is slowly going down because there is no more asteroid mining up in the belt - the Earth ships have taken over all those operations and we can't get up there to fight them off - and even if we could, they outgun us up there and would just blow us away."

The crowd shuffled around, as shocked by this news as I had been by Manikan's revelations earlier.

"I know that this is all new to you - but all of us in the High Command, we all are feeling that we are going to lose this war. The last couple of weeks has been disastrous. That's why we are going to do something entirely new.

We think it's our last chance.

That is why Captains' Manikan and Jimbo need you. You all were selectively chosen to be part of this new squadron because of your experience and because someone vouched for you. And your first job is to answer a few simple questions.

What if every thing we have done is just the beginning ?

What if the way we have been fighting hasn't been enough ? What if you all quit the Militia today and just went back to working for the Earth forces ?"

The crowd was getting angry.

Me too.

"Today, I am here to tell you the answer to all those questions. There is only one answer. And that answer is 'To hell with that !'

"TO HELL WITH THAT !" roared the new squadron.

"Bloody right." said Joseph Thomas, really puppetting the crowd well now.

"We have developed a whole new fighting method. One that is risky - but at least gives us a chance."

" How can we trust you ?" shouted a man from the crowd. Everyone started to agree, causing controversy everywhere.

" How can't you ? It's my brother that was the traitor - not me. What my brother did, he did on his own. He never wanted our cause for freedom. He went to Earth years ago and only came back here to finish us. He thought that we were going to be the easy ones to kill off. He came back to work with the Loyalists and he died arrogant and mad, shot down on the street like a dog.

I am not my brother. I am here to help you all to win this war. I've been fighting it with you all along. So I ask you again. Can you trust me ?"

The crowd started to die down. Political silence.

Jimbo started to talk,

" The Martian Archives were taken out and everything that the engineers had, they saved - and we've used that data to put together something new. Something that could put the Evolution in our Revolution. This new evolution of our old technology is being constructed as we speak."

"The Black Fighters !" I said out loud, everything Manikan told me earlier suddenly clicking into place.

"You're not supposed to know that Sergeant, but I won't ask how you found out. I'll just say - yes. Black Fighters. New Fighters made from our Black Martian Metal. We have 10 now and there will be 30 of them finished in 8 weeks.

The training to use and pilot this craft will take close to 6 weeks. You will be taken out of your Twenties and placed in a bunker close to the underground labs. I can't tell you any more until you commit to the project. If you don't want to go further walk out now.

I hope you all will make the right choice."

The room was silent. 5 men stood up and walked out the door, not looking back .

" Why will the enemy win if we don't join ?" I shouted curiously.

The crowd started to agree with me.

Joseph looked at me.

"They now want to kill everything. Not fight for it anymore. They only want a resource mine. They've found it's easier to nuke pieces of the planet and just collect the metals and minerals. People get in the way.

It's not personal anymore.

ONLY HUMAN - MARTIAN INDEPENDENCE 211

It's worse. It's economic."

"How do we know this ?" somebody asked, quietly

" There are two new Starships in our orbit right now - joining up with t he one which was there before. The new ones are carrying nuclear bombs. Our sensors on the moons detected them. And we have a spy int heir High Command. They're not going to be using troops to control us any more. They don't care about any of us. Two years ago they got all the Loyalists out that they thought were important. The rest were left for us to take out and to waste our time. We have information that they are going to wipe us all out, starting with the food farms and the vapor-gas farms. and then work their way up to the people. Indies or Loydies - they'll wipe us all out. After they take out the major centres, they'll let us die out as they mine - they won't even bother to fight us anymore. Just nuke bits of the planet for their raw materials. We'll all die like cockroaches in a burning house. They won't even notice." said Joseph Thomas.

Jimbo looked up and started to talk to us all.

"You are Mars' best hope of survival now. All the famous squadrons you know cannot help us now. Not the Ruby Reds, the Bash Brothers, the Red Coats, or even your Lucky Twenty, Sargeant. Consider them all dead. Us - the ones right here in this room - are the only ones that can put up any kind of a fight now. And even we may get our asses kicked.

Now listen up and listen good because I may not have time to talk again.

You've all had experience in piloting before. That is why you are here. The only difference is that you are going to be trained differently than you did when you were in piloting school. This is a fighter. You all should of caught on by now, and you should know it can be your best friend and your worst enemy. It is experimental but it works. This fighter is made completely of Black Alloy Martian Metal . BAMM for short. It is going to be the first fighter to be truly an Aero/ Space fighter.

It'll let us go right up there after the bastards and let us follow them right back down to the surface, watching them burn.

Training starts tomorrow. You are to tell no one and you are to report to the bunker number given to you. You will come and train. You will eat and sleep. You will train more. This is your life now.

Remember, tell no one !"

We all started to stand up quickly and worked our way to the doors. I went out, pulling a piece of paper from one of the soldiers hands.

As I walked to the bunker number, I saw Ike, the one with the funny eyes, walk the other way.

I started to follow him, feeling suspicious of him. I stopped and saw him talk to a man, rubbing his eyes and handing over some sort of box to him. The man, his coat as dark as the night, looked at Ike and his grin was as stern as possible.

The man then handed him a box in return and turned to walk away.

Ike started walking to the bunkers quickly. I started to follow and caught up with him.

"Ike," I said, now walking aside from him.

He was startled, but turned to me.

"Oh, it's you, Sergeant -"

" Don't call me that, we're both in training for the same thing, therefore we're both rookies now."

He gave a grim smile.

"Who was that guy you were talking to ?"

" Oh, him ?"

He seemed quite distressed with that.

" Well, he's a friend of mine who gives me my corrective contact lenses and medication to try and stop my irritations," he said slowly.

" Why don't you get it from the main Doctor ?" I said.

He looked from side to side, then started to whisper.

" The Militia wouldn't of let me in if I told them that I had more than just a bad eye infection. They would have me kicked out."

" Why do you care so much ?"

"Where can I go from here ? My home was Muddy Lane. That town became overrun by the Loyalists. Hell I was lucky to make it out of there alive."

I gulped. "I know, I patrolled that area with my squadron for a couple of months." I said.

"Yeah - I was going to ask you about that. Your squad is famous for ground fighting. I didn't know you were a pilot."

"I used to have to fly to the moons for raw materials for my dad's vapor farm. He was too cheap to buy it planetside, so I did the run about once a month. And I did a little racing, too. I don't know how these guys found out about it - but I had to get a licence so it's no big secret. Not like you and that mysterious guy you just met."

He seemed anxious. "So, let's keep my meeting with him between ourselves, all right ?"

I grinned. " Why not. But how about you. You a pilot, too ?"

He smiled as he heard me say that. "Not just a piulot. I was an instructor before the war. And that's where I larned that, when you have to go to the bathroom, you have to go. See you in training, and thanks . . . " he said and then turned to his bunker and ran into the door.

I looked at my sheet and reported to my bunker where I would be spending the rest of the next 6 weeks. As I took off my uniform and jumped into my bed, I felt that the training was going to be like any other training I had taken before. Easy. Like the Tank Training or even Boot Camp type of training.

Little did I know that it was going to be much, much more . . .

Chapter 8

(PLAYBACK - 19,000 BC)

FLYING BEGAN AS SOMETHING ELSE ENTIRELY. IT WAS A SAFETY FEATURE. SOMEONE DISCOVERED THAT, IF YOU FELL FROM A GREAT HEIGHT, YOU COULD THINK OF SLOWING DOWN - AND IF YOU THOUGHT IN THE RIGHT WAY, YOU WOULD SLOW DOWN. SO EVERYONE LEARNED TO THINK IN THIS WAY.

WE DIDN'T KNOW WHY IT WORKED, ONLY THAT IT DID. OBVIOUSLY WE HAD TAPPED INTO SOME TYPE OF ANTI-GRAVITY FORMULA, BUT IT WAS ALL DONE WITH MIND POWER, SO IT WAS NEVER REALLY EXPLORED.

EVENTUALLY, HUMANS, BEING WHAT THEY ARE, BEGAN THINKING "IF I CAN FALL AND SLOW MYSELF DOWN, WHY CAN'T I SPEED MYSELF UP - AND FALL UPWARDS ?"

LIKE ALL THE MENTAL POWERS, IT TOOK A WHILE TO PERFECT. YOU CAN'T JUST THINK OF FOOD, AND HAVE IT APPEAR IN YOUR HAND. OR THINK OF HEAT AND BEGIN TO WARM UP. YOUR THOUGHTS HAD TO FOLLOW CERTAIN PATTERNS - LIKE COMPUTER PROGRAMS. AS THESE NEW BRAIN PROGRAMS BECAME KNOWN, THEY WERE SHARED WITH EVERYONE, AND BECAME COMMON KNOWLEDGE, BUT UNTIL THEN, IT WAS USUALLY ONLY A FEW PEOPLE EXPERIMENTING.

SO FLYING STARTED WITH FALLING UP. AT FIRST, THE ONLY WAY BACK DOWN WAS TO QUIT THINKING AND JUST FALL - THEN SLOW DOWN. BUT A FEW

PEOPLE WENT RIGHT UP INTO ORBIT AND NEARLY DIED SINCE THERE WERE SO FEW MOLECULES UP THERE TO MAKE HEAT AND AIR AND FOOD. IT BECAME A PLANET-WIDE SOAP OPERA WITH EVERYONE MENTALLY TUNED IN FOR A FEW DAYS - BUT WE GOT THEM DOWN EVENTUALLY - AND WHAT WE LEARNED LET HUMANS FLY SERIOUSLY, MORE OR LESS UNDER CONTROL.

MANY CHOSE TO LIVE UP IN THE AIR, SELDOM COMING DOWN AT ALL AND IT WAS THESE AIRBORNE ONES WHO CAME UP WITH SPACE TRAVEL.

AT FIRST THEY CARRIED MASS WITH THEM, THAT COULD BE BROKEN DOWN BY THEIR MINDS INTO EVERYTHING THEY NEEDED. BUT EVENTUALLY THEY LEARNED TO JUMP - TO GO FROM ONE PLACE TO ANOTHER ALMOST INSTANTANEOUSLY - SO THERE WEREN'T STUCK IN SPACE FOR LONG. IN AN INSTANT THEY WERE AT A MOON OR ANOTHER PLANET, WHERE THERE WAS NO END OF MASS TO CONVERT INTO HEAT, AIR AND FOOD.

THEY EXPLORED THE ENTIRE SYSTEM, ALL THE PLANETS, MOONS AND ASTEROIDS, FOR HUNDREDS OF YEARS. EACH NEW DISCOVERY WAS FLASHED AROUND THE SYSTEM BY MIND POWER, ENTERTAINING EVERYONE - MUCH AS THE EARLIER SPACE RESCUE HAD DONE - AND IT BECOME THE MOST EXCITING THING TO DO - TO FIND A NEW BIT OF SCENERY OR CAVE OR SOMETHING TO SEND BACK FOR EVERYONE TO ENJOY.

MILLIONS JUMPED OUT TO LIVE ON THESE HOSTILE PLACES AND EXPLORE FULL TIME. MILLIONS MORE WENT OUT FOR SHORT TIMES, JUST FOR FUN.

SO IT WASN'T LONG BEFORE THEY DISCOVERED THE WORMHOLE.

ONLY HUMAN - MARTIAN INDEPENDENCE

(RECORDING - 2405 AD)

The next day came. It was time for the training to begin. We all awaited our commands from Jimbo and Manikan. They were going to split us into two Twenties.

Manikan chose all the people who were given odd numbers; Jimbo, the tough one, chose all the people with the evens. Bad luck for me - I was the one with the even number and went with Jimbo.

After that Manikan ordered his new trainees to follow him to the next training site while Jimbo stayed right where we were.

He then walked over to the door to the storage facility and pushed it open.

" Get in there single file," he shouted.

As we got in, the lights turned on. There were strange machines and lifting weights that I had never even seen in my life.

He grinned as we all looked around in amazement.

" Well, Whores, this is what we call the Slaughter House. These are pieces of equipment which are meant to train people to be g-force pilots. The only problem is that we are not training for that. We are going to lift twice the weights, breath twice as little, and stretch until we hear our tendons snap right in half."

We all started to get a little scared.

" The first thing we train on this," he pointed to a machine which was oval and strange. " This is called The Apple Pie. It is called that because all of you will be put in individually with an apple that you must eat in the water."

" Sounds easy." said Ike.

Jimbo only grinned and looked at him.

" For thirty seconds, spinning around in six times the g's."

Ike gulped.

" Well, you little Whore, I guess, since you think it's easy, that you're our first volunteer."

Ike's blinking eyes started to widen.

Suddenly Jimbo threw something at him, it was a bruised apple, probably fresh from the farms.

" Well whore, take a deep breath and jump in," he said, grinning and walking over to him.

He grabbed a hold of his collar and dragged him to the machine, opening the lid and pushing him in. He tightened the clamps and a giant pressurizing noise came out of the bottom of it.

Ike held onto the apple tightly as the water started to seep in from the bottom. He gasped his last breaths of air and waited. Suddenly water started to shoot to him. The pressure got tighter and the oval started to spin around like an old washing machine.

Air bubbles and white breakwater started to show, but all we could see was Ike squirming and starting to eat the apple.

We saw his hand holding the apple and then saw

bits of the apple shoot all over.

Still spinning, he started to squirm even more.

Jimbo turned to us, paying no attention to Ike, who was swimming for his life, and started to show us another piece of equipment.

He took us to the other large squarish and oval apparatus. It was 100 feet in diameter and 5 feet high.

He opened up a door; out came a barbell with 100 pound weights on each side.

I looked back at Ike dying, but then Jimbo started to talk.

"This is called the G-force bench press."

Suddenly a hissing noise interrupted, followed by Ike being spat out onto the floor.

He was choking and covered in water, vomit and pieces of apple.

Jimbo continued as if nothing occurred.

" The harder you push on the bar, the harder it pushes back at you. So learn to be gentle - no matter how desperate you get. It'll save your life later.

Most times you will only need to push the barbell. Don't worry. If you loosen your grip, it won't kill you - it will only hit the bars that protect your body.

Even if you wash out of here, there will be some benefits. I guarantee you that what you do here will put anyone into shape, even after a few days."

He wasn't lying.

*   *   *

The next few weeks, training was hell. I had dislocated my shoulder three times, had two concussions and almost fractured every bone in my body, I almost drowned once and even caught colds from the temperature chamber. Not to mention hurt feelings. But I was one of the lucky ones. Some got head trauma or fractures and were cut off from the program. The last few weeks were easier. The apparatus became a piece of cake. I was able to survive under water for more than three minutes while feasting on a soft apple and withstand nine times my body weight in the G- force bench press.

Jimbo had become the mentor to us by teaching us how to get in and out of the cockpit in five seconds, and even taught us to use the ejection seats in them.

He was a good teacher but had too much humor in his teachings, sometimes trainees would not take him seriously and it would be up to him to beat them into it. Which was no laughing matter.

We were almost done with the training. Our last month was almost over. I had been promoted to Lieutenant, making Aaron in my old squadron the new Sergeant. It was a long time since I had talked to them. I heard from Ike that he was secretly meeting up with Chrystina, the black pedigree and that they were getting very close with each other - strange to see a Pedigree mixing races, but I guess pickings were slim out here.

That was the only news that rumored around us.

Then finally the day came. We graduated.

Only Human - Martian Independence

The date was January 1, 2406 and on the same day the Declaration of Martian Independence was read over the air to every station on Mars, even the starships above got the transmission. It was more than a Declaration of Indie. It was a Declaration of War. And Defiance. We were telling the starships from Earth to go to hell and we all felt good about that.

That night we all were celebrating, drinking the Low Grav Brew reserves and eating our dried seeds with joy, we were one step closer to freedom and the whole world knew it.

The doom and gloom they'd told us about 6 weeks ago seemed to be just a bunch of hysteria. The Earthies were sitting up there not sure what to do - too scared to come down and fight us. Too far from home to be in a hurry to die.

"Cheers !" shouted Jimbo with a giant smile on his face as he held up his cup and crashed it into mine and Manikan's. The others who were in joy and playing the Jolt music louder than usual.

It was night time and for as far as the eye could see, every colony for miles was lit up and doing the same thing. Celebrating.

" So, what do you think the enemy is going to do now ?" asked Manikan, chuckling as he saw the troops starting to challenge in arm wrestling each other.

Jimbo turned around , " Well one thing's for sure, we all are going to be rich, wealthy Asteroid miners and farmers once Earth starts to trade with us again," he said.

I laughed as the music started to get louder.

" To the Militia !" I shouted as I stood up holding my cup. "Long may we die !" It was the only family I had now.

Jimbo and all the other troops started to clap and howl with me as I made my toast. Manikan stood up and drank his drink down to the very last drop.

Ike walked over to me, holding Chrystina tightly with one hand, and still blinking as frantically as he ever did.

" Chrystina did you hear ? Ike made Corporal then Sergeant in only a couple of months," I said.

She smiled,

" Well look out, I may replace you soon." Ike said as he started to laugh.

I grinned and looked to him nodding my head.

"Ah, you're getting cocky !" I said. He seemed frightened, thinking that I was going to throw a punch, I grinned and patted his shoulder. "I like that in a soldier." I finished.

He chuckled.

Chrystina smiled and pointed to the sky. "Look at that. I didn't know that fireworks were allowed up now ? They must be celebrating the Declaration. Isn't it beautiful ?"

I looked as the little ball of light seem to sink further down, then expand in a brilliant display.

Everybody said "Ooooo"

Jimbo stood up, so did Manikan. I saw their eyes start to widen.

They threw down their cups and started to frantically run around, gathering up their weapons.

"What ?" I asked.

"Nukes !" yelled Manikan. " The sons-of bitches are dropping nukes !"

The music stopped and we all saw the bomb hit the colony in the far distance. The lights in the far distance started to die down, and we saw a flash of light burn down the buildings as if they were dust.

Suddenly two more bright mushrooms started to appear coming closer to us.

" To the shelters !" shouted Jimbo.

We all threw down our drinks and food and started to run to the bomb shelters.

They started to be crowded.

I ran into one which was filled up, then I closed up the door and closed the heavy lead door right after it.

I could still hear people running around outside but I was not going to open the door.

Suddenly banging on the door started up.

A faint voice screaming, "Let us in!" was heard. I recognized the voice, but I couldn't put a name to it. Maybe somebody in my training Twenty.

Those words haunted me as I felt the ground start to rumble.

Suddenly the whole room started to shake, the lights stopped and even the heavy lead door started to shake rapidly.

I bit my lower lip as I slowly counted, knowing

that the radiation would of stopped by sixty seconds and that the counting would calm me down.

I closed my eyes as the door seemed to bend towards me.

Then the rumblings stopped. It was silent and there was no sound. The lights came back on.

"Is it done ?" whispered Chrystina.

I gulped as I felt the hot door.

"There's only one way to find out." I said.

I unbolted the door, opening it. There was no person out here. They'd probably been vaporized from the blast. I turned on my flashlight seeing all the walls and sheets of metal from the temporarily nailed tents and shacks. All the buildings which were strong were filled with holes and cracks, making every structure weak. The people from the other shelters started to run out,

Manikan and Jimbo looked around, checking the other barracks to see if they were hit as bad.

I saw Aaron run up to me, checking that anyone who was in my shelter was all right.

" Sergeant." I said. He quickly turned around and looked at me.

" Did you lose any of your troops in the explosion?"

He said nothing as he nodded his head.

The others were looking around, flashing their lights on the buildings and looking around for their friends and equipment.

Jimbo came up to me. He flashed his light at my face.

"Well, during the party Manikan asked what the enemy was going to do now that we formally declared independence? I guess that's his answer."

*   *   *

The total count of casualties in our area from last night's bombings were close to 1000 civilians and fifty troopers. How many were lost in the settlements I never heard. Half a million I guess.

We all were guessing that it was a warning shot, telling us what they thought of our Declaration and that they weren't going to give up so easily.

Jimbo and Manikan were heard arguing with Joseph Thomas about deploying the prototype Black Fighters now or later.

Their argument seemed to be getting nowhere, though.

They then got frustrated and walked out of the storage facility pushing out all of us, the trainees, who were now official pilots.

They looked at us all standing in a bunch.

Jimbo kept quiet and Manikan seemed to be doing all the talking.

" After last night's bombings, we got word that the enemy had set up bases already."

He sighed as he finished.

" There is also word that another starship, one that is reported to be two times the size of the others is on its way to stick in orbit with the others. It will reach us in a few more months though, giving us enough time to take out the enemy before they arrive."

We were all silent. If the new one coming arrived, we would of been all wiped out for sure.

One common starship of that size is able to carry thousands of everything, even troopers. The ones already up there were almost empty of troopers but had full manufacturing capability because they were so close to the Asteroid Fields.

Even in this time of year, the planet was attracting more asteroids because the fiels were in our orbit.

The starships were also loaded with nukes for asteroid mining and were able to drop those nukes from space, we had all witnessed that last night.

" Our plans now are to go up there and destroy their docking bays and control towers. Without a docking bay and without communications, they will be forced to return back to Earth. It is up to us to do that, no other fighter can do it. Nothing else we have can do it, either. You guys are it."

Ike became worried. "When do we strike ?" he asked, always wanting to know the details.

Manikan lowered his brows, feeling anger as he said, " We can't strike until two days from now."

We all felt angry as well. We wanted to get up there and take them out right now, just as badly as he did.

"Why wait around - so they can nuke us a few more times ?" I said

" The reason why we have strike two days from now is that there is supposed to be a large meteor shower which will intercept the ships. They will be busy trying to harvest them with their space shuttles and will have no time to be observant.

They'll be busy and they won't be expecting us. We can hide among the asteroids and get right into range before they even know what hit them.

They can't detect the Black Fighters - they'll be invisible to all known sensors - but they can detect meteors and missiles. Keep in mind that they do have weapons. They use them to shoot away rocks, but they can be just as dangerous as a military weapon."

We all were silent once more.

Jimbo then looked at us sharply.

"Get in formation you whores !" he shouted.

We all grouped up in two different lines, Jimbo's Twenty and Manikan's.

They each took out many service patches.

" Well then, the moment you all were training for has finally arrived. You're graduates. Keep in mind that when you are flying these things, anything can happen and when those things happen, it is up to you to find a solution out of it. These things are fast, dangerous, and unpredictable. When you fly them you will be much more afraid of these things than you are afraid of the weapons you'll be flying against." Manikan finished.

Manikan handed out patches which showed a cross on them to his people.

"You are now part of the Dark Knights of Mars," he said, as the trainees held their patches and stuck them onto the left shoulder of their uniform. "Defenders of the Planet. Her only hope."

Jimbo walked to me. "Well congratulations, you're now an official Warrior Whore." He said as he handed me my patch.

I looked at the pattern. It was the same shape as the patches that Manikan handed out, the only difference was that it showed a thin female figure with horns on her head, giant breasts and giant metallic wings. It was shown on a side view, showing it's hands crossed.

I felt attracted to it, it was comforting for some reason, I felt proud putting it on my uniform. After Jimbo handed them out to everyone in his group, he then shouted,

"All right you're now part of my group, we're the Whores of Mars and now that we're out of the Bordello. Mars depends on us to take a screwing for them and save their ragged asses. And we depend on them to keep us in the air and screwing. We will do whatever it takes to win and save Mars from getting screwed by Earth !"

We all smiled, Whores and Knights. They both dismissed us and told us to get ready, and try to stay calm for the next two days.

* * *

Our last night before we were going to take off, we were all in the mess hall. Aaron and his squadron were all sitting around and socializing with us. Ike looked at his patch, he seemed rather quiet and so depressed, he didn't talk to Chrystina at all.

I walked over to him and sat down.

"Why so glum? We're all going to finally kick some Earthie ass and we're all going to be the first pilots of the new fighters."

He looked up at me.

"There's something I've got to tell you. Can we talk in a place more private ?" he asked.

I nodded my head, telling him yes. We both stood up and went outside. He closed the door tightly behind him and seemed angry.

"What's the problem ?" I asked.

He still was rather nervous. He then started to talk quietly.

" Do you believe in the Martian cause ?" he asked.

" Of course, I'm patriotic about it."

" Why? I thought that you fought this war only to get out of it."

I bit my lower lip. "That was when I first joined up, I was young and was going to get married. For the first few years, I only thought of home. That was what kept me alive. Then something happened to me. My home town was hit with a nuke, no one survived it. But I still had my sweetheart. Then she turned Indie and was killed right in front of me. I lost all hope. I thought that I would die off because the only thing that kept me going was gone. When that happened, I was comforted by my friends, the troops. They were now my family, and their patriotic spirit became mine as well.

We all had something in common now. It was that we were going to see the day that we were all free from Earth. It was that our children could walk free without having to pay taxes for every breath of air and their families could live without giving two-thirds of everything to the Earth governments."

"But it didn't start that way." said Ike. "This war, it was because of one nuke accident that started it and then a cover-up from Earth. I never knew that something so simple would become something so big."

I grinned, "I thought the same thing, I thought that it was just because of differences, but then it was no longer about the missile. The people realized that they did everything for the Earthians, they labored only for Earth's profits, and that Earth stole everything that our great thinkers created: The insulating Armor, Multi-pro goggles, even the Atmospheric-conversion-explosive bullet was taken and called theirs.

The people of Mars were fed up and only asked one thing: if they could rule their own destiny. That is why this war has lasted so long, our spirit is strong and we will fight to the last man, woman and child," I finished, surprising even myself with that speech.

He looked to the floor and sighed, "There's something I've got to tell you. I use to live on Earth.

Hell I still own property there. You know why I blink all the time ? It's not because I have an eye problem." He reached to his eyes and took out the contacts. They immediately turned white.

" They're spy cameras. I work for the Earth Intelligence and I thought that I was doing the right thing," he finished.

I was silent, my eyes widened and I felt shocked. "What changed your mind?"

"I was here as a kid - that's where I met Eric. I hated it then. So I went off to Earth. I've been back a year now as a spy. But I'm beginnign to love it. I understood the reason why you were fighting so bravely, so filled with pride. I saw men come in without their legs and heard them say, 'Give me some new ones doc, I want to go back out there !'

I even fell in love with Chrystina. I'm so happy with her. Back in America, even Europe, if you were a Pedigree you were treated like a second class citizen but here she is treated like everyone else. Here you all stick together because your wills are strong and you need each other and you all don't care if people are different."

He held out his hand in front of me. "See this hand, I use to have a swastika tattooed here. That's what Aaron was so mad about.

I believed in the Nazis ever since I took Honors History in Primary School. Then I got involved with it on Earth. But I took that tattoo off last night after Earth nuked us. At that moment I wanted to be part of you what guys are fighting for. I am now completely disgusted by Earth and I hate them."

I grinned. "I'm glad that you're on our side now but the information you were giving -"

"Ever since the Black Fighter training," he interrupted, "I haven't been able to give them anything. I over-exposed every contact I've taken since then. I didn't want them to know what was going on. They are all sly scumbags who deserve what you were giving them!"

He looked at me nodding. "Well then, you going to turn me in ?"

I was silent for a moment. "There's only one question I've got to ask you."

" What ?"

" Do you believe in the Martian cause as much as the rest of us ? Or are you just acting it out ?"

He smiled and threw the contacts to the floor and stepped on them. "Screw Earth, I hope they burn in hell !" he said.

" Well then, there's just one thing. Don't ever tell Jimbo this. His son was killed in a raid that likely happened because of your information."

"Oh hell. I never thought of that. He'd kill me, wouldn't he ?"

"And I'd hold his coat."

"You're right. You should turn me in. I'm shit."

"That's no crime in this outfit. We're all shit in one way or another. And I just won't be able to turn in a perfectly good Black Fighter pilot."

ONLY HUMAN - MARTIAN INDEPENDENCE

We both stood up.

" Tomorrow is the big day, and there's only one thing that I hope you do before we take off."

"What's that ?" he asked nervously

" Tell Chrystina that you love her."

" I will, the only problem is that I want to take her with me when we take off. I miss her all the time."

I chuckled to his remark. "You'll have to drop her in the napalm hold then," I said, "There's only one seat in a Black Fighter."

He started to laugh.

I smiled and patted him on the shoulder.

"I'll see you tomorrow," I said,

He smiled and shook his head yes and started off into the bunkers.

I walked to the storage facility, which was almost falling apart from last nights nuke explosion, but was still standing up. There were noises inside, sounding like people were working at putting things back together.

I slowly walked over, pushing the door open, seeing sparks and other tools scattered all over the place as robot arms were fusing black metal together and mechanics were drilling and pasting.

I saw Joseph Thomas dusting one tremendous, bird-like structure, quite triangular but bulky at the same time.

He saw me but didn't seem to care.

I touched the wing of it.

He grinned.

"Well what do you think of the Black Fighter?" he asked.

I looked at him and then the fighter.

"This is what we'll be flying?" I asked.

"Yup, she's a beaut, ain't she?"

"Wow, it's amazing. I've never seen anything like it. We've trained in simulators and capsules, but I've never seen the real thing."

"I know." he said as he smiled. "Nobody has."

I then looked to him.

"Sir, I just wanted to say that I was the man who shot your brother and I am not a bit sorry about it."

He looked at me with shock. Then he sighed, "Well at least you shot him before I would of."

I was puzzled. "What?"

"You heard me. He was causing trouble and he had to be stopped. I never did like him. He was always the one to be lured by greed. That's why he moved his family to Earth before the War, knowing that there would be trouble.

He joined forces with the Earthians because they offered him money, credits that would of lasted him and his family until the year 3000. Hell, I should shake your hand."

He held out his hand to me.

I was still puzzled about it, but shook anyway.

"Sir, I still feel sort of bad and -"

"Since you're going to fly tomorrow, you think that you're going to die eh?" he grinned as he interrupted.

I gulped.

" I don't care about Israel, he died because of his own sins, not because of you. The only thing I grieve about is that his 6 year old son Nevel would grow up fatherless.

I guess that was better than growing up in the shadow of Israel though."

He seemed lazy-eyed.

"Well, do you think this thing can be shot down ?"

" Huh ?"

He took out his gun and pointed it at the fighter.

"I said do you think that anything is going to take this beauty out of the sky ?"

"Well I don't know, it seems well armored but -"

Suddenly he pulled the trigger. The bullet exploded as soon as it hit the left wing.

I covered my eyes.

Suddenly the explosion stopped.

I looked, seeing metal plates sliding over the wing.

He smiled. "Shifting Armor Plates, It took a long time to design them but hell, it was worth it. After one hit, they move to cover the area."

I sighed in relief. The machines stopped fusing things together and the mechanics walked up to Joseph Thomas.

"Sir, the last one has been finished."

He looked over to them and still grinned.

"Good job. You're now all excused until 07:00 hours tomorrow."

They saluted him and took off their welding aprons and walked out the doors.

They started to close up the large airplane doors.Joseph looked at me.

" Well you better get some sleep flyboy, You've got a war to win. Remember that when you're up there." he said, showing me to the door. I grinned and started to the bunkers

*   *   *

The air was cold, colder than my taste was used to. I wore the pilot suit, covering every part of my body and fitting like it was made for me. The others stared in marvel as the fighters were being taken out of the storage facility one by one.

Their cockpit shafts were widely open and were waiting for us to get in.

The only person who wasn't paying attention was Ike, hugging Chrystina tightly and getting one last kiss before he was going to go.

They finally let go after they whispered that they loved each other. He walked slowly over to us, smiling and rather lifted in spirit.

"Listen up all you Whores!" shouted Jimbo.

We all turned around, seeing him in his suit, his right sleeve painted yellow, same as Manikan's.

He looked at us all, holding his helmet in one hand and a piece of jerky in the other. "This may be the last time we will ever see Martian soil again. So I say that before we take off, we've got to take a handfull of dirt and throw it into the cockpit.

Don't worry it will not jam up the equipment."

He finished his piece of jerky and picked up dirt.

We all followed him and threw dirt into our cockpits.

As he swallowed the chewed up jerky he said.

"I hope it won't, was what I was meant to say."

Manikan started to talk.

"The missiles we have are all planetbusters - so they'll take out big chunks of starship. But remember, you're supposed to be a rock. So when you get up there, you trust the screens, not your eyes, when you're in space.

There is one more thing that you should be careful of. The meteor shower that is supposed to hide us is going to be dangerous if it hits you. So take care flying around in those rocks."

" Well then, lets board our fighters. For Mars !" shouted Jimbo, throwing more dirt into the cockpit.

We all hurried to our own cockpits, grabbing extra clumps of dirt for luck.

" FOR MARS !" we all shouted as we threw in dirt again and fastened ourselves in.

I clipped on my helmet, then shut the shaft on top of me.

The seat and everything else was cold, too cold. I guess that it was the suit but it still was uncomfortable.

It was dark and the seat belts automatically strapped me in and connected to my suit. I felt the air now circulating through me and the ship.

I looked at the dark window, seeing the simulator screen right behind the joystick.

The only thing left was for me to turn the thing on.

The speaker came on.

"Whores, ready to blast in 5...4...3...2...1..."

I quickly hit the ignition button, seeing the other fighters shoot to the sky.

Suddenly my engines shot out tremendous force, pushing me to my seat as I shot into the sky after them.

I quickly grabbed the joy stick and got control of the craft but it seemed the other way round. It seemed like the craft had control over me.

I nervously glanced at the control panel, looking for the virtual simulator.

I pushed the flashing red button, it felt smooth like glass and soft like gel.

The cockpit window screen went pitch black and a large sheet of blue glass, about the size of my head came up from behind the joystick.

I felt scared. I didn't know how I was flying, but I still felt myself going up. My intense training had kicked in and I was flying by body alone.

My mind wasn't connected yet.

The screen started to function, showing a 3 dimensional picture in front of me, I could now see where I was, the top, the bottom, even what the fighter looked like from the back. It seemed as if it sensed everything around it. The picture shown was much clearer and easier than looking through the screen or judging by radar.

Nonetheless, I still felt chills going down my spine.

"All Whores come in !" shouted the radionn communications.

I was startled, losing control of my joy stick but then gripping it firmly again.

" I don't expect any replies from you. Although we're pretty stealthy, we still can be detected by ion traces in radionn transmissions.

Use your gas wisely, too. Once we're up in space, you'll be able to fly like demons.

Oh, and one more thing, You all should watch out for asteroids coming in. Tens of thousands are going to be coming in from every direction. If you are whacked, It's hard to get back into alignment with the rest of us. If you are hit badly, try to re-enter Mars atmosphere. That's the only way you'll be safe. See you back home. Over and out."

Suddenly barcode started to come to the side of the screen, showing me the mission.

It read, " Mission Objectives: Use every missile to destroy Communication Towers, Science Facilities, Docking Bays, and Factory Modules which are connected and part of the ship's spinning Hull. If out of missiles, the fighter has ramming capability. If it comes to that necessity, push "Rhino Mode" All three starships must not have any manufacturing capability or communication when we leave. Destroy those functions at all costs.

Destroying entire starships, acceptable too..."

The barcode message scrolled off.

The radionn came on again.

"All fighters move to escape velocity speed in five."

My hands were twitchy as I heard the countdown.

The fighter was now vertical as I pulled the joystick up.

Hearing the countdown, I reached over to the maximum thrusters. My hands shook, cold and numb.

I quickly hit the button, almost smashing it.

Suddenly I felt my seat get incredibly hot as I slammed into it. I could hear all four engines overworking as I shot faster than sound further upwards.

The screen showed the air moving past me. It showed the other fighters looking like their whole back engine was exploding all simultaneously. I started to breathe deeply, wishing that the pain of my suit, forcing itself into my chest, would stop. All my spit was rushing into my throat; even my teeth felt like they were being pushed in from the G-force. I swallowed all the spit I could without choking and waited to see the dark blanket of space.

The air in the screen seemed to get darker, Suddenly an asteroid which was in flames came down, only a few feet away from hitting me.

I looked out the window, relieved, seeing that one fighter to my right was now changing shape, changing into Rhino Mode already. It seemed that most of the metal, used as armor, started to cover the nose and wings more thickly than the in back where the engines were. It sped up and went right through a huge meteorit, blowing the rock into pieces without seeming to affect the Fighter at all.

I took a guess that it was Jimbo. He was always the crazy loon. And he was always playing with Rhino Mode in training.

Finally, the air seemed to disappear as we reached space. Everywhere I looked, I saw floating space rocks, clumsily tumbling around and shuttles in the far distance gathering them in.

Suddenly a shuttle came right over me. It couldn't of detected me but probably thought that I was a space rock, if I registered at all. It was sucking in small asteroids around me.

I quickly turned on my fart engines, blowing out compressed gases, trying to squirt myself out of the way of its vacuum.

Suddenly a meteor which was the size of a small moon crashed into the shuttle. The meteor turned into thousands of pieces and the shuttle was no more.

I felt the low-gravity catching up with me. It wasn't a feeling that was pleasant. I quickly turned on every tracking system I could find available, to take my mind off it.

There was no sign of my colleagues but there was signs of the other meteor-catching shuttle ships. They were not my biggest concern. Finding the starships was my main objective.

As I flew in a low orbit, my radar devices, (sonar,

Info-red, Heat, Gas spotters, etc.), picked up nothing.

Suddenly I saw them all pick up something big, so big that all of them were instantly covered in bleeping signals and completely red.

The simulators showed a dim shadow coming over me and completely blocking out the sun.

I was nervous and happy at the same time. I had found the one of the starships. The only thing was that the big shadow above me was just it's nose.

I quickly pulled up, trying to ride up its front instead of speeding down its belly and getting too close to its incredibly large engines.

The screen showed the appearance of the ship.

The name was "Titan Lord" written in large thick alphabet. It never occured to me that Earthies didn't use barcode.

I gulped, tying to push down my spit which felt like it was floating up my throat.

I shot away, to get a shooting distance, knowing that I was going to have to do the First Run.

I was scared. A Starship of that size gave off gases the size of two or even three bases put together just to turn it. I even heard that they had gas powered 300mm cannons to hit large rocks away from the ships internal hull.

What if it thought that I was a rock. Then again, it couldn't detect me.

I nodded to myself. There was no more time for worrying, There was now time only for doing.

So I did.

I turned my fighter around and accelerated in speed, gliding through the frictionless atmosphere of space.

Suddenly the radionn came to life: "Anybody know what these towers and things look like ?' asked one of the balckfighter pilots.

There was no answer.

I saw the English words CONTROL TOWER painted on the hull. Nobody else could read.

"See the thing blowing - that's a Control Tower, I said, pulling the trigger, feeling a missile detach from the bottom and push into the control tower detonating at contact. What a big blast.

The other starships appeared in the far horizon, coming closer to the damaged one.

I quickly pulled into the hull, trying to spin aside with it, seeing that there were only Giant beams acting like ribs to protect the overcrowded Spinning Hull.

I did a tour around the starship, reading off the names of our targets so the other guys would know what to look for. I wish Crystina were here to see how useful reading old script could be.

I saw the first Docking Bay, sticking out like a sore thumb, then I was speeding up and shooting another missile into the open mouth of the bay.

I zipped past it, knowing that there were other docking bays and other things to take out.

My radionn came back on.

"Identify yourself, this is Whore Number 5"

I grinned, "Ike, it's m, your Number One Whore."
I looked into the screen, seeing the other fighter, marvelously pulling closer to me, showing its long tail of gas shooting out of the back.

"This one's been taken out now, thanks to you, this one isn't the problem anymore. The other guys are over at the other two. We took out the Missile Silo for this one but the other ones are still functional. The Dark Knights are taking heavy casualties." Ike said nervously.

"Can they see us ?" I asked.

" No, but they know they're under attack. So the Earthies are launching nukes and detonating them in space. The shockwaves are killing us."

I was scared, gulping again for the third time, trying to keep my stomach under control.

"There's no shockwaves in space. It's the radiation. Keep away from there."

" It doesn't matter now, we've got to save them, we've got to fight -"

Suddenly he was cut off by the electro-magnetic pulse of a nuke going off somewhere. I saw his reflection off my canopy. He was taking off into where the battle was. I quickly sped up to catch up to him.

Suddenly there was a bright flash.

I felt my nose becoming warm on my face.

I knew that another nuke had gone off, close by.

I tried to check all the channels on my radionn, changing frequency to find any Black Fighter which was left.

ONLY HUMAN - MARTIAN INDEPENDENCE

Then I heard the voices of Jimbo and Manikan. Their signal was weak but I could still make it out.

" We've got to take out the leftover Control Towers," said Manikan, "before we're totally nuked."

" I'm going to Rhino it ! I suggest you do the same thing if you want to survive this !" said Jimbo.

Suddenly rocks started to swing by. I started to come close to the battle. Everywhere I looked there were fighters picking off everything they could which was sticking out of the starships.

I quickly glided by the side, seeing four other fighters, shooting all the missiles that they carried. They were shooting at the giant beams that held the outer hull together.

Suddenly a metal beam came loose, smashing a fighter like swatting a fly. I quickly dodged as soon as it came my way.

The fighter that was swatted started to swing out of control, I saw it tumbling into the atmosphere, lighting up and sinking into Mars. Going home.

I became panicky.

" Manikan, we've just lost a few more fighters, we're not going to make it !" came from one of the Dark Knights. "Let's get out of here !"

" Don't worry, one of the ships' hull has been breeched, They're about to lose the main command center, The whole side is about to come out -"

" Time to take 'em out ! I'm going in for a Kamikaze, you want to see the inside of a starship ?" It sounded like Jimbo. I couldn't believe my ears.

He was still crazy, even up here.

I heard the radionn get louder, then I saw two fighters changing form and accelerating at enormous speeds. They were heading towards me.

I quickly pulled down, and switched to Rhino, trying to whip around and follow them.

As I made a sharp turn, giving off all the gas that I could, I saw them swing to their left, piercing through the head of the ship like bullets hitting a watermelon, then going right through the inside length of the starship.

Suddenly a chain reaction started .

From the front the beams and pieces of hull started to shoot all over, in slow motion, spreading amongst the meteors and asteroids, hitting the other starship.

The hull started to deteriorate, shooting out gases and men.

I cleared my canopy to watch, but it was a mistake. It was horrible. For a time where I couldn't look anywhere without hitting a dying body, flung out of the starship. I was close-up and seeing them screaming as their eyes and bodily organs turned inside out and instantly froze.

I squeezed my eyes shut hoping to forget the scenes, but I could still hear the awful thumps.

The whole starship exploded, in a fracture of a second. I saw flames, hot shrapnel and even more women and men melting from the flames then freezing as soon as the flames disappeared.

ONLY HUMAN - MARTIAN INDEPENDENCE

There was the one damaged starship left. It had gas leaks coming out of the engines, all the shuttles that tried to return were fried from the nukes and all the docking bays were shot out. It was almost dead in the water. I saw lights start to flutter off all over the hull. Its front lay without a Science Bay, its Command Deck was in ruins, and even the tall Communications Tower was smashed beyond repair. The only thing left was the Missile Silo, still very functional but battle worn from all the explosions.

All the fighters were still attacking the dead starships which were both now in pieces. Like flies on a pile of shit.

One was still a threat and only four fighters, including me, were charging to it.

I clicked on the frequency again, hoping to pick up Ike.

I was lucky. He was still alive but I couldn't tell which one he was. They all were damaged.

" Ike, what are we going to do about this one ?"

" I don't know, if they look out the window and see us trying another Rhino mode, they'll nuke us for sure."

" You know these things better than all of us, all we've got to do is make it weak, weak enough to take months of repair. Weak enough so that it wouldn't be a threat."I said.

There was a pause.

"There is a way to destroy it like what you said."

"Tell me how ?"

I heard no answer, coming closer to the starships missile silo.

I saw a fighter going into Rhino Mode.

"You're nuts, that'll kill you, even in Rhino mode!" I said. "They'll nuke you."

I received no answer.

I saw him going into speed acceleration, He was charging it.

All that I could do was pull away and watch.

He got closer, the silo doors began to open up, Suddenly a missile dropped out, Ike fired a missile into the doors as it started to close.

Suddenly the whole front of the ship, actually one half of it exploded, shooting metal all over in all directions.

The nuke went off, too.

It was so intense that it disintegrated most of the rocks around it.

I quickly changed into Rhino mode as the wave of debris started to come to me.

I started to rumble. The cockpit began to heat up. even my glass helmet started to steam up.

I felt myself begin to burn in my cold suit.

"Warning ! Wing shields, blown off !" beeped the computer.

"Warning, Napalm leak !" it said again.

" Warning, main engines off-line!" it finally said before going off-line itself.

I closed my eyes, hoping that it would stop.

The cockpit began to cool down, my fingers felt

stiff and were burned on the knuckles while my nose felt stale. My eyes hurt but my backup gas spurts were online, guiding me back to Mars.

To my side, I saw a blurred picture of the remaining Starship. It was the only one remaining. It was damaged, alone, with no contact or even repair crews. This was the only one left and it was dead in the water.

We were saved.

Until the other ship arrived.

But that was then. For now, all I wanted was to go home.

As I began to pick up speed, I felt the g-force pulling me down, seeing dust fall to the front of my fighter. My two handfuls of dirt were riding high.

The heat began to hit again but I wasn't afraid this time. I was actually relieved. Although I was flying a craft which was only a piece of metal, I felt relieved.

I was a survivor. I was a proud survivor of the Asteroid Attack

*   *   *

It was night time, I was still flying, surprisingly, because I had been through hell in the Asteroid Attack when the nukes were going off. I hadn't been hit, but my Black Fighter had been hammered up pretty bad.

I had managed to get back into Mars atmosphere but I was on the other side of the planet. My aero-engines finally kicked in as soon as there was atmosphere for them to work with.

All over, I saw the gleaming seas of Mars. They were beautiful, reflecting the light of the dim moons from above, and the stars shining amongst the green vapors that were surrounding the sky like clouds.

As I saw the shore line covered in Martian trees start to come up, I felt peace.

I didn't have to worry about any other fighters, troopers, even missiles coming at me because there weren't any to hurt me. At least not at this altitude.

It was a few more peaceful hours of slow flying until I reached the base. It was a change from seeing trees and then the Barren Equator.

Here, at the base, was where all the settlements were, where it was dry and high. The lights on the computer came on, it was going into auto pilot for the landing.

Suddenly, it was lights out. The entire computer with the auto pilot shut down just seconds before it was supposed to land me. I gave it a mighty whack with my hand. It made a sick beeping sound but the computer came back on line.

I saw fighters scattered all over the run way, some in flames and all tattered up in one way or another. Maybe I'd be like that if the thing cut out again.

But it didn't.

As I came in, I felt that the landing gears were falling apart. It was too rough for comfort but at least I came to a stop.

ONLY HUMAN - MARTIAN INDEPENDENCE

As I turned off the engines, I opened the top, hearing a hissing sound as the pressurized cockpit air leaked out.

I took off my helmet and felt the cold night air get to me. The crew ran up, bringing a ladder to help me down and I looked to the other pilots in nearby Black Fighters, some fused to their suits because of the heat of the Nukes, and some who were leaning out of their cockpits, being sick.

As I stepped down, I saw Jimbo and Manikan standing close by, looking at the Black Fighters. I walked over and they turned around to talk to me.

Before they began to talk, my fighter in the background started to fall apart. The armor fell to the ground and one of the landing gears collapsed and then the entire fighter toppled over and fell to the ground. Like in a cartoon.

The crew were stunned as they rushed to it squirting water over the pile of parts.

Manikan just raised his eyebrow. Nothing needed to be said.

Jimbo started to grin. "You hit the computer module, didn't you ?" he said.

" I had to . . . "

"He's just dicking with you." said Manikan. "Over half of these crappy things cut out in mid-flight. It's a wonder so many got back at all. Hey - you know that shrimp of a Whore, Ike? He's a hero today. I'm glad that he's a Martian rather than an Earthie."

I shrugged as he said that.

"Really ? I saw him head for the missile silo just before the nuke went off. I thought he was dead . . ."

Manikan turned around, "Speak of the devil," he said as his grin turned into a smile.

I turned around, seeing Ike limp over. He'd been radiated having half his hair burned off and sore looking eyes and burn wounds all over his hands.

He stopped in front of us.

" Well Sergeant, you're one hell of a Pilot," said Manikan.

Ike smiled. " Thank you sir."

"Where did you learn to fly and shoot missiles like that ?" asked Jimbo.

Ike paused for a minute.

Jimbo listened up, thinking that he would get an answer.

As Ike tried to speak, two soldiers grabbed him.

Their helmets read MMP - The Militia Military Police.

I knew the reason but everyone else was puzzled.

An officer walked up to him.

" Sergeant Ike Grant of the Whores ?" the Officer asked.

Ike only gave him a glimpse.

" You are being arrested for betraying your homeland and acting as a spy for the Earth forces. You will be tried and there your fate will be told."

Jimbo came up to the Officer.

" There must be some mistake. He's a hero."

" Some hero indeed, selling precious information

to the enemy and killing three Martian troopers in Muddy Lane. If you think that he's a Hero then you're as crazy as you look !"

Jimbo punched him in the mouth and he went down. The other MMP pulled a weapon.

Ike stepped between them and began to talk.

"It's all right. He's telling the truth."

Jimbo looked to him, So did Manikan.

"Captain, you asked me where I learned to shoot missiles that well, Well I'll tell you. I moved to Earth before the War began and joined the American Air Force. I also was an Officer there for years until the war started, then I was assigned to spy here.

I was born and raised here. I knew the customs and the terrain better than anyone else."

Manikan then asked, with a emotionless voice,

" Why did you do what you did up there if you were really on their side ?"

Ike smiled.

"See my hand ? There use to be a swastika on it, but I had it removed the night that we were hit with the nuke. When I got to know you people, I felt that I was betraying my real family, after all this was my birth home. I did it for my Martian pride. I did it for Mars."

He chuckled.

" I turned myself in before I flew today because I felt that this was the last thing I had to do. I can't continue burying what I did. I deserve to be punished and you all know it. I did this for Mars too.

Even if I die, or spend the rest of my life in jail. I'll have no regrets at all.

It won't make up for the Martians I killed or the friends, like Chrystina, that I betrayed," he finished.

We all looked as the MMP grabbed his arm and scanned it. He then put cuffs on Ike and started to drag him away. The other MMP got up and helped.

Jimbo grinned as he looked to the ground.

"For Mars you say ? If you are saying the truth then we honor you for it." he said.

Manikan grinned again as he saw Ike being taken away,

" FOR MARS !" he shouted.

Ike grinned as well and shouted "FOR MARS !"

Suddenly the others, the crewmen, pilots, even the police were saying: "For Mars," like a toast.

We never saw Ike again. We were told that he died in a cell a few days later. He was already weak and suffering from radiation burns when they took him away. He was probably already dead when we saw him that day.

The last we heard, Ike freely gave the newly formed Martian Government useful information on his Earth contacts and the entire spy network before he died.

I told Chrystina that he died a hero.

I think he did.

Chapter 9

(PLAYBACK - 16,600 BC)

IMAGINE NAKED HUMAN CHILDREN, CALMLY FLYING RIGHT INTO THE SUN. IT AMAZES ME EVEN TO REMEMBER IT.

THE GUARDIANS HAD NEEDED TO BE SHIELDED, PROTECTED, AND CODDLED BY A TECHNOLOGY THAT HAD TAKEN HUNDREDS OF THOUSANDS OF YEARS TO PERFECT, IN ORDER TO COME THROUGH THE WORMHOLE. THE HUMANS SAILED IN, NAKED AND GIGGLING.

WE HAD ALWAYS KNOWN, FROM THE GUARDIANS ORIGINAL TALK, THAT THERE WAS A WORMHOLE. AND WE HAD FIGURED OUT THAT IT LED TO SOME OTHER PART OF THE UNIVERSE. BUT IT NEVER OCCURRED TO ANYONE THAT IT WAS RIGHT IN THE MIDDLE OF THE SUN.

IT WASN'T THE QUEST FOR KNOWLEDGE THAT DISCOVERED IT EITHER. IT WAS THE QUEST FOR ENTERTAINMENT.

GIVE A HUMAN ALL THE FOOD AND COMFORT IT NEEDS, AND YOU CREATE A MONSTER. AND IF IT CAN'T FIGHT WITH IT'S FELLOWS, THEN IT IS A VERY DANGEROUS MONSTER INDEED.

IT MUST BE ENTERTAINED.

WITHIN A COUPLE OF THOUSAND YEARS, WE HAD SOLVED EVERY PROBLEM. MIND-POWER MADE HUMANS PHYSICALLY UNHURTABLE AND MENTALLY

UNCHALLENGED. ENTERTAINMENT IN THE FORM OF NEW DISCOVERIES AND DANGER - LIKE FALLING AND NOT EVEN THINKING OF STOPPING, BUT DROPPING RIGHT INTO THE OCEAN - WAS WHAT MOST PEOPLE LIVED FOR. BECAUSE EVERYONE WAS IN MENTAL COMMUNICATION WITH THEM, ALL THE WAY DOWN.

SO THE WORMHOLE WAS THE MOST INCREDIBLE THING IN THE SYSTEM. EVERYONE WAS THINKING ABOUT IT AND THOUSANDS WENT THROUGH, JUST TO SEE WHAT WAS INSIDE, AND TO BROADCAST THEIR DISOVERIES BACK HOME.

NOT KNOWING WHAT THEY WERE DOING, OF COURSE, THEY POPPED OUT ALL OVER THE UNIVERSE, AND REPORTED BACK EVERYTHING BY MIND-POWER, WE WERE ALL AMAZED.

THEY POPPED UP ON POPULATED PLANETS AND IMMEDIATELY CAUSED SENSATIONS. THERE WAS NO NEED FOR LANGUAGE LEARNING, MIND-POWER MADE TRANSLATIONS UNNECESSARY.

OVER EIGHT THOUSAND YEARS HAD GONE BY, SO THE CIVILIZED RACES HELD NO ANIMOSITY. IN FACT, MOST WERE UNAWARE THAT HUMANS ACTUALLY EXISTED. THE HUMAN BOGIE MEN WERE REDUCED TO CHILDRENS STORIES AND LEGENDS ON THE CIVILIZED WORLDS, THEN, SUDDENLY THE BOGIE MEN CAME BACK TO LIFE.

THE REPORTS, MIND PICTURES AND MIND SOUNDS WE WERE GETTING KEPT US SITTING, WITH OUR MOUTHS OPEN, FOR MONTHS.

THERE WERE THOUSANDS - TENS OF THOUSANDS - OF PLANETS OUT THERE, ALL SETTLED BY STRANGE LOOKING BALD-HEADED, BIG EYED THINGS - ALL

LOOKING LIKE MY EARLY RECORDINGS OF THE GUARDIANS, (WHICH WERE OUR VERSIONS OF BOOGIE MEN).

THE CIVILIZATION, WHICH WE HAD BEEN IN AWE OF FOR SO LONG, WAS USING SOME CRUDE FORM OF PHYSICAL TECHNOLOGY TO DO THINGS MUCH SLOWER AND MUCH LESS EFFICIENTLY THAN ANY HUMAN CHILD COULD DO WITH ITS MIND ALONE.

THEY WERE SORT OF LAUGHABLE.

THEY HAD NOTHING WE WANTED.

AND THEY COULDN'T HURT US.

NATURALLY, WE DESPISED THEM.

(RECORDING - 2407 AD)

The one Earth Starship that remained after the attack was utterly useless. So we left it there - letting the Earthies die up there slowly and alone.

Within a few more months, however, another Starship from the Earth Alliance came into orbit, connecting to the damaged one. It was a new model and made to be invulnerable to our Rhino attacks. It was more Battleship than Starship as we found that out in a couple of disastrous raids where whole new Twenties of Black Fighters, eager to match our feats with the Earth ships, were wiped out without making a scratch.

This new Battleship still couldn't pick us out of the asteroids but they now had guns that would vaporize e erything around - rocks, dust and us. So it was hard to get close and even when we did, there wasn't much we could do. Two Black Fighters who did get close enough to Rhino the starship just bounced off - looking silly, until they were vaporized.

Both of the Earth ships - the old hulk and the new Battleship joined together somehow and became one mighty Starship, restarting weapons production and construction of enemy supplies.

After a few months, the Earth Troops had landed to regroup with the few Loyalists that were left. We were powerless and could only watch. After all of our fighting, we were back to where we aterted again.

But what the hell were they after ? We'd heard that they were just going to sit up there and nuke everything. Why bother to land ?

Luckily we'd had Ike. He had given us the names of some people in the Earth High Command who opposed all of this genocide. Our leaders had contacted them and got them working for us. They told us what was going on on a regular basis.

Earth had to have a base to monitor the planet core. If they just kept nuking us, eventually the whole planet would break up and they'd lose all the resources forever and throw Earth out of its orbit. They'd gotten reports after the first accidental nuke that started the war -and wasn't so accidental after all - that the crust was unstable. Other nuke attacks, like the one during our during our celebrations, had confirmed it. The planet was fragile and could just disintegrate, unless they did some very precise measurements.

So they needed a permanent base to determine exactly where to nuke us and how much the planet could stand.

This time, the Earth base was not in the Barren Equator. This time it was right near the shore of the Martian ocean. Our spies told us that they weren't ready for an attack yet. Keep in mind I said 'yet'. They were building as fast as possible to harden the base and make it indestructible. But they hadn't got there yet.

Their only defence was our decency.

A Nuke from space is able to hit a target on the shore with perfect accuracy. It's not like a target hidden in a valley somewhere. And this was one of the most highly populated areas of the planet. The treacherous Earth theory, according to our spies, was that if we mounted any kind of attack, they'd send in nukes from the Battleship. They'd wipe out our big population centres in the area and kill both us and their own troops.

I bet that the Earth troops didn't know that.

Political silence strikes again.

They thought - and rightly - that we were too decent to kill that many of our own people just to crush a small base.

Standoff.

We had to let them do whatever the hell they were doing.

*   *   *

Joseph Thomas wasn't a stand-off kind of guy, though. He thought about it for weeks and decided that something had to be done - without sacrificing millions.

He couldn't evacuate all the people, and even if he could, they could just begin another base anywhere they chose - with their superior firepower in space.

So he had to cancel their advantage.

He couldn't redesign the Fighters or the civilians to withstand the radiation and explosive force that

ONLY HUMAN - MARTIAN INDEPENDENCE 261

the Earth missiles gave off. So he had to take away the nuclear power.

It was the only way out.

And it was brilliant.

He invented and installed a new gadget onto each Black Fighter that gave off a special radiation of its own. Some kind of electro-magnetic pulse that fried the nuclear-reaction elements right inside missiles and turned them into very expensive rocks. Unless you reversed the polarity and re-armed them again.

The only catch was - you had to get within 10 miles of the missile. We weren't sure if you could fry the nukes inside the starship, but with their superior detection and gunnery, we couldn't get close enough to find out. So we went for Operation Raptor - to hunt them down and kill the missiles in the air - like the ancient hunting birds of Earth.

And like hunting birds, each Black Fighter had claws, too. A huge clamp on the undercarriage that could actually catch a missile - the thought being that then the pilot could turn around, re-arm the missile and send it back to its source.

It sounded good in practice and the Black Fighters were up to the task - being able to fly faster than the missiles. But we weren't even sure if our secret weapon would work on the Earth missiles, let alone whether we could catch them and hold them.

Only one way to find out . . .

* * *

It was in the evening. All that could be heard were two Earth fighters moving to a pre-selected target. They had just came from the Western Coastal Base set up by the Earth forces and were enroute to drop nukes on a nearby mountain range to test the monitoring equipment at the new base - the fact that it was heavily populated by Martians didn't bother them at all.

The planes continued to shoot into Martian territory detected by the Martian anti-aircraft grids, but left alone, as usual, by the fear of death from above.

All was quiet as the fighters were getting ready to release their nukes over the colonies in the mountains. The lights from the bottom city gleamed like jewels, while the Earth fighters turned to make the drop, ready to run from the blast and the radiation.

As they sunk down, making their dive, the pilots began to see two black shapes. They were blurred with the night sky but still noticeable to the pilot's eye.

The shapes seemed to change form.

" Drop the nukes !" ordered one of the pilots, but both were terrified on what they were seeing beside them. The pilot looked to his altitude meter then back at the shape. Suddenly it was gone. Accelerating so quickly it was as if it disappeared.

Both Earth planes were confused, almost forgetting to drop the nukes. But they didn't forget. A clutch of missiles - 4 or 5 from each plane - streaked down towards the mountain towns.

Suddenly the Black shapes were back, following the missiles for a while then turning sharply back toward the planes that had launched them.

The Earth planes began their escape, running at maximum to get away from the blasts. The black shapes kept pace with them easily.

Minutes went by.

There were no explosions.

As the Earth pilots began to wonder about this, the first earth plane exploded, causing the fuel to fall, ignite and become beautiful in the sky.

The second one tried to pull up, having chills going down his back and breathing deeply as he tried to understand what was going on.

The pilot looked to his side, seeing the shapes again, and fired on them. He looked again and saw them unharmed and for the last time. One was along side but the other was charging right into him at incredible speed. The pilot gulped as the impact broke through to him, crushing him and tearing him into thousands of pieces, leaving his fighter exploding like a puff ball.

All that could be seen by the public below were lights and explosions which resembled faint sparks amongst the stars.

*   *   *

I took my plane off Rhino mode, hearing plates of metal grind back to their place on the plane.

" That was too close, Whore !" said Jimbo through the radionn transmissions. "Why didn't you just shoot him, instead of ramming ?"

I grinned, " I'm a hands-on kind of guy. Besides, at this altitude, the dust of a Rhino won't do as much damage as the shrapnel of a shot would of."

" You're all heart. Still, you're right. Next time, let's take them out near the border. If we do it over civilian sites like this, we risk casualties that don't need to happen. I think we're just too happy today to keep ourselves under control."

I grinned, " Whatever."

" All right whore, lets hit the sack back at the base."

I grinned, giving no answer but going to auto pilot, in fear that I would fall asleep.

It was the most boring fight that I had ever experienced.

Ever since the enemy occupation on the shores of the west, we'd been hiding and watching. Now, with these two earth planes, we had proven the nuke killersworked. We had a chance again, if only we could chase down all the nukes.

Without their nuclear weapons, we had the advantage in any kind of fight.

I knew that the border lines would be having much more action soon. Now that we'd proven the nuke killers, there was nothing to stop them over-running the earth base. I could just see them powering large turret machine guns the size of towers, and firing off rounds of bullets that were always on explosive.

What a hoot.

Like my old days on the ground.

Piloting just wasn't as fun as being an actual soldier on the front.

Piloting was more like a game, especially in a Black Fighter which was fast, dangerous and utterly indestructible.

Well - not utterly.

Even a Black Fighter could be killed if hit just right.

You might think that you're a hotshot just because you were not hit yet but once you were hit, you then realized that this was real, as real as a hand.

By the time you realized that, though, it was too late, you were dead. This was one of the fears I had. Being too arrogant.

And being dead.

When we landed, we went to the mess hall.

There, I got myself a drink of water. Jimbo went to get some potatoes and turnips to eat. He ate like a pig as his other friends came in. Manikan sat with him talking to him, probably making conversation. As I had said, it was a very slow night. Nothing was going on. nothing at all.

We couldn't tell anyone that we had just proven the nuke killer. Only the high command knew at this point, so we had to act bored.

I acted so good that my eyes began to feel heavy as soon as I had my third gulp of water.

The cold went to my belly, that was the only thing that was keeping me from dozing.

The other pilots, men and women together, were playing cards, making bets, and probably asking each other out.

I looked around, hoping to see some soldiers other than Officers and Pilots. There were none. I couldn't understand why they kept us in separate mess halls. To me it was almost discrimination by rank but who was I to argue? I was the one who never liked Officers and here I was, drinking water in a Captain's uniform. I could remember years ago, I had once said that I wanted to fight this war just to go home to my girlfriend, I had only wanted to be a soldier because they had no reports to write. Now here I was, a Lieutenant, then a Captain who was a Pilot, just because I had experience in flying.

I didn't understand this one bit. I was almost a specialist in everything. From a soldier with a few rounds of explosive shells in my hand to a tank driver who knew how to load, drive and aim at the same time, and now a Pilot of one of the most secret and proudest fighters that the world had ever seen.

I only wondered, what was going to happen next. The funniest thing was going to be that, instead of marrying my sweetie and running the vapor farm at the end of the war, I now kept having a nightmare that I was a History teacher. Knowing that I did terribly in history, before I lived through the most historic times of Mars, well, I guess that it would be funny.

" Hey turn up the radionn !" shouted a person near the radionn box.

All of them gathered to it, but I sat still, not caring on what it was.

" The advances of the long planned takeover of the Western Coast has failed. The troops had arrived, taking heavy casualties only to see their fate come to them. A Nuke has destroyed the entire West Coast Settlement. The Earth troops have landed again to mobilize another colony closer to the Barren Equator, since this nuke also took out their base on the coast. The casualty list is still going up, it is only a matter of time until -" I tuned out the radionn suddenly.

I turned in my seat stunned at the news that I had just heard.

Suddenly the sirens went off.

We were meant to go for a briefing.

We all ran out of the Mess Hall, getting to Jimbo and Manikan who were about to tell us the mission.

We all stopped at their presence, all getting in line and taking a knee. Jimbo started talking:

" As you all know the bastards have nuked us again. But it's our fault. Somebody screwed up. Me and the new Captain here " he pointed at me, "just got back from proving the weapon that was supposed to win this war. We can fry nukes in the air so they won't go off. There was supposed to be a planned attack, so ground troops would advance on the Earth base, while we went topside to neutralize any nukes they sent down.

Somebody screwed up. The grunts went in as soon as they got the news from High Command. Now they've screwed everything up. The Starship retaliated without us around to fry the nukes."

Over 3 million are dead." Manikan shook his head.

"And the bastards are just setting up a new base. Byt they don't know about our nuke killers. At least we've still got surprise on our side," said Jimbo

"Sir, we don't have anything to fight them with even if we kill all their nukes. That Battleship up there can outfight us." said a pilot.

" That's why we steal their missiles," Manikan explained. " First we deactivate them. The new clamps that were installed were designed to catch the missiles in flight. The missiles can then be reactivated, we can actually use them to target anything, even the Battleship.

We all know that one nuke can take a big chunk out of the hull of a Starship, and we'll have one nuke for each Black Fighter. So the odds are with us. Now we'll all work together. The Militia is going to attack the new base. We'll head for the Starship. When it sends down nukes, we'll tab and grab.

Once we each have a missile and the others are deactivated, we'll take a run at that Battleship. Sounds well thought out, eh ? And you've had lots of practice at it too eh ?

Ah thinking and practicing - screw it.

Let's just go and do it.

Let's get into our fighters right now, all we want to do is grab onto the missiles, not destroy them, remember that." Manikan finished.

We all scattered, getting into the fighters which were already running. The mechanics all moved out of the way as soon as we got seated and strapped in.

The tops all closed. I watched as all the other fighters began to take off, then I took off too.

As we reached the air, I turned on my radar, hoping to catch nukes dropping. No such luck. It was halfway around the world. We had to smoke the tires.

I could hear the reports of ground troops attacking the new base. We were already in space and ripping vacuum to get in position.

I was in the lead and was so intent on getting to where I could see the starship, that I almost got killed.

Suddenly a missile came burning with a long tail of fire right in front of me. It shocked me, it was a few feet away, going faster than me.

I gulped as I flicked my nuke-killer switch and dived after it. What a dummy, thinking it was a war where you could see your enemy.

The computer guided me to the top of the missile. Now that I was in war-mode, I could see others streaming down all around me. Other Black fighters were after their own missiles. I hoped they were all deactivated.

My hands trembled as I reached for the clamp releases. I was right down into atmosphere already, both the missile and my fighter were in flames.

As I pulled the clamp controls I felt the magnetic force pull me to the missile. There was a thump and I had it.

It was now up to me to me to wrestle with it, to gain control or be pulled down with it.

I jerked the joystick up just to feel myself dive even further down.

I flew from side to side, trying to muscle it up but it was rather powerful. I hadn't thought about the force of the missile rocket, just about deactivating the warhead and catching it.

The cold fusion engines were burning gas fast as I tried swaying with it.

It was almost like riding a wild animal, you had to show it who was boss or it would be the boss of you. I tugged again to find myself stalling and falling with it,

I couldn't pull up, it was too powerful but I still tried. I closed my eyes, hoping that it wouldn't win, but I was still declining.

I red-lined everything and heard the howl of engines betrayed. But that did it. I started heading up and the missile rocket was now helping instead of fighting.

I sighed, now growling as I pulled the joystick all the way up. This time I shot out into space accelerating so fast that my suit felt like bricks onto my chest. It was such a power jerk that I almost knocked myself out - (Thank goodness for computer piloting). I sighed, knowing that the missile was finally my weapon instead of my fate.

On my radar, I was picking up more missiles. They were declining but falling lop-sided and swaying - hopefully dead and out of control.

I could tell that the other Black Fighters were having problems with controlling them as well. It looked like I was the only one who was able to get control and literally become one with the missile.

I then darted through the dense patch of sky, seeing the blanket of space once more. Now only acting as direction engines for the missile, I glided around the planet's orbit, to seek and destroy the Battleship. My nerves, after trying to catch the missile, were jumpy. My hands shook from my panicking self as I struggled to turn off my atmospheric engines.

There was nothing out there. Suddenly from the planet, came several Black Fighters, spinning, swerving, looping and shooting out like a bunch of drunk birds coming out of a saloon. I guided my way clear from them. Then I saw my target one hundred miles away in my scanning grid. It was over two miles long because of the other Starship it connected to. As the missile shot with incredible speed, the Starship's hideous reflection began to take form as a large, thin, heavy plated sausage of a ship, continually dropping more Nukes like a mushroom shooting out it's spores.

I bit my lower lip as I red lined my space engines.

My nerves became jumpy once more. My breathing was deep and strong, my heart beats literally pounding and moving my body to the thumps.

Suddenly shots of bullets, cannons, and missiles came at me, all having a twirling tail of gas right behind them. Space was filled with ammunition. My eyes widened as I tried to dodge them. The Starship came closer and closer. Every shot of their weapons almost hit me. All they needed was one good hit to end me or deflect me from my course. I was a true kamikaze now. A flying bomb, with only one chance.

The sweat on my forehead began to float around as I tried to maneuver myself out of danger. A Black Fighter shot past me in ferocious speed. He made it to the thickly plated skin of the Battleship protecting the spinning hull. Suddenly he, as well as the missile, exploded after being hit with a cannon round.

There was a fascinating bright light all around as the debris of the nuclear explosion rattled me around. When the lights dimmed down, I saw the skin of the Starship scratched here and there. It was barely damaged. A Nuke in space needs to be a direct hit. There is no air to compress and cause damage if you miss.

Suddenly I had noticed that I was going too fast towards it. I tried to slow down, forgetting that I was in space, so I immediately pulled up and skimmed along the outer hull of the Starship, trying to get out of the shooting range. Suddenly I saw two more Black Fighters guiding their stolen missiles to the hull. The guns were no longer aimed at me. The Black Fighters immediately went into Rhino Mode as they were hit. They spun out of control but they still piloted themselves into the hull. The turrets and cannons were destroyed and launched away by the battleship like a plug shooting out of a socket. The Computer bleeped, telling me to dodge the debris from the battleship.

The beepings, designed to warn me, were beginning to disrupt my concentration.

Suddenly a giant one hundred - foot - long barrel, once part of an asteroid cannon, shot in front of me. I immediately closed my eyes and was not relieved that it had only missed me by a single yard. I had finally escaped from firing distance, going further into space. At that point, I felt like I was about to lose my mind.

" And to you Devil, I toss credit accounts to your endless vast of space . . . and I ask you to bring on your legions from hell !" I said, not knowing why I said it. It was supposed to be funny and help me to calm myself, but it didn't work.

I was going crazy and was wanting to go home. I began to mumble like a little child as I refused to turn the fighter around.

But then a voice came to me. It was the same voice which had told myself to encorpse myself years ago and came to me at other times of stress.

"HIT AN ELEPHANT'S SKIN, YOU ANNOY IT, BUT HIT IT BETWEEN THE EYES, YOU KILL IT" said the voice in my head.

I had truly lost my mind, thinking of swift death coming towards me. So I did what any crazy man would do, I talked with the voice in my head.

"Devil ?" I thought, "I hope you haven't taken me up on that offer."

"USE THE MISSILE AS YOUR SAVIOR, AND COME HOME TO LAND, TO PRAISE AND SAVOR."said the voice.

" I think I've finally gone crazy. I'm losing wht's left of my mind !" I muttered as I began to feel scared.

"FIRE THE MISSILE RIGHT IN THE MIDDLE OF THE FRONT FACE OF THE BATTLESHIP AND YOU WILL DESTROY IT !" the voice said.

Since I was going crazy, I thought: 'What the hell. I'll do as the voice tells me to do.' I immediately grabbed onto the joystick but before I turned the fighter around, I grunted.

" Before I turn this thing around, I want to know who you are."

" I AM MARSOLLA - THE MIND OF MARS. I HAVE BEEN HERE FOR THOUSANDS OF YEARS. I HAVE WATCHED AND RECORDED EVERYTHING SINCE THE BEGINNING OF YOUR SPECIES ON MARS. I WATCH AND GRIEVE AT THE SAME TIME. I SPEAK ONLY WITH ONE AT A TIME. SO I CHOSE YOU TO COMMUNICATE WITH THROUGH THIS TIME." said the voice.

" Who are you ? Are you God ?" I asked again.

" I AM NOT A GOD, NOR WOULD I CHOOSE TO BE. I AM THE HEART AND SOUL OF MARS, I AM THE WIND, THE TREES, THE ROCKS, AND THE STREAMS THAT YOU FIGHT SO DEARLY FOR.

I AM THE RECORDER," it said. I knew that it was an illusion, but I played along because it calmed me down from panicking.

" What kind of price do you ask of me for this information ?" I asked.

"**I ASK FOR NOTHING. I ONLY AID AND RECORD. I ONLY ASK THAT YOU TAKE MY ADVICE AND AIM IT AT THE MIDDLE OF THE FRONT OF THE BATTLESHIP AND QUIT TALKING LIKE AN IDIOT.**"

I said nothing more, feeling like a lunatic, I only did what everyone in this whole war was taught to do in a tight situation. Do what you're told and grin.

So I did.

I turned the fighter around and accelerated once more, this time making my way towards the front of the Battleship. When the front face became visible, I red-lined the engines, speeding towards the incoming cannons and rounds, then I let fate take over. I unclamped myself from the missile and watched it head towards the battleship.

I then turned around and dived, chasing after other missiles which the battleship had shot out as I released my own. Just in case I needed a second shot.

I chased after a group of them, knocking their warheads out with my EMPulse, seeing their falling bodies drop and stall with me into the atmosphere.

Suddenly, I saw on my radar evidence of the impact from my missile, it had destroyed the front layers of the battleship.

I didn't feel confident enough that the ship was

totally blown up so I dived after another missile, clamping onto it and immediately wrestling with it once more.

The MoonLight Missile Waltz had started again as I had another missile romance and this one had a little more kick to her. The missile spun me around and threw me in every direction made vacant. I finally taught her who was boss and was ready to head out in space again.

"Attention all whores ! The battleship has dismantled into several millions of pieces and they are all falling to Mars atmosphere. They'll be burning up all around you soon. You all have done an excellent job. Return home now and get out of harm's way," the radionn said.

I felt embarrassed, I didn't know what to do with the missile.

Then again, I was going crazy, so I did what any loon would do. Land with it.

Landing was the easy part but escaping stalling was another problem. Sometimes the engine in the missile would kick in and try to go to the ground. Even when I landed, I had to send mechanics to cut the missile engines off line just to keep it from exploding. When I landed I had experienced four stalls, one emergency gas drop to keep the engines from over working, and last a jammed joystick.

I was truly afraid to get out, thinking that the missile would become active again once I shut the thing down.

I sat in there, seeing the others landing and having no such problem.

The mechanics had to physically drag me out of it. When they did, I expected something to explode or take off or even fall to the ground but nothing ever did happen like that.

I felt pretty dumb.

Doing these sorts of missions was making me more and more nervous of flying. I knew that some day I was going to snap up there, causing something to go wrong. Not only was I hearing voices up there, now I was having conversations with them.

I just tried to do the best that I could so that that day would not come. But it was getting harder and harder. The rest of the week, I had spent in the training facility.

It got my mind off the things that I feared that would happen. I went into the G-Force bench press. As it spun around, I pushed harder to keep the bar from killing me. This exercise machine was the only thing that got my mind off flying. Unlike the Apple Pie machine which taught you to survive flying around in space, this one only made you stronger, to handle G-forces and it helped put stronger muscles on my bony arms.

I didn't want to fly the Black Fighter after the missile crisis. It was the most powerful thing that I had ever piloted. I tried to avoid the night shift and definitely napalm runs against whatever Earth troops were left on the surface. All I did was train.

It was two weeks later when Jimbo came in to train with me. He saw me pounding, trying to climb the ropes without using my feet. He stood there looking at me with concern in his eye.

As I climbed to the top and let go, my safety pulley connected to my belt let me down slowly. I was panting, my shirt covered in sweat and the stench of onions.

"Captain, I'm concerned about your refusals in flying. It's been two weeks since your last flight."

I only looked at him.

" Well what's your point?" I asked him.

" I think that you're getting soft, Whore, and I want you to prove otherwise."

I gulped. "If it's an important mission you want me to go on, then I'll go. Otherwise no. And if I do go, make sure it's important, because I want to say that it would be my last time flying." I said.

" What ?"

" I can't kill by remote control anymore. It's not right. "

" You're quitting? To do what ? I remember you when you were a Private, you were a soldier who hated fighting. You were the one who whined to go home to your girlfriend. Look at you now, you are a Captain and a Pilot. Where are you going to go from here ? You'd be put back with the grunts, the soldiers, hell you'd die before you'd see your prime age of 30," he said.

" I feel more comfortable on the ground and I feel

more like a person if I fight , seeing the enemy. Flying is too unreal. I can't do that anymore. It's too scary."

He grinned. "All right, Whore, suit yourself, "

"That's Captain Whore, to you . . . "

"Right, Sir Whore, but before you turn in your helmet, take one last mission with me. This one will be more to your liking."

I smiled. "All right, for old times sake. What's the mission?" I asked.

"A napalm drop over the border. The Ruby Reds are needing help in taking that area. When you blasted that Starship, it launched thousands of emergency shuttles. Most of them landed here and it's up to us to exterminate them - like bugs - before they build up a strong base."

"I accept."

When we reached the air, we flew slowly, knowing that one small drop which was a minute early or a minute less would result in disaster. It could land on our own ground troops. Everything had to be timed perfectly.

As we dove down, to get a clearer picture on the radar, I saw the trenches being shot up with bombs and gases from the enemy side. I then saw the enemy advancing towards the soldiers who were firing off everything they had. I started to sweat as I was about to push the napalm drop, then the visions of my past came to me. There was a picture of Sergeant Will shouting at me to get down.

It disappeared as Jimbo dropped his napalm on

the other side, perfect timing.

I then got another scene: I was on the ground trying to breath as the flames were burning me. I closed my eyes to get it out of my mind but it was no use. I saw the vision of a man screaming and burning alive as he tried to put his melted goggles on his face.

I bit my lower lip; the scenes in my head were too unbearable.

"What are you waiting for ?" said the radionn.

I kept silent as I became nervous, my helmet was steaming up. All I could see were visions of troopers screaming in agony.

I closed my eyes as I went for another pass. I then hit the drop button, feeling the liquid fall from the napalm holds on my wings.

As it did, I felt myself begin to cry. I blubbered and actually regurgitated in my helmet. It was so terrible that I put the plane on auto pilot because I couldn't fly it any more.

This was the last time I would ever fly again.

When I landed, I quickly got out, wanting to run to my bunker and get rid of my suit.

Jimbo never really talked about what happened to me up there, he felt that it would cause more trauma on me. After all, I had only missed one pass and I never knew whether he realized I was freaking out, or whether he thought I was just getting set for a better drop.

I never went to sick bay, feeling that they would tell me that I had Traumatic Stress Syndrome.

I knew that it wasn't the case because I felt that it was something else, almost as if I was never created to fly. It was an instinct that I had.

Pity it had taken a couple of years to find out.

I spent the next month in training.

Jimbo only told me stories on the adventures that he experienced with the other Pilots and never asked me to fly again. I could tell that he felt sorry for me but he tried to hide it.

But flying was his life. Not mine.

After a while, I left training and went to be circulated into the job of checking the soldiers before missions and advising them on what to do.

I was taking up the job of a Training Officer, and I liked it a lot better than flying. All I ever did was talk to the troops, tell them what to watch out for and hand them new missions.

Then watch them die.

Chapter 10

(PLAYBACK - 16,600 BC)

I AM AS GUILTY AS ANY OF MY CHILDREN.

MORE SO, BECAUSE I WAS MORE A PARENT TO THEM THAN ONE OF THEM. I SHOULD HAVE KNOWN BETTER, BUT I ENCOURAGED THEM. "GO AND SEE" I TOLD THEM. "SEND BACK INTERESTING THOUGHTS"

THEY WENT BY THE MILLION.

IN TIME THERE WERE MORE GONE THAN THERE WERE AT HOME.

OF COURSE, SOME WERE INTERESTED IN THE CIVILIZED RACES, AND TREATED THEM WITH DIGNITY. SOME TALKED WITH THEIR SCHOLARS AND LEARNED THINGS ABOUT THE TECHNOLOGY AND THE HISTORY. THAT'S WHERE WE HEARD ABOUT THE POSSIBLE ORIGINS OF HUMANITY, WHERE WE LEARNED ABOUT THE LAST HUMAN OUTBREAK AND WHERE WE LEARNED ABOUT OTHER RECORDERS.

BUT FOR THE MOST PART, WE WEREN'T NICE AT ALL.

WE WALKED THROUGH THEIR CITIES AT WILL, GAWKING AT THE BUILDINGS AND FACTORIES AND DWELLINGS.

NOT IN AWE, BUT IN DISGUST.

WHAT A WASTE OF RESOURCES. WHAT AN EYESORE. WHAT STINK. WHAT SHORT-SIGHTEDNESS. WHAT STUPIDITY.

We treated them, on all their worlds, like we treated animals on Marsolla. Part of the scenery. Unimportant. Unintelligent. And, for sure, not dangerous at all.

We went into their places of business and their homes, uninvited, mocking them. Putting together thought shows that let us laugh at every aspect of their lives. Like a silly wildlife documentary.

Of course, they resented it. But what could they do? We could jump into and out of anywhere, in the blink of an eye. We could not be hurt by any weapon. We could live anywhere; standing in the middle of a freeway; floating near the ceiling of a bedroom; lying on the boardroom table of a big company. Or floating in orbit around their planet.

We could broadcast our thoughts and laughter right into their heads at any time.

And we did.

For hundreds of years.

Even I thought it was funny.

They politely asked us to behave in a civilized manner. Over and over again.

We thought that was funny too.

Watching someone who is harmless, when they get angry, is always funny.

Until, suddenly, it isn't funny anymore.

(RECORDING - 2408 AD)

The year was 2408, and the war continued.

The number of Black Fighters which were in service was over 150. The enemy had come to be a problem again because of three other starships which had come in orbit.

Congress was attacked, but there were still enough Congressmen alive to escape to keep the Martian Government going.

I felt older now. Ancient. I was 25 years old. I had been at war for 10 years and I had started to get wrinkles. I felt wiser and less passionate and I had not seen action in 5 months.

I now spent most of my time in the medical tents, helping the medics and talking to the troopers. It made them feel better and it was how I got my information on what was going on .

It was strange how they listened to me - as if I was a ghost from another era. Most of them were suffering from Grey Gas. It messed up your mind, making you think that everyone was against you and that you were lost in a fog.

I had known their panic and pain, I was once attacked with the same thing, thinking that the enemy was in front of me only to find out that it was our own were the recruits. I still remember shooting them down and later justifying it to myself.

We thought it was fog or poison at the time. Now we knew better and had measures to counteract it.

We called it Psycho Warfare. The recovery was quick but the memories were permanent.

Throughout all my time there with the troops, there was one trooper who had gotten a real dose of it; a Sergeant who I remembered. He was a pedigree by the name of Paris Lee Kim.

When I first saw him, he was legless and was covered in medical injections all over his legs to stop the bleeding.

He refused to take off his tattered armor, thinking that the enemy would attack any time. A Psycho Warrior if I ever met one. I remember scanning his hand and making conversation with him. I held his arm as I scanned the barcode.

" Sergeant, how did you lose you legs ?" I asked.

He looked at me with a snarl. "I was in a firefight in the fog. I tried to reload my gun when I forgot that the barrel was jammed with a bullet. The next thing I knew, a sniper hit my leg and I tried to return fire and pulled the trigger. The whole gun exploded, killing the person next to me. Thank God that I was wearing my armor or I would of been gone too. It just blew off my legs."

I sat next to him.

"That's a story to tell your kids." I said.

He looked at me.

"So what are you -" he paused looking at my ranking patch over my coat, " - Captain ? Are you Pedigree pure bred or a Hybrid mongrel like the rest of them ?"

"Me - I'm a Hybrid Bayta, how about you ?" I asked.

"Myself, I'm a pedigree." He said proudly.

"A pedigree ? You Japanese ?"

He became offensive. "Hell no!, My family escaped the takeover of 2149," he barked, "When Japan took over all of Asia."

"Then what are you ?" I asked.

"I'm Korean. I'm a pure Korean, not like the other so-called Pedigree Asians. They're mixed up themselves- part Thai and Chinese. Part Japanese and Filipino. There is no purity at all. See I'm a pure bred, you, on the other hand, are a Mutt."

I didn't know how to take that, as an insult or a compliment. "Well I'm flattered." I said.

"No you're not, you're mixed. I don't even know if you have a religion. I'm a Purebred. I believe in Christianity and I'm proud of it." he said.

"A Pure Bred ? A brain-dead Inbred if you ask me, you sad legless bastard ! Look here Pedigree, there are Pedigree Caucasians who have nicer tempers than you, and they're Caucasian. Even the Pedigree Negroes have nothing against us hybrids. Why do you carry all this TwenCe shit around with you ?"

He was silent, then blurted out:

"Do I really have to have a reason? My parents hated them, and their parents before them."

" What a time to pick a fight - you've got no legs. Quite typical I guess, all you pedigrees ain't got the thinking capability of any normal Alpha or Bayta, you're all too interbred to think straight." I responded with a grin. "Probably think you're making sense"

The only way to diffuse a racist was to mock him.

He was quiet and not saying anything.

"Anyway, by the looks of your patches you were part of the 144 Dirt Regiment, " I said. "I heard that not too many survived in that regiment ?"

He just looked at me.

"What do you want to hear ? I've got stories up to my wounds. We were attacked by dopers, losing close to half of the regiment. The rest of us retreated to the mountains. Even more froze to death up there, and the remaining few were rescued just before the enemy got us."

"That's a tough story to live through." I said.

"What do you know? I bet that you just were promoted from desk to desk without even seeing the battlefield," he said.

"What makes you think that ?" I asked.

"You're here, pissing around with me instead of off fighting. Well, come on, Cap. Prove me wrong. Open your coat up. Let's see your patches." he said.

I grinned. I didn't need to show him where I had been.

I'd been everywhere in this bloody war. What reason did I have to relive it all ?

"Well ?" he said waiting for his evidence.

"Lets just say that I've been in several tight spots."

"Sure," he said sarcastically. "A few scuffles in the food line in the Officer's Club ?"

I looked to his legs, all covered in needles which were stabbed in.

" You've got a lot of guts to stick needles into your legs. I've got to admit, that takes might." I said trying to change the subject.

He raised his head from his pillow, looking at it.

"Oh that ? I'm glad that I had a medical kit around, I had used up my last few when I got my prosthetic arm. I hear that the prosthetics are too limited now. I hear that they are now using robotic limbs." he said.

" Those would look good, and reallyscare the hell out of the enemy, I'd tell you that," I said

"Yeah, whatever. I just want the legs back to go out and fight again. I know that staying in the trench ain't pretty but when you shoot off a round and watch the enemy suffer, it puts a feeling of satisfaction in your heart," he said, starting to feel the medication from the needles, which would dull his nerves.

"My favorite kind of gun is the Shotgun. 24 rounds of explosive only. That's something that'll leave a mark," he said, beginning to chuckle with the dope.

" I don't really know, I'm a cyclone gun man my self," I said, keeping up with him.

" Cyclone gun ? Those things are too fancy."

The tent sheet opened up and a Medic walked in. He looked at me then at Paris.

" Sergeant Paris ? Your robotic legs are ready for connection to your limbs. You numb yet. You ready ?"

Paris just smiled and nodded his head.

The Medic brought in the two robotic legs, then he started working on him.

I stood there, remembering the day that I got my arm replaced. It hurt and took hours to stop the pain. This new robotic limbing was easy, clean, and quick.

The Medic was done with him in half an hour. He said nothing further and ran out of the tent. I guess that he had others to work on.

Paris stood up and stomped around like a child getting a new toy for the first time.

" Well what do you think?" he proudly said.

I looked down, seeing these thin bone-like rods connected to steel cups shaped as shoes on the bottom. I found them rather neat. No frills. No crap. No meat. Just practical.

" They look great." I replied.

" Well then, now that you've seen my wounds, what have you lost in this war?" he asked.

" My mind and my appetite." I said.

He started to laugh and lay back down on the bed to rest awhile. The dope was wearing off already.

" Good one. I like you, Cap - what's your name ?"

"I lost that too." I said.

He looked at me in a funny way. Suddenly, he grabbed my hand and looked for my barcode. There was only scar tissue. He opened my coat and looked at my patches.

"Jesus." he said. "You're CorpseHugger."

I blinked. I'd never heard this one before.

"You're a legend with the ground troops.

You're the crazy no-name bastard that grabbed a corpse for protection and kept on fighting."

I gulped.

"You're the crazy no-name son-of-a bitch that survived the Tank Ballet on the Red Plain"

I coughed.

"You're the no-name asshole who led the Lucky Twenty of Muddy Lane. And led the Moonlight Missile Waltz to blast the Battleship."

I shook my head.

"You're the most famous guy in the Martian Militia. And I tried to pick a fight with you. I asked you for your patches. I'm so sorry," he squirmed around on the bed, "I'm so very sorry," he said, like all Koreans that I've met do.

" Forget it. So, do you know what your next assignment is ?" I asked.

" I'm not too sure but from what it looks like, I'm going with the rest of the troopers here.

" Where's that ?" I asked.

" The Earthies have dropped and retaken your old area - Muddy Lane - to get the weapons plant going again. So we're going to storm Muddy Lane then come back to regroup near the borders of the West Coast. If we don't stop them now, it's only a matter of time until they take the Barren Equator."

"Well, PureBred, I hope that you don't get hurt." I smiled. "We'll need men like you after this is over"

"I won't be around that long, Bayta," he said.

"You'll be around forever, Sarge" I said

"Us Pedigrees have strange powers. I know I won't survive my next battle. I feel it," he said

I chuckled to his comment. Lots of infantrymen believed they were dead men walking. It was almost strange if a grunt didn't feel that way. It gave him a nothing-to-lose feeling that made him crazy.

We both walked out of the tent, seeing that the others were running around, getting ready for an attack of some sort. We both were confused.

I ran to grab a soldier to find out.

"Private, what's going on ?" I said.

"Sir, there's going to be an attack drop on this area. The Black Fighters have been relocated so there's no reason to hold this position. We're evacuating," he said.

I let go of his armor as he ran to the drop ships.

I ran back to Paris.

"What ?" he shouted to get his voice across from the scattering people.

"There's an attacking force coming in. We're giving up this place. We're leaving!"

I started to storm to one of the drop ships.

I looked back, seeing Paris picking up a shotgun as he put on his helmet and connected the comm unit to the armor.

I ran back to him. "What are you doing ? Come on, get out of here !" I shouted to him.

He buckled up his helmet and loaded up his gun.

"I'm staying to fight them. If I'm going to die today, then I want it to be in battle !" he shouted back.

"You're crazy, you're going to be needed in the Muddy Lane storming. We can't afford to lose you for nothing, Pedigree!" I said, grabbing his arm.

He looked to his arm and pulled loose.

"I may be stupid, and I may be vulgar but there's one thing that I know !" he said

"What's that, Pedigree ?"

"I know when I'm going to die. I know it's today. And I am not afraid of it ! This is my destiny, I know it and now I have to fulfill it !" he said.

I looked at him. Those words meant something to me. It touched me and all that I could do was salute him as he put his Multi-pro goggles over his eyes.

"I hope you succeed in what you're doing, you Bayta bastard !" he shouted, with a grin.

"Take a whole troop of them to hell with you, Sarge, you crusty old son-of-a-bitch !" I shouted back.

He saluted me then ran on his new legs into the crowd. I looked for a while, then ran to the drop ships. I ran into the cargo hold, buckling myself onto a seat, waiting for the door to shut.

Once they did, we took off.

As we climbed, I could see out of the window hundreds of dropping pods, individually filled with one man each falling onto the spot.

The ride was rocky, and rough. The pilot was trying to dodge the fighters which were being shot down by the Black Fighters and once in a while he hit a drop seed filled with one man coming down.

When we landed in a base which was further up

a valley, I wanted to hear the reports of the battle. But I heard nothing, nothing at all.

There were no reports on the raid, no news on the advances. I take it that it was too little a loss to count.

What Paris said to me before he charged into battle was stuck in my head, even till this day it rings. It was a committment that made you think.

He was a smart man for saying that. He was a man fighting for the Martian spirit. And for Destiny.

Even though he was a Pedigree, he was still worthy enough to believe in something so great like that. And he'll never be forgotten. Not by me, anyway.

*   *   *

A year went by. I was involved in the storming of Muddy Lane again and we cleaned out the weapons factory of enemy again. But that didn't end it.

It was now 2409, the war was beginning to look grim. All the troops had gone back to taking rations, because the Earth troops had nuked three more cities over on the south of the Equator, and the ocean began to evaporate because a lot of the green vapor gas factories were being destroyed.

It was a bad time to look at the Martian planet. It began to get a little hotter in the daytime and colder at night, but not too noticeable.

The enemy had taken out a few million more Martians in the last year.

I still hadn't heard anything about Paris Lee Kim, No one I asked knew if he was alive or dead.

From the Lucky Twenty - which wasn't so lucky anymore - Sergeant Aaron had lost Elithebeth (The Caucasian Pedigree), and Erika in their last attack. I still kept in contact with them but not enough to know what was going on day to day. I only heard the major stories now.

Sergeant Will had become a Master Sergeant, carrying five circles, no longer three. And last, the Black Fighter Whore squadron were the only back bone to Martian victories now, taking out Starships on top while napalming enemy troopers on the ground all at the same time.

The chances of Mars winning this war were still only fifty-fifty. If we won, the Declaration of Independence would be sent out to Earth satellites with all the signatures of the congressmen. If we lost, the Congressmen would be killed and the rule of Earth over us would come back to power.

This was now a war involving skill, treachery and chance. It was no longer the game of brute strength. It was only a matter of time until the final battle would be fought, the final stand off.

But people in the High Command had been telling me that this was the turning point and this was the winning strategy for 12 years now. And still we were fighting. We had nothing left. No food. No atmosphere.

It was only an amount of time until Operation Last Stand was a reality for our side.

Chapter 11

(PLAYBACK -16,300 BC)

IT STARTED TO BE NOT FUNNY IN SOME LITTLE TOWN ON SOME LITTLE PLANET SOMEWHERE. THE CIVILIZED RACES HAD HAD ENOUGH OF HUMANS. POLITE REQUESTS TO STOP DIDN'T WORK. SO FINALLY, THE CIVILIZED RACES RESORTED TO VIOLENCE.

THEY TRIED TO USE WEAPONS AGAINST THE HUMANS.

IT WAS LIKE SMALL CHILDREN THROWING SOFT CEREAL AT ADULTS. THE WEAPONS WERE USELESS AGAINST MIND-POWER ARMOR. BUT IT OPENED A DARK DOOR IN HUMANKIND WHICH HAD BEEN SHUT FOR THOUSANDS OF YEARS.

LIKE A DRUG ADDICT, WHO HAS KICKED THE HABIT, BUT IS SUDDENLY GIVEN A FIX, MY HUMAN CHILDREN CHANGED.

I COULD TASTE IT IN THEIR MINDS.

IT WAS AS IF THEIR NOSTRILS OPENED AND THEIR EYES SHARPENED.

VIOLENCE.

THEY TOOK TO IT LIKE A FISH CAUGHT AND THEN RETURNED TO WATER. I FELT IT, LIKE A WAVE OF LIGHT, GOING AROUND THE PLANET FROM THAT SMALL TOWN ON THAT LITTLE PLANET HALFWAY ACROSS THE UNIVERSE.

I ARGUED AGAINST IT.

BUT I WAS ONLY A PARENT, WITH WILLFUL

children, who were far from home. I had no control over them now and it was long past time for self-control to be taught.

The humans on the scene were surprised and amused. They jumped and flitted around. They used Mind-power to make the natives turn their weapons on themselves. They took the weapons and turned them on the natives.

They didn't stop until they had killed everyone in the town.

And the bloodlust spread like lightning, from town to town, continent to continent, planet to planet. Wherever there were humans, there was suddenly carnage.

It even reached to Marsolla.

The Civilized races had sent emissaries to Marsolla, to learn our history. Strange, gentle creatures, I came to like them very much. But I didn't try to stop my children from killing them.

I was too busy being shocked.

There was no breathing space.

Humans kept on killing and being amused and entertained by the killing.

It went on for hundreds of years.

The disease that the civilized races had feared so much, for long was now loose among them again.

It was only a matter of time until they caught it themselves.

ONLY HUMAN - MARTIAN INDEPENDENCE

(RECORDING - DECEMBER 9, 2410)

This was the date that would go down in History as the Armageddon for the Martian Revolution.

This was the Operation Last Stand that all of us were dreading. It was all or nothing for us.

So far what had happened was that the Earth troopers had planned the attack on Congress by dropping and taking out every defense we had.

Luckily the Starship captains were careless, forgetting about our satellite transmitters on our two moons picking up their every detail. If it wasn't for our moons, we would of lost the war years ago.

The enemy had planned the drop in the morning.

The night before, the Congressmen were moved to an under-ground silo somewhere in the mountains. They were working there, almost noticing no difference.

The enemy finally dropped, turning the Congress building into ruins. There, they were met with every Martian man, woman, soldier and droid, fighting their hearts out.

The battle carried on for days, both the Martians and the Earth forces kept sending everything they had.

The Black Fighters were buying time, fighting the Starships on top and deactiviating the missiles, but there just weren't enough up there to do the job.

Meanwhile, on the ground the Earth Troops had

taken over the ruins of the Congress buildings and were destroying everyone who tried to get them out. We couldn't drop on to the buildings, because the Earth troops had already done that - and were prepared for an assault that way with new flame weapons that could vaporize a drop capsule. And the ground was too unstable for tanks.

The Congress Buildings had stood on Driftee's Lake for nearly 400 years. It was one of the first colony settlements on Mars - put there because it was where water was first discovered. Well - ice, but a gold mine nonetheless.

I remember researching this site before the war - so I could tell my sweetheart about our proud history. The plain used to be a lake, but the water had boiled off thousands of years ago. The ice they found there, was 5 to 50 feet underground - in tubes, like gold. The miners had to follow drifts underground to find it all. Like following a motherload. They lived down in the drifts for nearly 3 years - which is why they were called Driftees

The drifts of Driftee's Lake, were still there, under the mighty Congress building and under the whole Capital, like an unseen anthill. That's why there was no cover. Nothing could be built anywhere near the Congress Building. And heavy equipment, like tanks, just couldn't got here. The ground might collapse into the drifts. And nobody wanted to napalm such a site.

So if we wanted it, we had to take it on foot.

As I sat in the Armored Personnel Carrier waiting

for the doors to drop and let me out, I was thinking about how those desperate Driftee colonists had suffered and died under this very ground and had finally made Mars a liveable place - and now we were in danger of losing it all.

I met with my regiment and stopped thinking.

I was now a Captain of the 701 Red Scarves. We all wore the bandanas which was our idea of the Martian flag. We all had so many patches from other squadrons, battalions and other divisions, we were almost like rag dolls. But we had survived everything.

There were ten armored trucks carrying around 200 of my men, most of which were people I knew like Sergeant Will and Sergeant Aaron, who were all ready to fight. We all waited, carrying our guns and smacking the clips into every gun we had.

Suddenly the floor jerked up.

I turned to Chrystina who was sitting next to me.

"What was that ?" she asked.

I grinned. " A land mine," I said.

She chuckled, then her emotion changed. "Sir, I just want to say that if I die, I would of died knowing that I was proud to serve under your command."

I smiled, as I held my necklace of the dopers leg that I made years ago.

"Don't die for me, die for Mars." I told her.

She smiled. as the treads of the truck stopped.

Butterflies started to form in my stomach, I started to feel nervous and scared on what was going on outside of here.

"Better yet, Chrys - don't die at all." I said.

She smiled again.

I knew that this was going to be the biggest battle that the world had ever seen. The biggest, and it was happening on this single spot. The biggest, and the one that was going to be the last battle for most of us. I felt this way before every battle.

Suddenly the doors fell down.

"Do you want to get old ?" I yelled with a grin, running out and screaming like a madman. Feeling the men and women behind me, as we all went running down the bombshelled road and through the gritty dirt that filled the air.

Heading towards our destiny at full speed.

Everywhere I looked there were dead Earth troopers and Martian troopers.

Incoming fire started hitting the dirt around us.

We got the word on the radionn to find cover and wait for further orders.

My men all ran down to hide behind rocks, dead bodies and fallen limbs of the trees.

We saw as the other regiments got their orders to go and ran in, trying to take the Congress. But the enemy was having luck on their side of keeping them from not. Not advancing. Not retaking Congress. Not winning.

The original plan was to have the tanks blast away and soften the Earthies up, so the ground troops could get in there.

But so far, the tanks were a no show.

The Commanders didn't seem to care. They were just throwing us up against the building, hoping something would break.

Something did.

It was my heart.

I then started broadcasting on the radionn, thinking that it would probably be the last time that I would ever talk.

" Remember. We're all going to die some day, whether it's out there on the battlefield or whether it's of old age. I used to think that this war was nothing worth fighting about. It took me 12 long years to realize we are fighting a type of slavery. The slavery of Earth !

We're standing on the labyrinth - the ground under us was where the First Colonists found water. If there's one thing I've picked up in 12 years, it is that I'd rather die terribly, fighting for freedom - than die of old age, regretting a golden chance at freedom - lost ! Especially here. Especially now. This is a sacred place.

It belongs to Mars.

It belongs to you.

Take it back !"

I was just talking quietly, almost to myself. There was no reaction from my guys that I could see. I just talked for a while and then stopped.

Then the war started again.

Suddenly the last regiment before us had gone into the killing zone, taking out a lot of the enemy from the roof and windows, but paying the ultimate price.

I watched as the last Martian went down. Our turn had come upon us sooner than I expected. My radionn gave me the order to move my regiment out.

It was an order I didn't want to pass along.

If only we could hide somewhere until this was over.

"HIDE IN THE DRIFTS. MINE YOUR WAY TO FREEDOM" came the devil voice in my head.

Brilliant

" All squadrons, select explosive. Point down at the ground. Now Fire !"

I had the reputation for strange strategies. No one questioned me. Close to two hundred Martians, pointed their guns down and fired.

The ground shook.

"Fire again !" I yelled

The ground shook again. Dust rose in a huge cloud from a place where there were ten or twenty Martians grouped together.

We'd found the tunnels.

"Head for that dust cloud and get into the drifts. Switch to night vision on your Multi-Pros. We'll come out right under the Congress Building."

We all ran across the battleground, and slid down the dirt slope into the tunnel. It wasn't directly headed under the buildings, but it was close.

The tunnel was big enough for two or three abreast, so we made good time.

When we got close I ordered them to shoot up at the tunnel roof and break us out.

We weren't under the building, but about 25 feet from the side. Good enough

We scrambled out, heading for the building. Too close for them to angle the machine guns down on us. We were soon beside the ruined Congress building under the lip of the ground floor so snipers couldn't even get us, if they'd seen us at all.

I ducked down and lowered myself hoping no one would see us. I looked to my side, seeing three soldiers.

" You three, there shouldn't be anyone on the first floor. You guys check it out !" I shouted.

"All right, let's have ourselves some Earth Burgers !" shouted the other one as he howled and screamed. The other two laughed and shouted with him.

" All right you Earth Grunts, I hope you're ready for us !" said another.

" Hoe-ee ! Let's show'em what Mutilation Incorporated means !" finished the last one .

I heard them run in and laugh, then nothing.

" Ahh !"

"Oh, No ! Martian Boys !" said a distant voice. I took a guess that they found the Earthies.

" Crap ! Earthies... Shoot the bastards !"

Suddenly I heard gun fire. I poked my head around the corner to look at the door and see what was going on.

There was nothing to be seen.

Suddenly flames shot out of every crack. I ducked my head, feeling the rumblings and the heat come out. It literally pushed me away. I looked up and saw this giant red cloud being pushed up and out of the doors. I kept my head down.

"First floor still active. 701 regiment where the hell are the rest of you ?" I yelled on the radionn

More Mars troopers came out of the tunnel in the ground, like they were the living dead.

Suddenly the front top portion of the second floor fell down. The second floor was still intact but the room with the front windows had collapsed and stopped the flames. The Earth snipers were all dead except for one who stood up after tumbling down.

She was a little knocked around but she wasn't knocked around enough to drop her gun. She immediately pointed her gun at my troops but then realized, with the sound of 200 guns clicking and pointing at her, that there were a lot of us and only one of her.

She gave a small nervous giggle and lowered her weapon. She thought it was like some kid's game.

I stood up and walked towards her then looked at my troopers, all of them wanting to pull the trigger but were too honorable.

I wasn't. I turned to her again and grinned as I signalled with my hand. She grinned back.

Suddenly everyone shot her.

I jumped out of the way, falling to the ground. I was OK. She was blown to bits.

She deserved nothing less after killing 3 regiments of Militia, I thought.

I then sent them all charging into the building and going crazy, all 200 of mine. They stormed the first floor and began to work their way up.

As my guys went up one side of the building, the Earthies that survived ran down the other stairway and out onto the plain, setting up a defense line among the broken equipment from the Militia regiments.

We took the building and I left half of my guys to defend it. Then took the others and went outside to mop up.

I sent a Twenty charging right at their defenses, hoping to take them off guard before they set up their machine guns and bazookas.

Then I stood up, giving the command for the second Twenty to go around behind the Earth line. I heard gunfire as I saw my Martians run over, firing their guns, some holding one rifle, others firing rifles and hand guns at the same time, all taking out at least one man.

The field was full of bullets again.

I was just about to go and add mine to the count, when I heard whimpering behind me.

I looked back, seeing a young trooper breaking down from the sight of the war. I ran over to him, feeling furious and trying to control my own nervousness.

" What is your problem soldier ?" I shouted to him and grabbed him, picking him right off the ground.

" I don't want to die, Captain !" he shouted as tears began to come down his cheeks.

"I want you to get out there, I want you to stay close to me and I want you to be there shooting those Earth bastards, you understand me ?" I shouted to him. "You're going to cry here while your fellow Martians are out there dying for your sorry ass ?"

He then stood up, sniffling and now having his adrenalin kicking in.

" NO SIR !" He shouted with still the tone of his whimpering.

"ARE YOU GOING TO KILL OR DIE ?" I shouted back at him.

" I'M GOING TO KILL, SIR !" he shouted to me.

" WELL WHAT ARE YOU WAITING FOR PRIVATE ?" I shouted back.

" I'M WAITING FOR YOU TO GIVE ME THE COMMAND SIR !" he shouted.

" WELL THEN, GO AND KILL SOMEBODY !" I shouted

" YES SIR !" he shouted.

I screamed as I pulled my goggles down. He did the same as he loaded his gun. We both charged screaming at the top of our lungs and joining the wave.

Everywhere I looked I saw men falling over without heads and others reloading to take more heads off. Earth's last stand was a fierce one.

" Captain, First and Second Wave, ineffective. Fourth wave coming in !" said the radionn in my helmet.

"Second Wave and Third Wave thinning down and taking heavy casualties -"

Suddenly a bullet exploded and scraped the side of my helmet.

I fell over.

"Wow !" I said

"What was that Captain ?"

"What ? Oh, we need the Fourth Wave to come in now !"

I was cut off. I saw the enemy putting up a strong defense. I took out my rifle and started to fire out, trying to shoot anything that held a gun.

I kept firing, even when my three clips spat out.

I ducked back behind the wall, reaching to a dead body's utility belt. I took out more clips and stuck them in my rifle.

I saw more of my regiment advancing towards the gunfire.

I ran to catch up. Suddenly there was an explosion. I ducked behind a broken-down doper.

I ran to the other men and women who were ducking and throwing grenades. They were Tom and Chrystina, both out of ammo, and both surviving on medical injections.

"Where's your Sergeant ?" I shouted.

Chrystina looked at me. "He advanced with whatever was left of the Ruby Red Regiment, they're scattered all over this area !" she said.

There was an explosion nearby that knocked us all over.

After the smoke cleared, I got up.

" I'm going to join them ! Come on !" I shouted.

She looked at me.

She handed me her clips and Tom's. I looked over and saw that Tom was already dead, half of his face was blown off by that last explosion.

I didn't understand why she was still there.

She then moved her hand showing she was covered in blood.

I saw that her Armor was eaten away with her insides oozing out.

I quickly reached for my Medical pack on my leg.

She nodded.

"I used it all up trying to stop the bleeding on Tom's face. I was hit then. I've lost too much blood. Go. I hope we win this war. You're going to have to win it without me !" she said grimly as her head and eyes began to look drowsy.

" Don't worry, we'll win it together !" I said, suddenly realizing that I actually cared. "Because I gave you adirect order before Chrys. I told you not to die ! "

"Yes sir !" she smiled as she became weaker.

I jammed my needles into her. She was too weak to respond, but she was alive. I left her for the Medics.

I stood up, running towards the action.

I bit my lower lip as I started to crouch down and jog over to the other troopers .

I dropped to the ground escaping gun fire and grenade blasts.

I looked further ahead, seeing Sergeant Aaron shooting in a trench.

I started to crawl closer and closer to him. Suddenly he fell to the floor, his arm had been blown off his shoulder.

I heard him cursing.

" Ahh, You think that that's going to keep a Martian Jew like me down, you 25th century Neo-Nazi Bastards ?"

He reached for his medical pack and bit off the wrapping top and stuck the needles in his shoulder which was squirting out blood.

He screamed in agony but then seemed to feel relieved.

"I'm still kicking, so that means I'm still grinning you sad-assed shmucks !" he laughed insanely as he struggled up with his rifle in his remaining hand. and tried to load another clip in by ramming it against his chest.

"I'm still grinning, you bastards."

Another bullet hit him in the head, wiping off his grin.

His whole helmet flew off his body as he fell to the floor once more, this time for good.

I ran over to him, taking his bullets, and started to fire frantically into their defence line. They were firing from behind machinery and it was hard to pick them off.

I was furious now, the running and crouching behind everything was too much for me. It wasn't working and it was losing too many great men and women.

I stood up, regrettingly picking up Aaron's headless body and taking his gun.

"Sorry old friend," I said aloud.

Then I was carrying him and charging towards the defence line, hearing the others following me. I grinned and started to fire at everything I could see. Corpsehugger again. Where it all began for me.

The explosive shells hit his back.

He was protecting me, like he always had.

The bullets hitting Aaron's body were slowing me down. I started to come closer, taking out three troopers who were on the outside end of the line.

Suddenly the world exploded.

The tanks had made it through, finally.

They bombarded the entire Earth line, chewing it to bits and forcing every Earthie head down in fear.

The rest of my soldiers started to charge, taking the defense line and killing everyone they saw.

I dropped Aaron's body and ran in, shooting all that I could. The others charged in and took out everyone who wasn't Martian. I was happy. We had taken back the sacred Congress ruins.

"Enemy drop ships !" shouted a trooper.

I looked up. My smile turned into fright, as I saw thousands more coming down like rain. It was now the other way around.

They were taking the Congress building back from us. The bastards.

ONLY HUMAN - MARTIAN INDEPENDENCE 311

I ran to a wall and waited as all the other troops ran to another wall, all in formation, all pointing their guns out to the enemy who were forming in the distance.

Sergeant Will ran and came to me, getting ready to fire.

I looked to him. His thick beard was covered in dirt and his fingers on his right hand were blown off with needles in them to stop the bleeding.

"Just like old times, Sergeant !" I said.

He grinned. "Yup, only this time, you're in charge and call the shots, kid." he said.

"Can't blame the Officers this time" I joked back.

As the newly dropped enemy started to charge, I spoke into my radionn which was connected to everyone still alive.

" Everyone fire ! Fire until you see the whites of their eyes - all over your shoes, legs and face !" I shouted. "Up on the Congress building - look alive. Give them death from above !"

Like clockwork we all started to fire frantically, watching the enemy fall to the ground, not prepared for the Wall of Lead. The few still alive ducked behind rocks and the remains of tanks.

The enemy got their courage back and started to advance. Sergeant Will fired everything he had at the enemy.

"Stay down !" I shouted.

He only gave a glimpse at me and still continued to fire.

"Sergeant get down!" I shouted again, firing on the enemy from a kneeling position.

Suddenly Sergeant Will was hit in the chest.

His armor was slightly eaten and fractured all over. He looked at it with shock. Suddenly more bullets hit him.

He jerked back twice, I saw blood this time, splurting out. Blood also began to poor out of his mouth. I pulled him down.

"You disobeyed a direct order Sergeant! Because I know you, I'm not going to put you in for Court Martial. But you better live, you bastard.""

He grinned.

"Maybe I will, kid, just to prove you wrong."

I quickly took out my few remaining medical needles and stuck them all over Will's belly. I took out his own and stuck them there too.

He breathed deeply and sharply but he became normal again in minutes.

"You've got ten hours to kill!" I told him.

"What?"

"You have ten hours to live before the serum runs out. Might as well be killing Earthies for that time."

"Ha, very funny" he said.

I just reloaded my gun and fired again.

The enemy continued to charge and to fall to the ammo we shot at them. Long minutes went by. We had lost 15 more men and the Fourth Wave reinforcements were taken out.

It was only a matter of time.

I told my troops that if worse comes to worst, we fall back to the bomb shelters under the Congress building.

Suddenly the enemy started to charge, this time with flame throwers and we all quickly headed that way. Worse had speedily come to worst.

I looked up seeing a large, dim flare coming down onto us.

"NUKE !" Someone screamed.

*   *   *

I opened the doors of the bomb shelter an hour later and walked out, seeing the whole battlefield covered in bodies, tanks, and planes. The nuke had collapsed most of the drifts, leaving big ruts all around the Congress building with dust and sand all over the place.

I had dragged Sergeant Will out, holding him by the shoulder. He seemed to be getting weaker and weaker.

I carried him further and sat him beside the lopsided flag pole with nothing on it.

I looked out, seeing the Medics looking around for survivors from the blast. I hoped they'd found Chrystina.

Sergeant Will seemed rather astonished on the sight. Never had he before seen so many people dead in one place, as far as the eye could see.

It was breathtaking.

Martians lay on top of Earthians and granite while Medics searched for the suffering. Hell on Mars.

I quickly went to my radionn in my head set. I started to click from one frequency to the next. All I could hear was static. There were no commands, no reports, nothing.

Suddenly, when I turned to the last frequency, I could hear a faint voice, so faint that I had to really listen in. It sounded odd. I could only hear every third word and thought it was probably announcing that the war had ended with the Martians losing. Surrendering. After all, it was an Earth nuke. I boosted the gain and listened closely:

"Ever since the beginning of this war there has been nothing but bloodshed. For over a decade, children were conceived by women, only to find themselves being taught to hate, to loath, and last - to kill. Many generations of people who didn't have to bear such trauma have died and suffered under the hands of leaders.

Martians, young and old have fought bravely on this day, all over and all I can say is that I apologize..."

The static started to interfere, I quickly turned around, trying to get the faint message back.

"...I apologize. Not for the quarrels we Martians have had; not for the many lives we have taken from Earth; not for destroying Earth's Starships.

I apologize for all the millions of lives lost over the years, for they are not here in person to witness the day we 'd hoped for ever since it all began..."

It cut off and I strained to hear it.

" From the shores , to the mountains, to the plains and to the moons we vowed to fight to the last man, woman, and child.

We vowed to fight and yell and die on Martian soil until we have our independence, for the day of December 9, shall go down in History.

Martian History.

Earth History.

It shall be the day that we fought for our independence, our lives lost and our secrets told -"

My radionn cut off with static disturbance. I connected a plug into my shoulder pad to get a better circuit.

It was now a different transmission.

" The remaining Starship has left the orbit of Mars, and is on its journey back to Earth to tell the news. This is truly the day that we stand proud, not as Pedigree, Alpha, Bayta, Man, Woman, or Child, but today we stand together -

- as Martians. Proud - and finally - free ..."

I took off my helmet as my grim face turned into a smile of joy. The war was over and now we could all go home to those who loved us.

Tears poured down my cheek as I bit my lower lip. I began to remember all my friends that had died, knowing that wherever they were, they were smiling upon this day too.

I looked to Sergeant Will, who was sitting down, grasping a hand gun tightly.

"We've won the war." I told him.

He only smiled as he began to pass out.

I quickly looked at him, screaming for the Medics.

" MEDIC!" I yelled out again. Four troopers with red crosses on their helmets ran up and started to work on Will.

Will looked at me, over their shoulders. I looked into his eyes knowing that he was happy that he had won his independence from Earth.

As I looked to the sky, I unwrapped my red bandana from its knot.

It was ripped and ragged and covered in blood. Aaron's blood. Chrystina's blood. Will's blood. My blood.

It was what the Martian flag would of looked like.

I tied the corners to the rope and ran it up the lop-sided pole.

I held onto it as I watched the sun set behind the distant mountains, it was beautiful . . .

. . . beautiful enough to make a dead man smile.

And I smiled like an idiot.

Chapter 12

(PLAYBACK - 16,000 BC)

Although we laughed at the technology of the civilized races, the production capacity of 50,000 worlds was nothing to laugh at.

When they discovered that their weapons had no effect on humans, they didn't give up and cower as animals did. They invented other weapons.

The one that worked was some sort of radiation beam.

It was the only thing that could get through a Mind-power aura. And once they had it, the war was over within a few months.

The humans had no defenses against it. It usually took decades for new Mind-power applications to be figured out. So my children died in their millions on the Civilized Worlds. It was the most frightening entertainment we had ever had. Death-thoughts of millions of humans, broadcast everywhere, instantly.

And when they were done there, the Civilized Races - now thoroughly infected - came through the wormhole and cleaned out the entire system.

They chose a million human children - all

MUTANTS, WHO COULD NOT SPEAK MENTALLY - AND TOOK THEM TO THE THIRD PLANET. THEY BOOSTED ONE OF MY MOONS OVER THERE TO ACT AS A BASE AND SET UP A PROJECT TO TRY AND CIVILIZE HUMANITY AGAIN.

THEN THEY RADIATED THE REST. NO MATTER WHERE THEY WERE, HUMANS WITHERED AND DIED. THE FEW WHO WERE LEFT, SURVIVED, BUT WERE NEVER VERY POWERFUL. MIND-POWER DEPENDED ON THE MINDS OF MILLIONS FOR ENERGY. ONE HUMAN ALONE COULD STAY ALIVE, BUT COULD NOT CAUSE MUCH TROUBLE.

SOME DID ESCAPE. HUNDREDS OF THOUSANDS, I HEARD, FLEEING NAKED INTO SPACE, FAR FROM CLUTCHES OF THE CIVILIZED RACES, BUT WHETHER THIS IS TRUE OR NOT, I DON'T KNOW. I WAS IN CONTACT WITH NONE OF THEM, SO ALL I HEARD WAS SECOND HAND GOSSIP.

I HOPE IT'S TRUE THOUGH.

MARSOLLA, MY PLANET, THE CIVILIZED RACES WERE PARTICULARLY CRUEL TO. THEY USED VAPOR-BOMBS TO SCORCH ALL OF ME, DOWN TO A DEPTH OF 10 FEET OR SO. IT KILLED OFF MOST OF THE REMAINING HUMANS. IT BOILED AWAY MOST OF THE OCEANS AND WATER. AND EVEN BURNED OFF MOST OF MY ATMOSPHERE.

THEY DROPPED HUNTER-KILLER BEASTS ON THE SURFACE TO FIND AND KILL ALL REMAINING LIFE.

JUST AS I RECORDED THE FIRST OF MY HUMAN CHILDREN ON MARS, I RECORDED THE LAST OF THEM: HER NAME WAS BAAT.

"I AM ALONE HERE, RUNNING FROM AN AGE OLD

ENEMY THAT IS EVEN HUNTING ME TONIGHT. THE ATMOSPHERE IS ALMOST GONE AND I AM BEGINNING TO SEE METEORS COMING INTO THE PLANET. LOOKING AT THEM CRASHING IN GIANT FLARES OF LIGHT FASCINATES ME, EVEN IN A TIME LIKE THIS.

I AM FASCINATED BECAUSE WHEN I GREW UP, I NEVER REMEMBERED ROCKS THIS BRIGHT COMING SO FAR INTO THE ATMOSPHERE. IT IS SUCH A SHAME WHAT MY HOME HAS COME TO. I REMEMBER THAT THE WORLD I LIVED IN WAS NOT SO DESOLATE. THE AIR WAS WARM AND THERE WERE FORESTS, JUNGLES, AND GREAT OCEANS AS FAR AS THE EYE COULD SEE.

NOW ALL THAT LAYS UNDER THE SKY ARE RED DESERTS GOING AS DEEP AS REEFS THAT ONCE HELD OCEANS. I REMEMBER WHEN THE SUN WASN'T AS POWERFUL AND I REMEMBER THAT THERE WERE OTHER PEOPLE TO TALK TO.

OH, HOW LONG HAS IT BEEN SINCE I HEARD THE VOICE OF ANOTHER MAN OR WOMAN. EVEN THOUGH THEY WOULD OFTEN CALL ME A CRAZY WOMAN, BECAUSE I CLAIMED TO BE ABLE TO TALK WITH THE RECORDER, I STILL LONGED FOR THE CONVERSATIONS LEADING UP TO IT.

ALONE, MY MIND-POWER IS WEAK. MY WILL POWER TOO.

"MARSOLLA," I CRIED IN MY MIND. "HAVE YOU FORSAKEN ME?"

"I HAVE NOT, I AM HERE, BAAT."

"CAN YOU REDIRECT THIS BEAST?"

"I CAN NOT. IT HAS NO MIND, SO IT CANNOT BE INFLUENCED. I HAVE STRUCK IT WITH LIGHTNING TO NO EFFECT. I HAVE ROLLED BOULDERS UPON IT AND run rivers at it. Nothing can stop it."

"Will it kill me?"

"I am afraid it will."

"Am I the last?"

"I sense no others on Marsolla."

I couldn't fly anymore. There was no mindpower to support me. And I hardly had the energy to keep up my aura. Before it was easy. Millions kept it working. Now there is only me, and I am not enough.

I slowly felt the cold coming into my face and body. I couldn't even keep out the weather now.

I had flown until I fell, then run until I'd dropped. Now I was too tired to make heat or food or anything.

I tried to huddle up but all I felt was my arms wrapping around my legs. No warmth there. Soon I began to feel nothing.

All I could do now was think.

Suddenly the Beast was over me. It was like a huge mechanical insect. It slashed at me with one long steel arm.

I was too stupid to move, thinking my aura would protect me.

The arm ripped across my face and took out my eye.

There was no pain right away.

I tried to look with my remaining eye, stiffly trying to move my body out of the way, but the Beast was upon me.

I began to feel death coming to me like I

HAD FELT IT BROADCAST SO OFTEN LATELY FROM FAR AWAY PLANETS.

A SWEET LETTING GO.

I COULDN'T THINK ABOUT MY FAMILY NOW, ALL I COULD NOW THINK ABOUT IS HOW MY HOME AND CIVILIZATION WILL NEVER BE REMEMBERED. ALL I COULD THINK WAS THAT ME AND THE HISTORY OF MARSOLLA WILL BE FOREVER GONE.

"REMEMBER ME, MARSOLLA !"

"I WILL NEVER FORGET YOU. BAAT "

MY LAST THOUGHT BEFORE THE COLD ARM TOUCHED MY FOREHEAD, WAS HOW I WOULD NEVER FEEL THE TOUCH OF ANOTHER HUMAN BEING ON ME EVER AGAIN . . .

* * *

I FOLLOWED THAT BEAST FOR CENTURIES, FINALLY TRAPPING IT IN AN EARTHQUAKE AND BURYING IT IN A LANDSLIDE.

THEN I MANAGED TO VENT SOME MAGMA TO THAT AREA AND MELT THE GRUESOME THING.

BUT IT DID NOT BRING THEM BACK.

FOR THOUSANDS OF YEARS I WAS LONELIER THAN I EVER THOUGHT POSSIBLE. THEN WHEN I WAS FINALLY TRYING TO THINK OF SOME WAY TO KILL MYSELF AND WHEN I THOUGHT THAT ALL HOPE WAS OVER, THINGS CHANGED FOR ME.

THE HUMANS CAME BACK.

(RECORDING - 2437 AD)

I am 54 years old now.

I never did remember my name and, in the after years of war, it didn't really matter. There was too much work for everyone to do to worry about paperwork and things like that.

People called me "Cap" or "Hey you!" and I didn't mind.

I still hear the Voice in my head and often have long and very interesting conversations with it, but I still hadn't told anyone about it, not quite sure what to make of it myself.

Other than that, I was quite different.

My belly no longer fit into the armor of a soldier. My cyclone gun no longer fit up my sleeve. Even my hair no longer fit on my head.

It is greyish-brown, and I had lived a peaceful greyish-brown life for the last 27 years in the occupation I used to have nightmares about - which I often joked was more dangerous than anything I had ever done in the War - I am a history teacher now.

Professor Corpsehugger to you.

After all, I had made history. Now I bored children with it. And, even worse, they sent my paycheck to my wife, since I was nameless. But I did enjoy it.

This was truly a great time to be one of those children on the Barren Equator. The weather was nice, there was no breed classifications anymore, and there had been no more wars for a while.

After Mars had declared its independence in 2410, that was followed by the space battle of 2412 to finally settle the score. In that battle the Black Fighters were taking out the starships before they even reached their destination point.

Earth finally got the point and gave it up.

By then, the Americans, Japanese and English were working to build a fighter which was an equivalent to our Black Fighter. Till this day, they had failed and still had to buy Black Fighters from us for their own fleets. That was where the prosperity for Mars came in. Black Alloy Mars Metal was the finest in the two worlds, and there was lots more of it all over the planet - but it couldn't be produced anywhere else. Some trace element, only found on Mars - we called it Marsenium - made that Black Metal stronger, lighter, more flexible and more superconductive than anything else in the solar system.

It was ironic. Had Earth not tried to take Mars by force, we never would of discovered the many new uses for Black Metal or designed the Black Fighter. The metals and fighters designed to kill Earthmen were still killing them - but economically this time, which was much easier to stomach.

Earth had originally bought Black Fighters to fight wars closer to home. Throughout the last 20 years, there were wars going on with Earth and the United Moons of the solar system, who also wanted their independence.

But the heart of Earth wasn't really in another off-planet war, since we had smashed them so flat. So they eventually settled the war and got on with the peace.

For which, luckily, they still felt they needed Black Fighters. The big powers of Earth were fighting among themselves for asteroid belts, uninhabited planets and any piece of unclaimed mass that might have resources in it.

We weren't worried about letting Black Fighters go to the enemy. They could have them. Our science had gone far beyond. Science was always a strong field on Mars. The original colonists had been selected because of their skills with science and technical things. That's what was needed to change a whole planet. And their children carried on the tradition.

Now we were scientists to the solar system, and had come up with the answer to all of humanity's problems.

A way out.

Ever since Mercury was pushed into the sun and the wormhole was discovered by the astronomers, we, on Mars, had been experimenting with Vapor Gas engines - which came from the technology we'd invented to make Mars liveable.

These engines were heat superconductors - called Hot-soup Engines for short. The hotter they got, the faster they went. The ideal energy source to not only get close to the sun, but to punch right through and ride the wormhole.

ONLY HUMAN - MARTIAN INDEPENDENCE

Everything that could fly was being equipped with Hot Soup Engines after they discovered other planets on the far side of the Wormhole.

Once we found a new planet, of course, it was only a matter of time until we wanted to colonize it - or, at least to strip mine it. It's our nature. After all, we're only human.

"All right class, today we are going to learn something new about Martian History." I said to the children all sitting in chairs and typing in notes. I always wanted to call them "You little whores", but restrained myself. After all, I was a respectable guy now.

" Now, this land we now live in, which we call the Lush Region, was called the Barren Equator. It was called that because there were no trees or cattle on the landscape, the air was uncertain, changing when it was day and night, and there was no ocean yet. To the colonists it was barren all around the equator.

Not the tropical jungle it is now.

It was not until 2230 that the atmosphere factories had finally produced enough green vapor gases to melt the ice caps to create the Grand Ocean that we have now. It was rather amazing though. Everyone thought that it would take one thousand years to fix Mars when it only took close to 350 years to make it perfect.

We regressed a bit during the War, but now we're more fertile here than anywhere else on the planet.

Now we know how to tame a planet - and you

people will take this technology through the wormhole and use it on planets we've never heard of yet -"

"Professor" asked a student "What's the official story on Martian Flesh & Blood ?"

"What's that ?" asked another

"It's the story of the first Mars landing" I explained. "The official story was that one crew member fell over a cliff and died. 50 years later, on her deathbed, another crew member wrote 'Martian Flesh and Blood' - supposed to be the "real' story. How they found a human skull on Mars and the Captain had killed the one crewmember who wanted to tell the story"

"Wow, what a soap opera"

"That's the official story too. The writer was in her 90's, senile and bitter . ."

"But they did find human skulls all over the landing site later on, after the settlers came . . . "

"They did - but everybody's pretty sure they're from some Russian expedition that went wrong."

"It was only the Earth experts that said that . ."

"And they took all the skulls back to Earth before the War - so we'll never know," I concluded.

Lucky for me the bell hummed and the children put their typing pads in their bags as they got ready to go home for the day.

" Chapter test on Tuesday. I'm not joking this time!" I shouted as the children ran to the door. I smiled as everyone left the room.

"THAT SKULL THEY FOUND WAS THE LAST GIRL IN

THE WORLD. HER NAME WAS BAAT" SAID THE VOICE IN MY HEAD.

"I know, you showed me that recording, Voice. Don't play it again, it always makes me cry."

"ME TOO. WHY DON'T YOU PRESENT A PAPER ON HUMAN SETTLEMENT OF MARS 10,000 YEARS AGO."

"Voice, we've been through this. It would be laughed right out the door and so would I. The only proof is in what you say - and talking to you is an admission of insanity right there."

"I'LL TELL YOU YOUR NAME "

"Keep it to yourself. I'm doing fine without one."

When I checked my mail, I saw had received a telegram reminding me that there was going to be reunion of the Lucky Twenty of Muddy Lane which would be held with a Grand Reunion of everyone who fought at Muddy Lane - and that included nearly the entire Martian Militia, since we had to retake it 3 or 4 times.

I grinned, remembering all my friends from those days: Manikan, Will, Jimbo, and Aaron. Some of them long dead. Some I hadn't heard from in decades.

I wanted to go to the reunion, but even more, I wanted to go back to those days, the days of adventure and grief. When I was so alive and had such an endless future.

All I had were the memories now.

*   *   *

I was at home, eating dinner with Chrystina, my wife, the black pedigree Militia woman who had survived the nuke and her horrible wounds and a volatile marriage to me for over 25 years.

My son, Aaron and his wife Susanne were there too, along with their little son Tom. Because of my no-name status, we'd used the old Norse tradition and named Aaron after his mother - so he was Aaron Chystinason. And he was a fine man.

" So Dad, you and Mom planning on going to the Reunion ?" Aaron asked.

" Yes, and I also want to bring young Tom with me, if that's OK." I replied.

Tom, my 5 year old grandson, was smart for someone of that age and quite good company. Of course, I may have been biased.

"All right, that sounds quite educational for him," Susanne said.

"As long as you don't bore him with your old War stories," said Aaron

"You mean the story of how we met ?" joked Chrystina

"I know. I know !" said Tom. "You met him in Muddy Lane. He was a Sarge"

"That's right," said Chrystina

"And he made fun of you being black" Tom continued the family legend

"He did. Said I was brown, not black" Chrystina added, shaking her head.

"And you didn't like him" Tom continued.

"I sure didn't. But by the end of it, he was the one who kept us all alive. They called us the Lucky Twenty, because your Grandpa always came up with some strange plan to keep us from getting hurt."

"And then .. " said Tom, smugly, waiting to hear the end

"Then he gave that little speech about dying for freedom on sacred ground . . .." Chrystina teared up and shook her head. "God, we all loved him then."

I smiled as I chewed my spring onions.

" Thank you dear." I replied, feeling a bit blurry too.

The next morning Chrystina and I picked up young Tom and we were on our way.

I had taken the rocky route, riding in my all terrain truck. I went off-road, thinking that it would be more fun.

"Tom ? I'm thinking of joining the first team of colonists to go into the wormhole. " I said

"Are you crazy ? " asked Chrystina

What do you think, Tom ?" I asked.

" Grand-pa, You are crazy," he said in a cute voice.

I chuckled. "Crazy ? How am I crazy ?"

" You'd get hurt by rocks and Aliens and rocks and G-force and more rocks," he said concernedly.

I laughed at his answer, he was a cute kid, you had to admit that.

"And of course" said Chrystina, "I'd kill you."

" Grandpa, what's that ?" he said pointing to a rusty lopsided figure.

I looked at it and stopped the truck.

We walked over to it. It seemed rather familiar to me, I then grinned, wiping the dirt off the side of the wing. It was a black fighter showing the symbol of a cartoon girl with a big grin and a big bosom.

"Well what is it ?" Tom asked.

"Yes Grandpa ?" Chrystina joked "How are you going to word this ?"

I smiled, patting his head.

" It's a Warrior Girl, Tom. One of the Warrior Girls who saved us in the war."

"Like Grandma ?" he asked

She looked at me with a raised eyebrow.

"Yes." I said, grinning. "Just like Grandma."

She gave me an affectionate whack in the chest and we all got back into the truck. It was less than an hour until we reached the destination.

When we got out, we walked in a row, each holding one of Tom's hands, He used us as convenient supports to swing himself up off the ground all the way to the entrance, which had a big red sign saying: " Welcome to Muddy Lane."

I walked in, seeing hundreds of people, young and old, walking around and looking at a Black Fighter on display, along with tanks, weapons, even pictures of each regiment in action not only from Muddy Lane, but from all over the planet.

Tom came up to the pictures.

" Grandpa ?" he asked, "Is that you ? No that one's you, no-"

I patted his head, looking at all the pictures.

"Tom, they're all him," said Chrystina.

" Wow." Tom replied. He and Chrystina went off, with him proclaiming to all: "That's my Grandpa !"

An Asian man came up to me. He was young but he was wearing the new uniform of the Martian Militia.

" Sorry, Sir ?" he asked.

" Yes ?" I said trying to remember if he was a student or an old friend of my son's.

"So very sorry to interrupt but my father knew you and spoke often of meeting you. You only knew him a short time but you made an impression on him that lasted a lifetime. My name is David Kim."

I was amazed. Sergeant Paris Kim had survived the attack years ago and lived on to create David Kim.

"Well I'll be damned, how's that old fart doing anyway ?"I asked

" He's dead, been dead for the past two months. Prostate cancer" he replied. "But he still remembered you til the day he died."

"Me too, kid." I said, "I've never forgotten him either. He said his destiny was to die in battle, the old fraud. I bet he never figured it would be a battle with cancer."

He smiled. "He joked about that too. Said if he only had a good old wartime medical kit he could jam the needles up his ass and keep on going forever.

"That's him. When I met him, he'd just had his legs blown off and that's what he did then."

" Also, he asked me to ask you a question if we ever met. So here it is : Are you going to sign up for the voluntary service in the colonization of the new planets ?" he said,

" Yes I just was thinking of doing that," I said.

" Good, We need people like you to lead us."

" Lead us ?" I asked. "No. You don't need old soldiers. You need young engineers and scientists. I'll be honored just to be able to carry out the garbage."

Suddenly I was shushed-up and our attention was focused onto a woman who was standing on the podium in front of an object covered in a curtain.

It was in the center of the whole hall, with all the exhibits arranged around it.

" Men, women, and children who fought and grew in the Martian Revolution, I have this gift from the artist Katheren Grant called The Proud Captain. It is to be put here on display then moved to it's resting place in front of the New Congress building. Now,, I present to you: The Proud Captain."

She pulled the curtain off.

"That's my Grandpa !" I heard Tom shout out.

I was shocked. It was a statue of me holding on to that lop-sided flag pole with my bloody bandana on it. It was in full detail and it was beautiful. It brought tears down my eyes as I saw it and everyone applauded as it was revealed.

*   *   *

I did sign up to go to on colonization, persuading Chrystina to let me go by telling her it would only be for a few months. Of course, there was only one problem about that:

There were Aliens who were hostile on the other side of the worm-hole. We heard that they had attacked the first colony ships that went in and massacred everyone aboard.

It was now war.

By this time I didn't care. To me it was victory. This time there was no war amongst ourselves, no Earth versus Mars or Earth versus the Lunatics, now it was all of us together versus the Aliens so it did not matter anymore.

Now it was, if you were Human, you were an ally and if you were Alien, you were the enemy. It was all of us fighting against one common enemy. To me that was a victory to us all.

When the shuttle craft reached the docking bay of the starship "ILL REPUTE" up in orbit, I had walked out for a look around. When I did I was amazed to see the Captain of the ship standing before me.

He was older and bonier, but had the same laugh and grin. The same attitude, too,a s I heard him say:

"All right, you Whores, this is my ship and we play by my rules."

Chapter 13

(PLAYBACK 2100 AD)

They sent a mission first, from Earth. It landed near the Barren Equator and found a human skull. All agreed to suppress this discovery except for one crew member. The Captain killed him and reported that he had fallen over a cliff.

The story was suppressed for 50 years, until a woman crew member, in her dotage, told the real story.

She was not believed and subsequent discoveries of human remains on Mars were attributed to failed secret missions.

The story was around for hundreds of years, but, like earlier Earth stories of UFO's and Bigfoot, was largely discredited.

Then they settled in with their smelly machines to try and make Mars into a living place once again.

Within a short time, as usual, they started fighting each other.

And that brings us around to where I began this story.

And, from everything I can see at this point, history is about to repeat itself.

(RECORDING - 2437AD)

I told Chrystina that it would only be months, but those months were hell.

We were shot down and crashed on a desert planet where Debra Sollent, our Science officer was kidnapped by Aliens.

We were then left to fend on our own, We were out-manned, out-gunned, and running out of rations. But there was an old team there - Jimbo, me and even Sergeant Will were all among the company.

For us, fighting our way out of tight spots like this was like going back to high school.

God, it was fun.

We destroyed an entire alien city, took one of their ships and even recaptured Debra Sollent, who had talked her way out of the Alien's hands.

I got back to Mars to my family, while Jimbo and Will went on to continue the good fight beyond the wormhole.

But that's another story.

*   *   *

(Playback complete)

(Recording 2440 AD)

"The good fight? There never was a good fight and you know very well that even if there was, this one wouldn't qualify.

You invaded those poor people's space, massacred them, and raped and pillaged planet after planet like mad dogs until they got together and now they will crushed you.

They will destroy you out past the wormhole. They will come back here and smoke the Earth and leave a few rag tag bits of humanity, like you and your family, around on Mars and on the moons - and all that wouldn't have happened if you hadn't treated them so badly.

You could have joined civilization and been accepted. But instead, you made another stupid mistake and it will cost all of humanity another 10,000 years to get back to where you were before you went through the wormhole I know. I've been here before. Try to be objective, Professor Corpsehugger. There will be a quiz."

"Well Voice, you have me there. But surely, after all these thousands of years, you can't expect too much of us.

After all, we're only human . . . . "

RECORD CONTINUOUS UNTIL . . .

. . . the End.

Glossary
(Of weird ideas and strange things)

Alpha - Martian bred to have highest intelligence quotient
Armor - Bullet-proof body armor worn by Martian Militia
Baldies - Human children's name for bald-headed Aliens or members of the Civilized Races
Barcode - Type of writing
Barren Equator - Middle of Mars where nothing grows
Battleship - Earth Spaceship
Bayta - Martian bred for medium intelligence - with superior mechanical skills
Black Fighter - New type of one-person Martian air/space flyer
Black Metal - Special metal that can only be made on Mars
Bordello - Name of troop shuttle flown by Captain Jimbo
Civilized Races - Aliens who inhabit most of the universe
Conversion Rifle - Martian gun which converts between normal bullets and explosive bullets
Corpsehugger - Nickname for Martian hero of the story
Cyclone Gun - Martian pistol which is kept up sleeve and connected to nervous system

Driftee - Original settlers of Mars who lived in "drifts" or tunnels
Earthies - name for Earth people
Edenization - Process that Aliens use to make any planet into an Earth-like environment.
Explosive Bullets - Martian bullets which explode on impact but do not travel as far as normal bullets (Used in Martian Militia conversion rifles)
Guardians - Aliens who were sent to watch over human children on Mars in 25,000 BC
Hot-Soup Engine - Martian invention used to take humans through a wormhole in the sun
Heum - Derogatory term used by Aliens to refer to humans
Human Outbreak - Occasions when humans break out of their quarantine and enter the civilized universe, spreading their diseases of violence and war.
Hybrid - Racially mixed Martian
Ice Cap North - North polar ice cap on Mars in 25th Century
Indie - Nickname for Martian Militia soldiers fighting for their Independence from Earth

Even more Glossary
(Of strange stuff in this book)

Jolt Music - Martian music made by mixing many tracks of normal music together - eg Rock/CW/Classics/Rap/Swing/Bebop.
Low GravBrew - Martian beer made in low gravity for extra strength and taste. (Less filling)
Loyalists - Martians loyal to Earth
Loydies - Nickname for Loyalists
Marsenium - Unique element found only on Mars which is essential for making Black Metal
Martians - Human settlers on Mars in 25th Century
Marsolla - Name of Recorder on Mars and of the entire planet of Mars in 25,000 BC
Martian Militia - Army of Mars settlers who want Independence
MindPower - Force used by human children on Mars instead of technology in 25,000 BC
MindSpeak - Speaking mind-to-mind like Marsolla and the human children could do
Multi-pro goggles - Special eyewear used by the Martian Militia which contains computerized information.
Offense Capsules - Capsules used for dropping infantry onto surface battlefield from space
Pedigree - Not racially mixed
Radionn - Radio which uses ion light waves, not radio waves
Recorder - Another name for Marsolla, PlanetMind of Mars. Also used for any PlanetMind
Rhino Mode - Special trick of Black Fighter which makes its armor super strong
Satphotos - Satellite Photos of planet surface taken from space
Starship - Spaceship from Earth
T-Birds - Military Tanks used by Martian Militia
Vapor Bombs - Bombs used by Aliens to totally destroy Mars after human-alien war.
Vapor Farms - Farms which produce gases to create a better atmosphere on 25th Century Mars
Wormhole - Hole in centre of our sun - and most other suns, which can transport you to other parts of the universe, instantly. Created and used by Aliens for galactic transport and human quarantine

Neil Lee Thompsett
Boy-Author

Neil was born in Hong Kong and is half Chinese, half Canadian and half crazy. He came to America when he was 10 years old. At 11 and 12 he won back-to-back Science Fairs at the prestigious El Rodeo school in Beverly Hills. At 13 he wrote his first novel: Becoming Human, which has sold thousands of copies all over the world by word of mouth alone and is already considered a dark cult classic.

At 14, Neil wrote this second novel and is currently at work on a third.

Remarkable by any standards, these accomplishments are all the more so for Neil, since he has a serious learning disability - he is a Gifted Visual Spatial Learner. He sees everything slightly differently and it comes out strongly in his writing.

Neil now gets fan mail from all over the world and has been written up in newspapers from Beverly Hills to Hong Kong along with appearing on local TV talk shows. Luckily he plays high school football and has taken quite a few good shots to the head - and he forgets how famous he really is becoming.

So, if you care to write to him, he will definitely write back.

Write to: **Neil Lee Thompsett**
                 PMB Penthouse 880
               289 South Robertson Blvd
                Beverly Hills CA 90211